# Burglary Blues

## A Lexie Sarconi novel

G.K. Parks

and Elisa Archer

This is a work of fiction. Names, characters, places, events, and other concepts are the product of the author's imagination or are used fictitiously. Any resemblance to actual persons, living or dead, places, establishments, events, and locations is entirely coincidental.



A Modus Operandi imprint



ISBN:
ISBN-13: 978-1-942710-38-7

*For my muse*

Other Books by G.K. Parks
BOOKS IN THE LIV DEMARCO SERIES:

***Dangerous Stakes***
***Operation Stakeout***
***Unforeseen Danger***
***Deadly Dealings***
***High Risk***
***Fatal Mistake***
***Imminent Threat***
***Mistaken Identity***
***Malicious Intent***
***Controlled Burn***

BOOKS IN THE ALEXIS PARKER SERIES:

***Likely Suspects***
***The Warhol Incident***
***Mimicry of Banshees***
***Suspicion of Murder***
***Racing Through Darkness***
***Camels and Corpses***
***Lack of Jurisdiction***
***Dying for a Fix***
***Intended Target***
***Muffled Echoes***
***Crisis of Conscience***
***Misplaced Trust***
***Whitewashed Lies***
***On Tilt***
***Purview of Flashbulbs***
***The Long Game***
***Burning Embers***
***Thick Fog***
***Warning Signs***
***Past Crimes***
***Sinister Secret***
***Zero Sum***
***Buried Alive***
***Trouble Brewing***
***Balance Due***

BOOKS IN THE JULIAN MERCER SERIES:

***Condemned***
***Betrayal***
***Subversion***
***Reparation***
***Retaliation***
***Hunting Grounds***

BOOKS IN THE CROSS SECURITY INVESTIGATIONS SERIES:

***Fallen Angel***
***Calculated Risk***

# ONE

"Alessandra Sarconi?"

I looked up at the sound of my name, the ridiculously long, ethnic sounding moniker my parents had stuck me with as a tribute to my father's grandmother. I had an Italian heritage, in case the brown hair and olive skin didn't give it away. But I didn't speak Italian. I couldn't even pronounce half the desserts or cheeses. But like a bad cliché, I became one of the city's finest.

"Sarconi?" The lieutenant looked around the room.

"Here," I mumbled. I'd worked patrol before. It was a decent posting until I figured out where to go since transferring out of vice.

"Alessandra?" He must not have heard me.

"It's Lexie, sir," I corrected, speaking louder.

"Whatever, Sarconi. I just wanted to make sure you were here." Lieutenant Peterson continued through the list, passing out assignments as he went.

While I waited to see who my partner was for today's tour, a detective I had never seen before entered the room. He had broad shoulders, a narrow waist, and under that fitted navy shirt was the outline of washboard abs. Studying his face, I found piercing blue eyes, a strong jaw with two days' worth of stubble, and short, dark brown, nearly black, hair. It was longer than a crew cut. Frankly, it was just long enough to give a girl something to tug on. Shaking off my thoughts, which were traveling into the gutter, I blew out a slow, calming breath. What was he doing in the middle of roll call?

The detective turned his back to us as he spoke to the lieutenant. Peterson flipped through the call sheet and held it out to the detective. He pointed to a few names, shaking his head. The men glanced in our direction every few seconds.

"Are you sure?" Peterson asked, and Detective Strong, Dark, and Ruggedly Handsome nodded. "Okay. But these are our newest additions, so don't come crying to me when they screw up your investigation." The lieutenant looked up, surveying the room of bored uniformed officers seated in front of him. "Hawking, Kemper, and Sarconi, follow Detective Riley. You're not patrolling today. He'll brief you on what you'll be doing instead."

I followed the other two officers out of the room. No one said a word as we went up the stairs and through the doors to the gangs unit. I read the gold nameplates on the desks, trying to familiarize myself. The only unoccupied desk boasted the nameplate Detective Michael Riley, the man who freed me from the tedium of walking a beat.

The other two desks were occupied by Detectives Jack Lightman and Samantha Preston. Even though I'd never met Lightman, he had a reputation around the station as a hardnosed, no-nonsense cop. And Preston was the only female detective in the unit. She and Lightman barely looked up from the paperwork as our posse entered the room.

"Are those our gofers, Mike?" Lightman asked.

"You said we needed help, so I brought help. I'm sure they're up for whatever tasks we throw at them." Riley noticed my gaze and winked.

If only I could disappear.

"Okay, here's the deal, people." Lightman pointed to a map pinned to a board. "There has been a string of B&Es around this neighborhood. The intel suggests a motorcycle gang is responsible, but we can't prove it yet. A few homeowners were attacked, but they aren't talking. So until we figure out who's responsible, we gotta knock on some doors, ask some questions, and be a pain in everyone's ass. Since some of us have better things to do, like investigate the liquor store and gas station robberies which appear to be connected to the break-ins, we need you to knock on those doors. It's called canvassing. Maybe you heard about it in the academy."

Officer Hawking, the oldest of the three of us, nodded. He had served in the military and knew to be respectful to a superior. Officer Kemper was smart enough to follow his buddy's example, but I had a chip on my shoulder that I'd never been able to shake. Working for vice had only made it worse.

"Canvassing?" I asked. "Don't we need equipment for that? Maybe a couple of paintbrushes and some acrylics?" I turned to Kemper and Hawking. "Unless you guys rather work with oils or watercolors."

Hawking remained stone-faced, but Kemper smiled. Detective Riley turned to read something on his desk to hide the snort that escaped his lips. At least someone was amused.

But my victory was short-lived when Lightman took a step toward me. "Do you think it's funny that hardworking people have been coming home and finding their apartments cleaned out? That they've been assaulted when they've found the crooks still inside?"

"No, sir." One of these days, I'd stop being a wiseass.

"Then get to work." He pointed to the open manila folder on top of his desk. It contained the addresses of the buildings that had been targeted.

The three of us piled into a squad car and headed to the location. In recent months, this neighborhood had become a hotbed for crime. A few automobiles had been jacked, but the real problem was the home invasions.

I didn't know much about motorcycle gangs or MCs, like they usually referred to themselves, but rumor was they were initiating new members into their crew, and the going price for admission was jewelry, electronics, and cash.

Weapons, particularly handguns, were all the rage. And the vast majority of stolen items fell into one of those four categories.

Lightman hadn't told us which crew they suspected was behind it. But without proof, we'd never be able to build a case and put a stop to it. Why hadn't the victims spoken out? Were they that afraid?

The neighbors who'd been home at the time were either asleep or pretended to be. They didn't want to get dragged into the investigation or forced to testify in court. And I couldn't blame them.

Gangs were scary, whether we were talking a bunch of street thugs or organized crime. In this neighborhood, drive-bys were commonplace, and payback was indeed a bitch. These witnesses and victims weren't crooks or part of the criminal lifestyle, but if they spoke up, they'd jeopardize themselves and their families. But this would never end unless they helped us. I tried to impress that point upon the people I spoke to, but so far, I hadn't gotten a single bite.

I double-checked the address and knocked on the door. "Police," I said. "Open up."

A woman came to the door with a toddler clinging to her leg. The child held a stuffed cow in her free hand.

I smiled down at the kid. "Hi, there."

The woman gave me an uncertain look. "What do you want?"

I straightened, turning my attention to her. "Last night, your neighbor's apartment was broken into." I pointed down the hall. "I wondered if you saw anything."

"Not a thing."

"Are you sure?" I peered around her. "That was the seventh break-in in the last ten days." Toys were scattered on the floor. Dishes were on the kitchen table, and the TV played in the background. "Have you noticed anyone suspicious in or around the building lately?"

"Nope."

"Do you mind if I come inside?"

She put her hand against the doorframe, blocking my entrance. "I do. It's almost Sasha's lunchtime. Now, if you don't mind."

"One last question," I said as she tried to close the door in my face, "do you own any firearms?"

"Why do you care?"

"The thieves are looking for cash, jewelry, electronics, and guns."

She picked up her kid and bounced the child on her hip. "They're not going to find any of that here."

"Be careful," I said. "If you have any concerns or you remember something, please call it in."

"Yeah, whatever."

After that final interview, I went down the steps, but I didn't spot a single security camera. Why couldn't this be easy?

I caught up to Hawking and Kemper. "I got nothing. How'd you guys do?"

"I got spit on," Hawking said. "I tried to ask a simple question, and this old woman spat on me."

"She must not be a fan of the uniform," Kemper said. "I got a lot of doors slammed in my face. But there was this smokin' hot chick in 2B who couldn't take her hands off me. I think she watched that stripper movie one too many times because she kept asking if I was wearing a thong."

"Are you?" I asked.

Kemper sashayed his hips and rubbed his palms down his chest suggestively. "If you want to find out, that'll cost you. Tuck the dollars in my belt."

Hawking let out a huff. "Did the two of you learn nothing from this morning? Lightman doesn't want us joking around. You need to watch it, Sarconi, unless you want to get demoted to meter maid. You too, Kemper."

"Have you worked with Lightman before?" I asked.

"Once. Keep your head down and do the work, and you'll be fine," Hawking said.

"Lightman sounds like a ton of fun," Kemper muttered.

"We aren't rookies," I said. "I thought we got picked to assist for a reason."

"The reason is they needed a few uniforms to knock on doors," Hawking said.

Kemper bumped up against me as we headed back to

the car. "I thought it was because we're special. I don't know about the rest of you, but I've done some things. My first week flying solo, I stopped an armed robber from knocking over a grocery store."

"Were you on duty?" I asked.

"Nope, but I was lucky enough to have my off-duty piece with me." Kemper gave me a sideways look. "Lexie Sarconi." He let my name roll around on his tongue. "Didn't you do something exemplary before you got kicked back to patrol?"

"I didn't get kicked back. I asked to be reassigned. And I'm not sure I'd call what I did exemplary. I worked as a decoy for vice, trying to sell my ass and arresting anyone who took me up on the offer."

Hawking stopped and turned, his brow furrowing. "You helped vice bust that serial killer."

I shrugged. "I was just doing my job."

Hawking's expression said he'd misjudged me. After all, the crack I'd made earlier hadn't been the most tasteful, but I'd only been trying to break the ice. He gave me a curt nod. "No wonder they picked you to assist. When are you taking the detective's exam?"

I hadn't mentioned that to anyone outside of my chain of command. "I don't know."

"Surely, after that arrest, they must have tapped you," Hawking said. "It wouldn't hurt for you to get a foot in the door at one of the other units. Gangs is a pretty good one, if that's where your sights are set. I'm guessing you don't want to go back to vice."

"Hell no," I said. "Stopping predators is important, but the work is taxing, emotionally, mentally, and physically."

"This must be a breath of fresh air compared to that." Kemper gave Hawking a look. "Okay, Mr. Big Shot, why did you get picked for this plum duty assignment? Did you save the mayor or something?"

"I follow orders and keep the quips to myself." Hawking got into the driver's seat and took us to the last location on the list.

Kemper mocked Hawking, making faces behind his back, and I gave Kemper a warning look. *Stop that,* I mouthed.

When we arrived at the final building to canvass, we split up.

As I stepped onto the third floor landing, I heard a commotion coming from the end of the hallway. A man and woman were screaming, but their words were garbled. A few seconds later, the voices quieted. I gave their door a wary look, but it wasn't on our list.

Returning to my task, I knocked on the first door to the right, apartment 307, the scene of another recent break-in. No one had been hurt that time, but the owner might know something about the thief.

According to the police report, a television, blu-ray player, laptop, and two tablets were stolen from inside. The apartment owner had been picking up an extra shift at work when the break-in occurred, which may have saved his life.

"Sir, this is the police," I called through the thick door. "I have a few questions."

At my words, the door at the end of the hallway swung open. A man wearing a dark hoodie bolted from the apartment. He raced past me before I had time to process what was happening. He wore dark colors and a hood. He must have been one of the thieves.

"Stop," I yelled. "Police." I keyed the radio, requesting backup, as I darted after him.

As I raced down the two flights of stairs, Kemper came down the steps from the floor above. "Sarconi?" Kemper asked, unsure if he should run after me or wait to see what would happen.

"A suspect is fleeing the scene. He just committed another break-in. Apartment 314. Make sure no one was hurt," I called up to him. I wasn't sure if that had been the apartment where I'd heard the yelling. Why hadn't I bothered to check it out?

"On it," Kemper shouted before disappearing onto the third floor.

The suspect burst through the front door and ran to the left. I sprinted after him, gaining as we went down the next street. He was approaching a crosswalk. Just when I was close enough to take him down, an unmarked cruiser rolled to a stop in front of him. The suspect collided with the car and fell backward, his bag of loot spilling onto the ground.

I pounced, holding the suspect down while I frisked him.

"Officer Sarconi," Detective Riley greeted, taking over and handcuffing the suspect, "I believe you called for backup."

"Uh-huh." Inhaling ragged gasps, I put my hands on my head and forced my lungs to fill completely.

"Who is this guy?" Riley asked.

"I don't know, but he heard me announce I was police. That's when he burst out of another apartment and made a run for it. Given that bag," I tapped the backpack with the jewelry box hanging out the open flap, "I'd say he was in the middle of clearing out the place when I showed up."

"That was a stupid move, pal." Riley pushed the handcuffed man into the back of the car as Kemper came up behind us.

"Was anyone hurt?" I asked.

Kemper shook his head. "No one was home. We cleared the entire apartment. Hawking is keeping watch while we wait for additional backup units."

"Good job securing the scene." Riley picked up the backpack and shoved what had spilled out back inside.

Kemper held out an evidence bag that contained a velvet satchel. "He dropped this. It was in the hallway, near the stairs."

Riley narrowed his eyes at the bag before taking it from Kemper. "Nice catch. Stay here and wait with Hawking. Sarconi, you're with me."

# TWO

Detective Riley pulled the cruiser to a stop underneath an overpass and turned off the engine. The thief was handcuffed in the back, but that didn't seem to matter. Riley's attention was focused on the food trucks parked in front of us.

"Sarconi, it's lunchtime. Why don't you get us a few hot dogs?"

"Do you think now's the best time for lunch?" I asked, confused by his casual suggestion and lackadaisical attitude. "We have a suspect in custody. We need to take him in. He has to be processed and booked." I narrowed my eyes at the radio. Riley never called it in.

"You really don't need to go to the trouble," the man in the back seat said.

I turned to look at him. "Evidence suggests otherwise."

"What evidence?"

"The jewelry."

"You can't prove that's mine." The suspect's eyes darted back and forth. "For all I know, you planted that."

"Hey," Riley pointed at him, "be nice, Frank. Or I'm not buying you lunch."

"Oh, Big Spender." Frank jangled his cuffed hands. "You didn't even ask what I wanted."

Before I could say another word or ask a question, Riley turned in his seat. "What would you like, Frank?"

"Turkey dog with kraut and mustard and make sure

they hold the relish," the suspect replied. "The last time I said no relish, they gave me extra relish."

"What the hell?" I shifted my confused look back to Riley. "Who is this guy?"

"Don't worry about it, Officer Sarconi," Frank the Suspect said from the back seat. "Mikey and I go way back. That's why it's his turn to buy lunch."

"So you're a frequent flyer or a CI or something?"

Riley hid his laughter in a phony cough. "Jesus, Frank, tell her the truth. She's gonna be working with us on this case."

The suspect leaned forward and pulled his hands free from behind his back. The handcuffs hung ineffectually from his left wrist, and he offered me his hand. "I'm Frank Devereaux, the one stop shop for all your undercover needs."

"So you are a CI?" I asked, confused.

Frank grinned. "I'd show you my badge, but I don't have it on me."

"You're a cop?" I didn't believe it.

"Yeah, same as Mikey." Frank patted Detective Riley on the chest before holding out his wrist with the dangling handcuffs. "You mind taking these off now, Mike? Or does this give you some kind of thrill?" Frank looked at me. "Be careful around this one. He's into all sorts of kinky shit. His last girlfriend had the leather and lace thing going on, complete with whips and chains." He shivered. "Lots of freaky shit like that. I, on the other hand, am a gentleman and a generous lover."

"Mariah wasn't my girlfriend. She was an asset." Riley sighed, unhooking the bracelet from Frank's wrist.

"She had very nice assets, if I remember correctly. But I'm not into pain. But whatever gets your engine going, Mike."

Riley rolled his eyes. "Shut up before you embarrass yourself further, which doesn't seem possible at this point."

"Do you think I should be embarrassed?" Frank asked me. "I'm out working while this guy's doing what? Riding around in a fancy car and playing with the siren?"

"Do you always work undercover?" I asked Frank.

He shrugged. "I do it a lot. The brass thinks I'm pretty damn good at it, which is why."

Riley let out a displeased grunt. "This guy will toot his own horn all day if you keep asking him questions." He pulled a twenty from his pocket and held it out to me. "You mind grabbing us some lunch before Frank says or does something that will make me regret not taping his mouth shut?"

"See, kinky shit. I bet he's got a ball gag hidden in his closet," Frank said.

"Frank," Riley snapped, "stop scaring her." He turned back to me with those blue eyes that froze me in place and offered a friendly smile. "Lunch is on me. Get whatever you like. And make sure they give Frank extra relish."

"Sadist," Frank muttered. "That's why you and Mariah would have been perfect."

"Shut it, Frank." Riley turned back to me with an apologetic smile. "Lunch, please?"

Taking the offered cash, I slid out of the front seat and headed to the nearest food truck. By the time I made it back to the car with a sack of hot dogs and fries, Riley and Frank were having a heated sports discussion. I ate in silence while I listened to them talk about last night's baseball game.

Neither mentioned a word about the current case or why an undercover cop had broken into an apartment in the building we were canvassing or had fled the scene. None of it sat right with me, but I didn't know enough about the situation yet. After all, I was only helping out for this one shift, or so I thought.

"Okay, the coast is clear," Riley said after Frank finished his lunch. "Watch yourself out there. If we arrest you again, we'll have to book you. Today, you were lucky Sarconi didn't cuff you before I arrived, or someone would have spotted you on the street and expected to see you in lock-up. So stop being stupid, and think before you leap. If you hear us outside an apartment you're in, by all means, stay put. Don't go running out like some shit-for-brains banger. That's how they get caught, and that's how you got caught."

"How do you know it wasn't part of my cover?" Frank

asked.

Riley gave him a hard look. "Do you want us to book you?"

"Not today, but I'll let you know if I change my mind." Frank waited for Riley to open the back door and hand him the backpack. "I'll catch you guys later. Nice meeting you, Officer Sarconi. Remember what I said about this one." Frank disappeared down the street.

"Crazy day, huh?" Riley said, getting back into the car. "I'm guessing you weren't expecting this."

"We're cops. When do we ever know what to expect?"

"Never." He checked the time, dug into the lunch bag, and retrieved a handful of fries. "For the record, I've never dated a dominatrix."

"None of my business," I said.

He cocked an eyebrow. "Are you into that sort of thing? It's okay if you are. No judgment here."

"Why would you ask me that? Is it because I worked vice?"

He shook his head. "Sorry. I didn't mean anything by it. I wasn't thinking. Frank's got me twisted around. Let's start over. Why don't you tell me about yourself, Alessandra?"

"I prefer Lexie."

"Interesting." He chewed on a fry. "How do you get that from Alessandra?"

"The short answer, my parents are insane."

"They sound like mine." He held out the bag of fries. "What's the long answer?"

I helped myself to a few, wondering why we were wasting time when the gangs unit had been swamped and needed to recruit additional officers to lend a hand. "When I was little, my parents called me Alessi. In kindergarten, the teacher had an accent, so it sounded like Alexi. The other kids started calling me Lexie, and it stuck."

He thought about it while he chewed. "Whatever works. Speaking of," he jerked his head toward the back seat, "how much experience do you have chasing down suspects?"

"Enough."

"You're fast. Frank wasn't expecting that."

"I like to run."

"It shows. But regardless, you took the whole thing better than I thought you would. Do you have any experience working undercover?"

I narrowed my eyes. "Didn't Lt. Peterson mention I transferred back to patrol from vice?"

"Uh-huh." His eyes told me he knew, so I didn't know why he bothered asking.

"Yeah, so I'm used to acting as a decoy and seeing tons of weird shit. I'm pretty sure whatever fetishes you have, I've seen and heard before."

"I don't have any weird fetishes," he said.

"Whatever. No judgment."

He snickered. "I walked right into that one."

"Yes, you did."

He wiped his mouth and tossed the napkin into the bag. "You look like you want to say something else. Go ahead."

"Don't we have work to do?"

"We are working."

"How? By guarding the food trucks?"

"We have to eat, and Frank needed some time to decompress. You were a decoy. You know what it's like."

"Sure, but Kemper and Hawking are still at the scene." I blinked. "Fake scene. Shouldn't we tell them?"

"We will eventually, but for now, we have to make it look real in order to keep Frank's cover intact. It's also why you and I are taking our time here. We don't want the other cops to realize it was a rouse or they'll make a half-assed attempt at combing the scene. Someone will blab. It'll get overheard, and word will get back to the gang. We don't want Frank to be compromised."

"You're overthinking," I said.

"Are you sure about that?" Riley stared at me. "My badge says detective. This is my regular unit. Don't you think I know what I'm doing?"

"I sure as shit hope so."

He chuckled. "Me too."

I cracked a smile, finding his infectious. "Sorry. I'm not used to this. We didn't run our plays like this in vice."

"It would have been weird if you did. But I'd think with

that Jack-the-Ripper-esque serial killer case, you might have."

"Don't remind me."

"Hey, you've got something right there." He leaned in and ran his thumb across my bottom lip. Instantly, my heart fluttered, and I stared out the windshield, afraid he would notice my blush. I wasn't used to being touched like that at work, unless it was by someone who'd end up cuffed and in the back of a squad car. Riley pulled his hand away, inspecting his finger. "Ketchup," he announced. "Apparently, there was a fatality involving a tomato. My prime suspect is," he picked up the ketchup packet and read the name, "Mr. Hunt."

"Cute."

He gave me a sideways look, possibly expecting more from that exchange. "Yes, you are. That's why they had you working vice, isn't it?"

I shrugged.

"Did you ask to go back to patrol?" he wheedled.

"I'm an officer," I said. "It's not like I have my pick of assignments."

"But you could, if you make detective."

"We'll see." Why was everyone obsessed with my career goals? Most days, no one asked such questions. Today, I'd been asked the same thing twice, and we were only a few hours into shift.

"I'm sorry about the bogus bust. Lightman likes to play ops close to the vest. Frank was supposed to have cleared out by the time you showed up, but we must have gotten our wires crossed somewhere. I'm sure no one will hold today against you."

"Against me?" I sputtered. "I didn't do anything wrong."

He held up his palms. "You don't have to convince me. I was there."

"You arrested Frank, not me."

"Technically, I cuffed him. We never arrested him. That would have required a lot of additional paperwork. I try to avoid that as much as I can. But if I hadn't gotten there in time, you would have arrested him, and Frank would have been in a big mess. You would have been the one who jammed him up. So you're welcome."

"Unbelievable."

"I am, and thank you."

Sometimes, I wondered why I even wanted this job. "Someone should have warned us."

"Us?"

"Kemper, Hawking, and me."

"Like I said, Frank wasn't supposed to be there. But I'll make sure you have better intel in the future. Okay?"

"Fine."

Riley played with the key in the ignition. "It all worked out. No harm done."

"You just said—" I shook my head. "Never mind. Shouldn't we get back to the station? Don't we need to fill out a report or something?"

"I guess, but be careful what you write." He put the car in gear and pulled into traffic. "Why'd you become a cop? You could have done something else. Lawyer, doctor, artist, professional runner."

"Yeah, I had plenty of options. It was either this or work in my parents' luggage shop. And frankly, I hate luggage. This makes more sense. The work we do is important."

"Did something happen to you?"

"No, but growing up, my family didn't always live in the best neighborhoods. A lot of our neighbors and friends were targeted. The neighborhood shops had to pay protection money to stay in business. Occasionally, someone would just vanish. It wasn't a good situation."

"Where'd you grow up?"

"On the southside, before it was gentrified. Organized crime was on the way out, but a few of the established families hung on as long as they could. Not to be a bad joke or cliché, but you know how things go in the Italian neighborhoods."

"I hear it's like that now in Little Moscow and parts of Chinatown. OCU has its hands full with all sorts of things. You must have learned to be tough at a young age."

"I never really thought about it. It was just how things were. My parents moved out of the neighborhood when I started high school, and we left that world behind."

"Not all of it. Something stuck. That's why you're doing this job."

"Maybe." I fell silent, contemplating how my life might have gone differently if I hadn't always been driven to right the wrongs I had seen as a kid.

"Why'd you leave vice?" he asked.

"Why are you asking so many questions?"

"Side effect of the detective's badge."

"I never wanted to work vice, but that's where I was assigned after I finished training."

"You didn't like it?"

"Being female and a cop comes with enough objectification, but those perverts take it to an entirely different level. The serial killer thing didn't help."

"Yeah, I heard something about that. What did they have you doing?"

"They sent me out as bait. I was alone in a room with the killer for what felt like an eternity. After that, I needed a change." I chuckled. "It's funny since that's the only case I ever worked that really seemed to matter. The rest of them were just demeaning. So a transfer was in order, but most of the guys around the station like to make jokes about vice cops, especially the decoys. At this point, I'd prefer if people didn't know who I was."

"You shouldn't let them get away with it," Riley said. "If someone's being a dick, report him."

"In that case, watch yourself."

He cocked an eyebrow up at me. "You think I'm a dick?"

"Jury's out."

He ignored the quip. "I'm serious. Don't put up with that crap. There's no reason for it."

"You're right, but we both know how it'll turn out." We remained quiet for a few minutes, and then I asked, "How long have you been on the job, Riley?"

"It's Michael." He dazzled me with a bright smile. "If we're going to be working together, we should be on a first name basis."

"Working together?"

"Gangs needs more officers to fill in since we're spread so thin. I'm looking for someone to ride with. Usually, it's

Sam or Jack, but we can't focus our manpower like that with so many crimes coming in all at once."

"That's why you've been asking so many questions. Was this a job interview?"

He shrugged. "You didn't think this assignment was just for the day, did you?"

"I thought it might be."

"No, it'll be for the duration." He tapped his fingers on the steering wheel. "To answer your question, I've been doing this for six years. Actually, it's almost seven. It's the family business. My dad was a cop, his dad, and his dad. Both of my brothers are cops. It wasn't a decision so much as a way of life." He stopped at a traffic light. "Anyway, getting back to business for a sec, if Frank had been an actual perp, you would have made a fantastic collar. You have skills, and your reputation precedes you. So what do you say? I'll ask Jack to assign us to work together, if you're cool with it." A thought dawned on him. "Were you hoping to partner with Samantha Preston? I don't see Jack agreeing to it, but you could ask. Still, I picked you. That should count for something."

"Why me?"

"You show promise and initiative, at least more than Hawking or Kemper. As far as I'm concerned, that makes you special. I'd like to see you in action."

"Do you use that line on all the women?"

"Are you always such a ball-buster?"

I pinched my pointer finger and thumb together. "A little bit."

He parked in the back lot. "All I'm offering is a chance to get out of uniform and see what life's like as a detective. What do you say?"

"Yeah, okay."

"Great. Now the real fun starts."

# THREE

Despite being invited to work the investigation with the detectives, Lightman and Preston kept me at arms' length. I was an officer, on the job for a little over four years, and unless they wanted me to take my clothes off and solicit sex, they saw no practical use for me. Kemper and Hawking weren't treated much better. They were unlucky enough to have to ride with Preston and Lightman. The only tasks they were assigned involved taking notes and scouting scenes. Riley was the exception. He let me spitball ideas about means, motive, and opportunity. Agreeing to work with him had been the right choice, and he had no problem reminding me of it on a daily basis.

The break-ins still hadn't stopped. They'd only gotten worse. I was a week into this posting when another call came in. The thieves hadn't hit an apartment this time. Instead, they broke into a storage unit. Four handguns and two hunting rifles had been taken, along with estimated cash and property worth twenty-two thousand dollars.

"How do you think they found out about this place?" I asked as we surveyed the outside of the ransacked storage unit. The lock had been cut off, and the metal roll-up door had dents, as if the thieves had backed a truck into it.

Riley peered inside. "The better question is why didn't they take everything?"

"You said they're interested in specific items." I slipped

on a pair of latex gloves and stepped inside. "Are you thinking this was done by a different crew?"

"I don't know. The MO's different. This storage facility is out of range of the suspected gang's territory. Then again, we have yet to prove the MC is responsible for this spree." He crouched down, examining something on the ground near the door. "I'll see what the security footage shows. Maybe they rode their bikes here when they ransacked the place."

"What do you want me to do?"

"Solve the crime spree."

"While you're gone?"

"Sure, why not?"

I muttered a few things about the arrogant detective under my breath while I moved deeper into the storage unit. On the bright side, no one had been injured, but this wasn't just a break-in, it was also a drive-by. The rental office had been sprayed with bullets. The manager said it happened before the break-in, but given how close this unit was to the office and front gate, I suspected the events occurred almost simultaneously. There was no better way to keep people from interfering than shooting at them.

The thieves wouldn't have had time to take everything because the shooting put them on a clock. They knew the police would respond. They didn't have long to wait.

I called dispatch. The nearest patrol car was seven minutes out when the call came in. I wasn't sure how the thieves would know that, but they could have been clocking patrol or testing response times with their other crimes to see how much time they had. But what was so special about this unit? How did they know this was the one to hit?

I looked around. The storage unit had the typical things I'd expect to find. Old furniture, baby clothes, decorations, and outdoor equipment. How did they know they'd find cash, jewelry, and guns in here?

Pulling out my notepad, I read the name from the rental agreement. S. Stanfield. The name rang a bell, and I flipped back to my other notes, finding that Stuart Stanfield had been listed as next of kin for a victim in one of the previous home invasions. Four days ago, Kathryn Stanfield had returned home from work to find two men in her apartment. They brutally beat her and threatened to kill her. She must have told them about her husband's storage unit.

I opened one of the boxes and peered inside. It contained a wedding dress, shoes, and bridal accessories. Replacing the tape, I opened another box. This one had dozens of photo albums. The boxes weren't labeled with what they contained, but they were labeled by room. This one said den. The one with the dress said bedroom. "That's how they knew which boxes to take."

"What was that?" Riley asked, returning from his trip to the manager's office. "You figured it out already?"

"Would that surprise you?"

"Not at all." He fought to keep the satisfied smile off his face. "I knew you were special."

I told him everything I'd discovered. "It has to be the same thieves. They beat Kathryn Stanfield until she told them where to find guns and money. But I'm wondering how they knew her family possessed such things."

"Let's deal with one mystery at a time. Right now, we know these two crimes were committed by the same thieves."

"You're sure?" I glanced at the security office several yards away. The camera out front must have recorded everything. "Were they on motorcycles?"

"Nope." Riley held up a USB drive. "Footage shows an SUV committed the drive-by."

"Okay, so how is that a good thing? Did you get a plate?"

"No."

I didn't understand. "What about a clear shot of the driver or whoever was inside the vehicle?"

"They wore masks."

"Then why are you so happy?"

"*We* finally have proof." He tucked the device into his pocket for safe keeping, a smug look on his face. "I knew I picked a winner."

"Excuse me."

He shook away my comment. "The gang was smart enough to remove the plates from their SUV, but they weren't smart enough to cover the VIN. The exterior security cameras caught it on video. The car's registered to William 'Big Bill' Dempsey."

"Who?"

"You'll see." Riley called to the members of the crime scene unit, letting them know we were done so they could resume what they were doing, and opened the car door. "C'mon, Lex. Let's go."

Once I was settled in my seat, Riley whipped the car around and headed back to the neighborhood I'd canvassed. "Big Bill runs the Street Bishops. They're a small operation. He's got a dozen guys under him. They operate out of a bar, Bishop's Bar. It's a seedy place. Pool hall. Strip joint. It's where you'd expect a motorcycle club to hang out."

"I'm familiar with such establishments."

"The Street Bishops usually keep to themselves. The trouble they cause tends to be isolated to the neighborhood. This is out of the norm for them. I wonder what's going on."

"You work for gangs. Shouldn't you know?"

"That's my point. Big Bill shouldn't be running an initiation like this. He's never been interested in expanding his ranks this quickly. Something's going on. Something we don't know about." He squeezed the steering wheel a few times, the muscles in his forearms bunching. "When we get there, stay on your toes."

"Copy that."

When we arrived at the bar, Riley blocked the alleyway with the car. Eight or ten motorcycles were parked in two neat lines. Two bikers eyed us as we stepped out of the vehicle. The look they gave us said two words: *Fresh meat.*

"Evening, gentlemen." Riley waved at them as he pulled open the door to the bar. "Has happy hour started yet?"

"I smell bacon," one of them said.

Riley sniffed deeply. "Don't get my hopes up. I'm a sucker for the stuff."

"Fuck off," the man on the left said.

Riley gave him a contemptuous smile. "You too." Then he stepped inside.

The two men eyed me, but they didn't say a word. I followed Riley into the bar, aware of them entering after me. Those were basic intimidation tactics, but it'd take more than that to scare me.

I scanned the room. Eight guys were inside, drinking. Three were at a booth near the back. Another three were throwing darts. And two were watching an overworked woman in tasseled pasties and a thong twirl around a greasy pole near the back of the room.

They sat on a ripped leather couch that would light up like a Christmas tree under a blacklight. The bartender was the only one not carrying, but something told me he had a firearm concealed beneath the bar top.

"What can I get you?" he asked as Riley and I made our way to the bar.

The two men from outside remained behind us. They didn't close the distance, but they'd make leaving a problem. I didn't bother mentioning it to Riley, since I was sure he knew, but I didn't like the odds of us getting out of here without drawing down on them.

"I'm looking for Big Bill," Riley said.

The bartender narrowed his eyes at the shiny gold badge hanging from Riley's neck. "He's over there." He pointed to a booth in a dark corner, where two other men kept Big Bill company. The bartender filled a glass and shoved it toward Riley. "If you're gonna talk to him, bring him that."

Riley gave the whiskey a look and picked up the glass. "Sure." He turned around. "C'mon, Lex. We're gonna serve."

"That's right, pig," the goon from earlier muttered.

Riley pretended not to hear him, so I followed the detective's lead. I never worked gangs, but I knew the members of the unit had their own rhythm and way of handling suspects on the street. But the tiny hairs at the back of my neck stood at attention.

The stripper slid on the stage, her heel making a scratching whine that sounded like nails on a chalkboard. The man playing darts missed, and the idiot with the pig comments cringed, covering his ears.

I glanced at her, but from what I could tell, her skid

hadn't been intentional. Riley didn't even turn at the sound. He had his sights set on the man wearing the ten gallon hat and shiny black cowboy boots. No wonder they called him Big Bill.

Riley put the glass on the table while I lingered near an empty booth, keeping an eye on the two men who had followed us inside. They had remained at the bar, their eyes on us. They had tucked their weapons into the front of their waistbands for easier access. They expected trouble. But shooting cops would be the worst thing they could do. They had to know hell would rain down on them, but that didn't stop them from making the unspoken threat.

"Take a walk," Riley said, giving the two men with Big Bill the evil eye.

Big Bill nodded, and they slid out of the booth.

Riley gave them a bright smile as they pushed past him. "Thanks for keeping the seat warm." He glanced at me, his gaze darting to the empty table across from the booth.

Taking the hint, I sat down, my back to the wall, the rest of me angled to see the bar. Every eye inside was on us. Even the men watching the dancer had lost interest. This wasn't good.

"What do you want?" Big Bill asked, picking up the whiskey and taking a sip.

"I have a question for you." Riley leaned back, appearing relaxed and in control. "Where's your SUV?"

"My what?"

"Give me a break," Riley said. "That big thing with four wheels that you drive around in when you're not here or on your bike. Where is it?"

"Why do you care?"

Riley gave me a look. "Do you want to tell him?"

"It was used to commit a drive-by. We have video footage to prove it," I said.

"Oh." Big Bill rubbed his chin. "That SUV. Yeah, it was stolen. I didn't get a chance to report it yet."

"Well, since we're here, how about we take your statement?" Riley said. "When's the last time you saw it?"

"I don't remember."

"Uh-huh." Riley looked around. "Do you think any of

your friends might remember?"

They stared at each other for a long time. Big Bill sipped his drink and gestured to the bartender for another one. "Nope."

"Are you always this quiet?" Riley asked.

"I don't have much to say. I parked it in the alley. When I went to use it. It was gone. Simple as that."

"Where were you when the drive-by occurred?" Riley asked.

Big Bill chuckled. "I was here. Ask anyone. They'll vouch for me."

"That's funny," I said. "We never told you when the drive-by happened."

"That doesn't matter, doll," Big Bill said. "I'm always here. I work here. I live here. I never go anywhere."

"Seems like that violates some kind of health code," I said. "You live in a bar?"

"In an apartment upstairs. Why's it matter?"

"Can we see it?" I asked.

Riley glanced at me before returning his attention to Big Bill. "My partner's into all those house hunting shows. What do you say? Give her a thrill?"

Big Bill eyed me up and down. "I'd be happy to give her a thrill."

"Great," Riley gritted out.

Big Bill got out of the booth. "Hold down the fort. I'll be back in five. If I'm not, you know what to do."

The men who'd been sitting with him nodded.

Big Bill sized up Riley before gesturing that I go ahead of them. "The stairs are to the left, right behind that curtain, sweet face."

After glancing at Riley, who nodded, I got up from the table and pushed through the curtain, expecting to be jumped or attacked. But no one was hiding in the tiny, dark hallway.

The stairs were where Big Bill said, and I went up them, feeling claustrophobic at how narrow they were. Big Bill clambered along behind me, reached around, pushed the door open, and ushered me inside.

Moving silently into the dark apartment, I rested my

hand on the handle of my weapon as I looked around the studio apartment. The fold-out couch remained open, the sheets tangled and hanging over the side. An overflowing pile of dishes took over the sink and counter. A container of milk remained open and sideways, creating a funk that would take days to clear away. But it was overpowered by the scent of microwaved cheese, day old fish, and ass.

I spotted an open duffel bag on the floor with a video game system, a few games, and a tablet. “Hey, Riley,” I pointed down at the bag, “take a look at this.”

“Those are gifts. I was shopping for my girlfriend’s kids. I got receipts around here somewhere,” Big Bill insisted.

Riley sifted through the open bag, but without any way to ID the owners of the items, we didn’t have enough to make an arrest. “Cut the bullshit. What’s going on, Bill? You normally fly below our radar. You take care of your business and don’t get in the way. You leave everyone alone, and we leave you alone. But you’ve broken our unspoken agreement. What gives?”

“Nothing. I told you my SUV was jacked. I got nothing to do with anything.”

Riley made a tsk sound. “We know about the initiation. We know you’re responsible for the home invasions and knocking over the local shops. It’s just a matter of time before we arrest someone who’ll roll on you. I suggest you call off whatever this is and tell us which of your biker buddies committed the home invasions. They’ll face charges, and you can get back to business as usual.”

“I can’t do that,” Big Bill said. “I don’t know nothing about it.”

Riley moved closer until they were practically nose to nose. “Yes, you do. Tell me what’s going on.” He narrowed his eyes. “You’re sweating. You’re scared. What are you afraid of?”

“Nothing,” Bill grunted. “I’m not a snitch.”

“He’s afraid of someone,” I said.

Bill’s eyes went wide at my words, and Riley caught on. “She’s right. I thought you were running the show. What happened? Did someone else take over? Is that why you’re expanding your reach beyond the neighborhood?”

"Unless you got enough to arrest me, I want you out." Bill pointed to the door.

Riley stepped back. "We'll be back with a warrant, unless you want to save us the trouble."

"Bite me," Bill said.

"You invited us up here for a reason," I said. "You want to tell us something. You wouldn't have done it otherwise."

Riley grinned. "She's right again. Every time she points out the obvious, your eyebrows lift in surprise. Tell us something. If you send us away empty-handed, we'll be back with reinforcements. And no one wants that."

"The Street Bishops want no part of this. You want to blame someone, look at the V-7s."

"Why?" Riley asked.

Big Bill shook his head. "I told you what you need to know. Now get out of my place."

# FOUR

"None of this makes any sense," Riley muttered.

I glanced at the bar. "Don't you think we should get out of here? We have an audience."

"That's why we're hanging around."

"Are we waiting for someone to shoot us?"

"Relax. They're not stupid enough to do something like that."

"You wanna bet?"

He almost smiled. "Don't you trust me?"

"I'm not sure."

He snickered, pulling out a paper map from the glove box and spreading it out on the hood of the car. He ran his finger along the street we were on and looked up. Removing the pen from his pocket, he marked the locations of everything from the home invasions to the hold-ups at the liquor store and mini-marts. "The Street Bishops never preyed on innocent people before. Until this latest crime spree, they used to stick to these three blocks and take care of the neighborhood and the people in it. I'm not saying it wasn't their own brand of justice, but incidents weren't this widespread. The people they targeted owed them or had done something they took issue with. If they are behind all the recent break-ins and robberies, that means their way of conducting business has changed."

"Are you sure it's them?" I lowered my voice. "Big Bill suggested otherwise."

"Right, because criminals always tell the truth."

"I didn't say that."

"I know, but the SUV was his. No one would have the stones to steal it. That means the storage unit was knocked over by his crew. I have no doubt about that. I'm just wondering why he's venturing so far out of the neighborhood. Half of these incidents occurred beyond his normal reach." Riley drew on the map. "These areas are controlled by other gangs and motorcycle clubs. Violating the boundaries could result in a turf war. Big Bill knows that, which makes me wonder why he'd risk it."

"Could the MC be under new management?"

"If it is, we haven't heard about it."

"What about Frank?"

Riley shook his head. "He hasn't gotten as deep as we'd like. He wouldn't be privy to changes going on behind the scenes."

"Word is the Street Bishops are initiating new members, right?"

"Yeah."

"So if they're hurting for cash or guns, they send out fresh blood to get it however they can. The newbies aren't part of the club yet, so they wouldn't have to follow the same rules. They could steal from innocent people, perform drive-bys, and avoid setting off a turf war since they technically aren't part of the Street Bishops."

"Maybe, but that's splitting hairs. I'm not sure the other gangs would buy it." Riley blew out a breath and glanced back at the bar. "I've never seen the bar this empty. Usually, there are a lot more bikes and a lot more bikers. Something has definitely changed."

"Is this the only place they hang out?"

"As far as I know."

"Maybe Big Bill decided to open a second location. Isn't that the American dream? You start with one place and eventually end up with a few dozen. That would explain why he needs additional capital and why most of the club isn't hanging out here. Perhaps he franchised."

Riley laughed. "That must be it." He tucked the map away and surveyed the area. A few men from a rival MC watched us from the end of the block. "Maybe we should see if they have anything to say on the subject of the Street Bishops' expansion."

"Who are they?" I asked, falling into step with Riley.

"Those are the Southside Slingers."

"Not the V-7s?"

"The V-7s control the area two blocks north of here."

"You weren't kidding when you said the Street Bishops controlled three blocks?"

"Nope."

"That's a very small operation."

"Which is why this is troubling." Riley glanced both ways before crossing the street. "Big Bill never struck me as the type to have a Napoleon complex, so I'm wondering if he's been threatened. If someone else is moving in on his turf—"

"Like the V-7s?"

"He'd have to encroach on someone else's turf or defend his territory by increasing the number of rank and file. That may also explain the sudden recruitment campaign and the need for cash and firearms."

"Why can't we arrest him for the drive-by?"

"You heard him. He'll say the SUV was stolen, and every biker in there will swear to it. It won't get us anywhere. We need more. Something irrefutable."

The conversation dropped away as we approached the two rival bikers. One of them smoked a cigarette, blowing smoke rings while the other stared in our direction as if in a stupor.

"Hey," Riley said, his hands on his hips, "how's it hanging?"

The one blowing the smoke rings grabbed his junk and readjusted. "A little to the left," he said, his eyes on me.

Riley moved a step forward, blocking the biker's view of me. "Is anything going on I should know about?"

"I can't think of anything." Smoke Rings nudged the guy beside him. "What about you? You think of anything this cop should know?"

"Nothing comes to mind," his pal replied.

"See? Nothing doing," Smoke Rings said.

“Word is a war’s coming.” Riley glanced at the Street Bishops’ bar before returning his attention to the men.

“If it is, it has nothing to do with us.” Smoke Rings sat up a little straighter. “The Slingers want no part in anything. We keep to ourselves and take care of our own.”

“Can I have your word on that?” Riley asked.

Smoke Rings nodded. “Whatever pops off has nothing to do with us. We got no part in this.”

“What is this?” I asked.

Smoke Rings blew a puff in my direction, but Riley dissipated the lopsided circle with a wave of his hand. Smoke Rings looked disappointed but let it slide. “Did you not hear us say we keep to ourselves?”

“Any idea who might be causing trouble?” Riley asked.

“You just spoke to him.”

Riley tucked his hand into his pocket before extending it to Smoke Rings. They shook, and Riley took a step back. Smoke Rings tucked the cash for the intel into his vest pocket.

“Are you sure you don’t remember anything else? Maybe something has come to mind,” Riley said.

“I told you everything.”

“All right.” Riley exhaled. “You hear something, I expect you’ll get in touch.”

# FIVE

"Mrs. Stanfield?" I knocked gently on the door to her hospital room. "I'm Officer Sarconi. This is Detective Riley. May we have a word with you?"

The woman nodded to us, muting the TV. Her arm was in a cast and her face was bruised. The doctor said she had a few broken ribs to go with the broken arm.

"How are you feeling?" Riley asked. "Is there anything we can get you?"

"I'm okay," Kathryn Stanfield said. "What do you want? I already gave you my statement."

Riley placed his hand on the small of my back, gently pushing me forward. He wanted me to take point on this interview. I hadn't expected that, but I didn't let it throw me.

"Mrs. Stanfield," I sat in the chair beside her bed, "did anyone inform you that your husband's storage unit was robbed?"

She stared at the flickering TV screen. "Uh-huh. Stuart went to the station to answer questions and file a report. It's crazy how we could be victimized twice in one week."

"Is it?"

She fidgeted with the hem of the blanket. "Do you think this was intentional?"

"We do, ma'am," Riley said. "Do you know why you'd be targeted? Do you owe anyone money?"

"No," she insisted. "When we could no longer afford our

house, we put our things in storage and moved to that apartment. We've been working our asses off to save as much as we can, but it looks like that was a waste."

"Did you take out insurance on your storage unit?" I asked.

She nodded. A millisecond later, her eyes met mine. "We didn't do this. This isn't a scheme. I swear."

"No one thinks that," Riley said. "Would you mind taking a look at a few photos?" He held out a tablet with the mugshots of the Street Bishops. "Did any of these men attack you?"

She flipped through the photos, barely glancing at them. "I don't remember."

"Have you or your husband had any run-ins with the Street Bishops?" I asked.

She stared at the blanket. "Who?"

"They're a motorcycle club," I said. "They have a bar a few blocks from your apartment. Maybe you've been there."

"No. No way. We don't ride. We never have. Why would we go anywhere near there?"

Riley gently nudged me, urging me to move on with the questions.

"When these men broke into your storage unit," I said, "they only took firearms, cash, and jewelry. According to your husband, the estimated worth was twenty-two thousand. Why were you keeping valuables in your unit?"

"Stuart doesn't trust banks. He's weird about that. He always has been. My paychecks go into our checking and savings accounts. He kept his savings in a lockbox in the storage unit."

"Who knew about it?" Riley and I asked at the same time. He chuckled, and I looked up to see if he wanted to take over the interview, but he shook his head.

"No one," Kathryn Stanfield said.

"Really? Because your belongings weren't ransacked. The thieves broke in, found exactly what they wanted, and left. Most of the boxes remained untouched. You said this wasn't an inside job, so we'd like to know how they knew where everything was stored."

Footsteps sounded outside the door, and the blood drained from her face. I turned to see who was there, but it was an orderly making the rounds. Riley moved to the doorway and peered into the hallway. Once he was satisfied danger wasn't lurking outside, he pulled the door closed.

"Did someone threaten you?" he asked.

Mrs. Stanfield shook her head. "No. I just don't know anything. I don't know how they knew."

"Mrs. Stanfield," I patted her hand, hoping to comfort her, "I know how scary this must be. Those men broke into your home. They stole from you. They attacked you. They beat you." I paused, seeing her chin quiver. "Why did they do that? What did they want?"

She swallowed, shaking her head.

"You told them about the storage unit," Riley said softly. "We can protect you. We'll make sure they never harm you again. Just tell us who they are and what they wanted."

"Nothing." But it was a lie.

"Please, we'll keep you safe." I gave her hand a squeeze, but she pulled it free from my grip.

"You said they wanted money, guns, and jewelry. They cleaned out our apartment, but we don't keep a lot of our valuables there. They were mad that they wasted that much time and energy for next to nothing. That's why they beat me. That's it. That's all there is to it. Now if you don't mind, I'd like to rest." She turned the volume up on the TV and lowered the incline on the hospital bed.

"We're sorry we upset you," Riley said. "But I don't want the men who did this to get away with it. And I don't want them to hurt anyone else."

She nodded, but she wouldn't look at us.

"I'll assign an officer to stand guard," he said.

Her eyes brightened, and a smile tugged at her quivering lips. "Thank you."

"Sure." He tapped me on the shoulder. "C'mon, it's time we let Mrs. Stanfield rest."

I got up from the chair. "I hope you feel better soon."

Once we were back in the hallway, Riley made the request to have an officer stand guard. When he concluded his call, he tucked his phone away. "She's scared. I think whoever attacked her paid her another visit and told her to keep her mouth shut."

"I agree."

Riley headed for the nurses' station and flashed his badge. After updating them on the situation, we were pointed in the direction of the security office. We made our way through the labyrinthine hallways.

"Let me do the talking," Riley said.

I held up my palms and took a step back.

He knocked on the door before trying the knob. A man in a suit sat behind a desk. Behind him were a dozen monitors mounted to the wall. Riley updated the head of security on the situation.

"This is a healthcare facility. Patient privacy is important. I'll need a court order before I can turn over that information."

"I'll get right on that." Riley turned, frustration creasing the corners of his eyes and tightening his jaw muscles.

I followed him out of the hospital, where he sat on the closest bench and made a few calls. While I waited, I scanned the vicinity. Several people were on their way inside. A few were visiting. Some appeared to be checking in. A rumbling engine caught my attention, but now that the sun had set, it was hard to see the parking lot. On the plus side, it didn't sound like a motorcycle.

"Dammit." Riley squeezed his phone, resisting the urge to throw it. "We don't have enough for a judge to sign off. We have no proof Mrs. Stanfield was threatened or coerced. We'll have to speak to her husband and see if he can shed some light on this. If he'll go on the record, then we can get a look at the hospital footage and see who may have threatened Kathryn Stanfield." He got off the bench, circling a few times with his hands on his head. "I hate this. While we wait, who knows how many more households will be victimized. We've been fortunate that the casualties up until now have been kept to a minimum, but it's just a matter of time. Violence begets more violence."

"Is that a commandment?"

Riley growled at me.

"I have an idea." Digging out my phone, I took a breath.

"Give me a sec."

"Why? What can you possibly do that I can't?"

"For one thing, I can run in high heels. For another, my best friend is an administrator at this hospital. Keep your fingers crossed she has enough clout to get us a look at the security footage."

# SIX

I put my phone away.

"Well?" Riley asked.

"She thinks she can get us something unofficial, if we want it." I eyed him. "Do we?"

"Absolutely."

"That's what I figured." I checked the time and cast my gaze at the entrance. "It'll be a few minutes. She has to sweet talk Barry into doing her a favor."

"Barry?"

"One of the security guards," I said.

"How is she going to manage that?"

"My best friend can talk anyone into anything. She should have been a realtor or salesperson. Instead, she went into the medical field, only to realize she hated blood and bodily fluids, which is why she went into administration. She could work as a nurse, but she prefers telling them what to do." I snickered. "My best friend's always been bossy."

"I can't imagine anyone bossing you around."

"Really? Haven't you been bossing me around since we met?"

Riley rubbed his mouth to hide a grin. "You like to push back." A devious thought flitted through his mind. His pupils dilated slightly, and he looked away.

"What?"

"Nothing." He looked shy, which was new for him. "I

was just thinking I like a woman who pushes back."

We stared at one another, the air charged around us. Did he find me as attractive as I found him? I dismissed the possibility, breaking eye contact and glancing at the hospital doors.

"I'm gonna wait in the lobby. Amber said she'd bring a copy of the files down to us."

He ran a hand through his hair. "I'll wait here and update the team." He pulled out his phone and dialed.

Once he turned his back to me, I went inside, confused as to our odd exchange. It was getting late. We were nearing the end of our shift. We were just tired. That's all it was.

While I waited for Amber, I bought two coffees from the cart. One for me, and one for Riley. He liked his with a splash of hazelnut creamer. If they didn't have that, regular cream would suffice, but never mocha. We'd only been working together for a week, but I already had his coffee order memorized. Clearly, we were working too much and spending too much time together.

"Lexie," Amber called as she stepped out of the elevator, "is that for me?" She pointed to the paper cup beside mine.

"No."

"Well, fine. Be that way." She held the stern look as long as she could before giggling. "I'm just messing with you." She held out a USB drive. "Here's the footage. All I could get you was the front door. Nothing else."

"What about a list of visitors? We need to know who paid Kathryn Stanfield a visit."

"The hospital doesn't keep records like that unless we're dealing with the maternity ward, ICU, or one of the locked floors." She narrowed her eyes at the untouched coffee. "Who's that for?"

"The detective I'm working with."

She made a show of looking around. "Is he invisible?"

"He's outside. On the phone."

She nodded at the cup. "Did you spit in his drink?"

"Amber," my eyes went wide, "no. I'd never do that."

"How's he treating you?"

"Fine. Better than how the other detectives have been

treating us."

"Us?"

I wanted to explain, but now wasn't the time. "We'll catch up soon. I promise."

"Call me," she insisted, walking backward toward the elevator. "We haven't hung out in months. I miss you."

"I miss you too. I'll call you in a few days."

"I'm holding you to that." She pointed at me. "I love ya, Lex."

"Love you too."

The man at the coffee cart gave me a strange look.

"What?" I asked. "Don't you tell your best friend you love him?"

"Uh...no." He rubbed the scruff on his cheek.

I picked up the two cups. "Well, maybe you should." And then I went out the door.

Detective Riley drank his coffee while I told him what the footage contained. "Once we know who came to the hospital, we'll take it from there. Set up surveillance, knock on some doors, and remind these bastards they can't intimidate witnesses or victims."

"Why do you think they'd risk it?" I asked as we made our way through the parking lot. "If they were so concerned Stanfield would identify them, why didn't they kill her?"

He didn't answer. Instead, he drained his cup and tossed it into a nearby trash can.

"Is that why you think they'll escalate?"

"It's human nature to learn from your mistakes," Riley said. "Unfortunately, I don't think they learned crime is wrong. Instead, they learned it's best not to get caught. My guess is they wore masks when they broke in and attacked her. CSU didn't find fingerprints or hair at the scene. So they were careful. When we originally questioned her, Mrs. Stanfield said they were covered from head to toe, that she couldn't see their faces, and didn't recognize their voices."

"But if they came back to pay her a visit, she would have had a better chance of identifying them because someone would have noticed a man walking through the hospital in a balaclava, so they must have exposed their identities to her when they warned her not to talk."

"More than likely, whoever threatened her still had on a mask, but it may not have been enough to completely conceal his identity."

"You're thinking he had on a face mask, like the kind the medical staff and some of the patients and visitors wear."

Riley pointed at me. "Bingo."

He pulled out his phone to make a note, and that's when the engine from earlier rumbled again. It let out a sputtering growl. It was close. Too close.

I looked around, but I didn't see headlights. Without any nearby streetlights, I didn't spot the car. Scanning the rows of parked cars behind and beside us, I didn't see brake lights or backup lights.

But the squeal of tires and the smell of burning rubber made me react. A reflection bounced off the side of the dark-colored car as it sped toward us. It was running dark.

"Riley," I shouted, knowing my warning would come too late.

He looked in my direction, but there was no time.

I dove at him, knocking into him so hard he lost his footing and we banged into the trunk of the nearest parked car as the beater sped past us. We slid off the trunk, landing on the pavement. I lifted my head, staring into the darkness at the disappearing car. It made a sharp turn out of the lot and onto the main road. They never turned their lights on.

"Lexie?" Riley brushed a strand of my hair which had fallen loose from my bun out of his face and tucked it gently behind my ear. He stared up at me. "Are you okay?"

I looked down, finding myself on top of him. "Yeah. You?"

He tilted his head back to see if the car had gone. "Did you see the plates?"

"No."

He rubbed a bit of dirt off my cheek with his thumb. "I don't usually ask women this question, but would you mind getting off of me?"

I got back on my feet and offered him a hand up. "Sorry about that."

"Another time and place and I would have been

perfectly content letting you stay like that all night." He searched the ground for his phone. After dusting it off on his pants, he examined the screen, which had survived the hit thanks to the protective case. "At least we know one thing."

"What's that?" I asked, my eyes on the dark horizon where the car had vanished.

"We're on the right track."

# SEVEN

Preston perched on top of Riley's desk, watching as he worked on his report. "Someone actually tried to run you over? And you didn't see who it was?"

"No, Sam." He gave her an annoyed look and went back to pecking at the keyboard with two fingers.

"How can that be?"

"It was dark." He slammed his palms down on the desk, too frustrated to type. "If Lexie hadn't been there, I would have gone splat. Then we wouldn't be having this discussion. Would you have preferred that?"

She glanced in my direction. "Lexie?"

I pretended not to notice, but I watched their exchange from the corner of my eye.

"Don't start," he warned.

She held up her palms and slid off his desk. "I'm not. I'm just glad you're okay."

He assessed her. "Thanks."

Putting some distance between them, she returned to business as usual. "After watching the hospital footage, Jack sent a few units to sit on the Street Bishops. If any of them go anywhere, we'll make sure we maintain eyes. It looks like we may finally get these bastards."

"What about Kathryn Stanfield?" Riley asked.

"Ask Jack." Preston pointed to the detective as he emerged from the stairwell and entered the squad room.

Lightman gave them an odd look. "Ask me what?"

"What are we doing to keep Stanfield safe?" Riley repeated.

"Officers are posted outside her room. No one's going near her without us knowing about it. Our biggest problem is finding out who tried to mow down a couple of cops outside a hospital. Traffic cam footage of the area caught the car. Dark-colored, older model, two door. But the plates were missing or blacked out. We couldn't see them, and we never got a clear enough view to identify the driver or pull the VIN."

"Let me guess what direction the car was headed." Riley got up and went to the board where a map with all the crimes had been marked. He stabbed the Street Bishops' territory with his pointer finger.

"Good guess." Lightman joined him at the board. "We can't tell for certain due to too many gaps in DOT footage between the hospital and there. But I'd say it's a safe bet."

"Do you think they followed us to the hospital?" I asked.

Everyone in the squad room turned to look at me.

"I didn't see anyone tailing us," Riley said.

"Did you mention where you were going or that you had to speak to a witness?" Preston asked while Lightman continued to stare at me, as if he hadn't expected a lowly officer to say anything when the detectives were speaking.

"No." Riley squinted while he considered it. "But maybe they were already at the hospital when we got there. Kathryn Stanfield seemed freaked out, and I don't think it had anything to do with the orderly."

"The hospital footage showed two members of the Street Bishops entering the hospital thirty minutes before you got there. You could have just missed them," Lightman said. "They weren't wearing face masks, but who knows if they disguised themselves when they spoke to the witness."

"If they spoke to the witness," Preston corrected.

Lightman glowered at her. "If, when, it's all the same."

"Who are they?" Riley asked.

"Isaac Bertrand and Chris Skilven," Preston read from the open file.

My fingers flew over the keys. Besides their motorcycles, Bertrand had a pickup registered in his name, and Skilven had a car.

"We don't have enough to arrest them. We can't even prove they spoke to Kathryn Stanfield. A judge won't sign off on anything yet, but I'm sure they threatened her. They may have even been behind the initial assault and home invasion," Lightman said. "The best we can do is have units keep watch on them. At the moment, they're at the bar. When that changes, patrol will let us know."

"What kind of cars do they drive?" Riley asked.

Before I could answer, Lightman gave me that cold look, like I shouldn't speak when the grown-ups were having a conversation.

Preston skimmed the file. "Skilven has a black Toyota."

"Two door or four door?" Riley asked.

"Two."

Riley reached for the report the techs had composed concerning the hospital footage. After checking the timestamp, he scribbled something on a sticky note and stuck it to the board. "They tried to run me over."

"Were they at the bar when you spoke to Big Bill?" Preston asked.

Riley shook his head. "I didn't see them."

"They must have been on the way to the hospital," Lightman said.

"Did you see them, Lex?" Riley asked. "Either at the bar or at the hospital?"

I got up from my desk to get a better look at their ID photos which were taped to the board. "No, I've never seen them."

"That proves they didn't follow us," Riley said. "Big Bill could have called to tell them to do whatever it takes to shut down our investigation once and for all. They could have been waiting for us to show up at the hospital."

"How would they know that's where we were going?" I asked.

"We questioned Big Bill about what went down at the storage unit. It'd make sense we'd follow up with the victim," Riley pointed out.

"Do you think they'd go so far as to kill a cop?" I asked.

Before Riley could answer, Lightman interrupted.

"Don't you have paperwork to do, Officer Sarconi?" He folded his arms across his chest. "We don't need your help theorizing. We're capable of doing that on our own."

For the first time in a long time, I held my tongue. This wasn't the hill I wanted to die on. "Sorry, sir." Quietly, I slunk back to my desk.

Kemper and Hawking gave me sympathetic looks.

*Good job,* Kemper mouthed.

We updated intel and ran reports for the next hour while the detectives theorized as to what was going on and who could be responsible. While they did that, I finished my report and typed up my notes.

As soon as they called it quits, Preston made a beeline for the exit. I spotted Kemper looking pointedly at her retreating back. I typed the last few words from my notepad into the word processing program and saved my file on the computer.

After making sure Lightman had left, Riley rolled his chair next to mine. "I'm sorry about that. Jack's...well, he's Jack."

"Yeah, I noticed." I shook it off. "It's okay. I shouldn't have overstepped."

"You weren't. You're part of this. You saved my life. You should get to offer input."

"I didn't save your life."

Riley looked like he wanted to argue but decided now wasn't the time or place since Kemper and Hawking were only a few feet away. "Why do you do that?" He pointed to the word processor opened on my screen.

"It makes life easier. Everything is one click away," I said in my best infomercial voice. "If I need to reference something in my notes, I search for a key phrase, and voila."

I reached for the keyboard to demonstrate, and our fingertips touched. Again, I felt the same electric intensity I did the day we first met. Riley must have felt it too because he ran his pointer finger up the back of my hand to my wrist, sending wonderful tingles throughout my body.

"Sorry." His voice sounded hoarse. "Can you print a few extra copies of your notes out? I like to keep things organized in the file folders. It's easier for briefings and reviewing the intel when everything's in one place." He glanced behind us, but Hawking and Kemper remained.

"Sure, no problem." I hit print and waited for the ancient community printer to fire up. When it started whirring, I went to collect the pages. "Here ya go. I made three copies. Is that enough?"

"It's excellent. And with that, I'm calling it a night." He stuffed the sheets into the case file and locked it inside his top desk drawer. Slipping into his jacket, he pulled the hem free from his holster. "Would you like to grab a drink? After the day we had, I figure you could use one. I know I can." My mouth must have dropped because he quickly added, "A bunch of us are going across the street to the bar."

"Oh, um," I must have resembled a deer caught in headlights because he was clearly amused by my expression, "I have other plans."

"A date?"

"Excuse me?"

"Do you have a date?"

"No. Nothing like that. Not that dating is bad. I just don't. I mean...I'm not dating anyone." Sighing dramatically, I laughed at my own idiocy. "It's not like you asked or even care."

Riley cocked his head to the side. "I wouldn't be so sure about that."

"It's been a while since I've been on a date." *Shut up now*, my mind screamed.

"Someone should rectify that very unjust situation." He gave me a final look, seeing my two fellow officers buried behind their computer screens. "If you change your mind about that drink, meet me across the street."

"Thanks, but I won't."

After he was gone, I got up to examine the board. A few interviews had been scheduled for the morning. I didn't know what else we'd have to do, but hopefully, Riley and I wouldn't be walking into enemy territory again or dodging speeding cars. After making sure I had everything completed and filed for the night, I shut down the computer and grabbed my things from the bottom drawer.

Kemper joined me at my desk. “I’m so jealous you saw action today. You saved Riley.”

“Little good that did. Lightman still treats me like a law enforcement reject.”

“Don’t let it get to you.” Hawking stood and stretched. “Tomorrow’s another day.”

We bid him goodnight, and he disappeared out the double doors.

“Aren’t you going to get your drink on?” Kemper asked. “I heard Riley’s buying a round for everyone. Half of shift will be hanging out. It’s a great way to get to know your fellow officers.” He waggled his eyebrows at me. “Plus, you’re the hero of the story. I bet everyone will be lining up to buy you a shot.”

“Not tonight. And I’m not a hero. I pushed him out of the way. I never saw the plate or the driver. I didn’t even see the car until it was almost too late.”

Kemper slung his arm over my shoulders. “You’re being too hard on yourself. Come on, Lexie, it won’t kill you to have one drink. You hardly ever come out with us.” His eyes held a challenge. “Is it because you can’t hold your liquor?”

“I can hold my liquor just fine. But we have an early morning, and I want to be sharp.”

“I bet you’re a lot more fun when you’re tipsy.” Kemper’s lips curved into a devious smirk, and he snatched my purse off the desk. I had been in the process of emptying my pockets and putting the necessities like my cell phone and shield inside when he took my bag. “I’m not giving this back until you agree to one drink.”

“Kemper,” I lunged for my purse, but he held it over his head so I couldn’t reach it, “give it back. I’m not in the mood.”

“One drink.” He cocked his head to the side questioningly. “Please?”

“Fine.”

He looked victorious, practically letting out a cheer. “Great. Let’s go.” He hooked his fingers around my elbow and dragged me toward the stairs, still holding my purse.

On our way out of the station, we encountered Riley on his way back inside. The detective's gaze shifted from Kemper to me. I stared at the floor, embarrassed by the way I was being dragged to the bar.

"Lexie," Riley asked, "is everything okay?"

"Yeah. What are you doing back here? Did we get a call?" I hoped for an excuse to get out of drinks with Kemper.

"No. I just thought of something and wanted to run a check before I forgot." His gaze went back to Kemper, sizing up the other man. "Where are you two going?"

"To get drinks, man." Kemper smiled and offered a fist-bump to Riley. "I had to take this little lady's purse hostage to get her to agree to one drink. Can you believe that?"

"Maybe I would have tried that if I was channeling my twelve-year-old self," Riley retorted, and I snickered. Kemper didn't catch on, which made me laugh even harder. "I also don't think any woman likes to be called little lady."

"Whatever. Lexie doesn't mind, right?" Kemper bumped against my shoulder. "We'll see you over there, Mike," he called as Riley continued up the steps.

# EIGHT

The bar was crowded. Every officer and detective who had gotten off shift had gone for a drink. Aside from the uniformed officers' girlfriends and a few badge bunnies, the only civilians inside worked there. Kemper ordered two beers, and we sat down.

"Are you enjoying being Riley's pet project?" He took a long pull from the bottle.

"I'm not his pet project."

"Well, it's not like Hawking and I have gotten to ride with him. We've been inside, running background checks, examining surveillance feeds, and processing evidence. You actually get to go outside and see the light of day."

"And nearly get run over in the process."

"That's not what I meant, Lexie. Why are you always so defensive?"

"I'm not."

He drank more of his beer. "It seems that way to me."

"What is your problem?" I narrowed my eyes at him. "Jesus, you're jealous. You wanted to ride with Riley. You wanted to walk into that biker bar and almost turn into roadkill. Don't you understand those aren't good things? This job is dangerous."

"No shit." He turned to a group of our fellow officers assembled nearby. "Did you hear Lexie saved Detective Riley's life tonight?"

They raised their glasses, and one of them put my next round on his tab.

I let out a bitter laugh. "So that's it. You're a glory hound. You wanted the free drinks and the pats on the back. Maybe you should have thought of that the first time gangs asked us to canvass. If you'd almost made that arrest, Riley would have partnered with you, not me."

"I doubt that." He took a deep breath. "Look, I'm not trying to sound sexist here, but isn't it possible Riley thinks you're hot and that's why he picked you?"

"Right, that must be it. It couldn't possibly be that I'm good at my job."

"Well, you did save his life, so there's that. But I'm talking about before that."

"Oh my gosh. For the last time, I didn't save his life." I raised my voice so the group behind us would hear. "Not that it's any of your business, but I've worked with vice for over a year. So until you have a few more commendations or long-term postings in your file, I suggest you shut your mouth. Hawking may have spent the most time on the job, but I've spent the most time working closely with detectives building cases. I have experience. That's why Riley chose me."

"Whoa, easy. I don't doubt that, but I want you to be careful. Mr. Hotshot Detective might expect a favor in return for showing you the ropes, or he may want to show you just how grateful he is to be alive. That's all I'm saying." He glanced around and lowered his voice conspiratorially. "Word is that's how Preston got to where she is."

I scoffed at his pathetic argument. "That's unsubstantiated gossip. It has no bearing on any of this. And I think you ought to mind your own business." I climbed off the stool. "If you take my purse again, I'll shoot you."

Returning home, I trudged up the steps to my apartment, unlocked the door, and slammed it shut. I was pissed. Too much had happened today for me to think clearly. I shouldn't let it get to me, but I couldn't shake that tiny bit of self-doubt that always kept me company. What if Kemper had a point?

Maybe the only reason Riley humored me was for what

he hoped to get in return. It happened in a lot of professions, and I didn't know him well enough to know what kind of guy he was outside of the job. Depending on how true the rumors were concerning him and Preston, bedding his co-workers could be part of his repertoire.

But tonight changed things. We were in the trenches together. Still, I found myself replaying everything, from leading the way up the steps to Big Bill's apartment to questioning Kathryn Stanfield. It wasn't common practice for a detective to let an officer take the lead. Maybe Riley had been hoping to trade favors. After all, we did have that weird exchange outside the hospital before I got the footage from Amber. Had Riley been flirting, or was that an act to make me think he cared in order to get me in bed?

Searching for my cell phone, I wanted to call Amber and ask for some advice, but I couldn't find my phone. It had to be on my desk at work. At the moment, I despised Kemper for sullying my self-confidence, ruining my evening, and making me leave my phone at the station.

"Dammit." Stomping into my room, I changed into workout clothes and pounded out a few miles on the treadmill. After that, I took a soothing shower and crawled into bed, forcing myself not to think about anything related to the job.

Eventually, I drifted into an uneasy sleep. Less than an hour later, I woke up with thoughts of Big Bill sending his thugs to my apartment to teach me a lesson. Eventually, those thoughts were replaced with more self-doubt. What if Kemper was right about Riley? What if I liked Riley a little too much to care?

As a rule, I despised women who allowed handsome assholes to sweet talk them into things. In truth, I'd been that woman before, and I promised myself I would never be her again. But was that what was going on here?

Working myself into a tizzy over the what ifs, I opened my nightstand drawer and grabbed my e-reader. It blinked on, flashed the charge button, and powered itself off. Nothing was working tonight.

I rolled over, beat my pillow into a preferable shape, and twisted and turned for another twenty minutes. No matter how hard I tried to force my thoughts away from work, they found a way to circle back. This was all Kemper's fault.

I stared at the ceiling until my eyelids grew heavy. Maybe now I could sleep.

The constant pounding at my door dragged me from bed. It was two a.m., not that I'd fallen asleep. But I'd been close.

Grabbing my robe, I tied it around my waist and went into the living room. Criminals wouldn't knock before breaking in, right? After a quick peek through the peephole, I glanced around my living room, making sure nothing embarrassing was in view before opening the door.

"Hey, Lexie." Riley leaned heavily against my doorjamb. He reeked of tequila. "I thought you could use this." He held up my cell phone but seemed to forget what to do with it and put it back in his pocket. "You have such pretty eyes."

I pulled my robe tighter around my waist. "How much did you have to drink? Did you drive here?"

"Just a little bit. And no, I took a cab." He shook his head, focusing again on the reason he was outside my front door, fished my cell phone out of his pocket, and handed it to me. "You left this at work. 'Cuz if you hadn't, I wouldn't have found your address stored in the phone's memory and wouldn't have known where you lived. I guess I could have called to tell you you left your phone instead of showing up. But I didn't know if you had a landline. That would have made this easier. I should have looked in your personnel file. Damn."

"You came all this way to bring me my phone?"

"Uh-huh." He gave me a huge, lopsided smile. "Okay, good night." He staggered backward.

"Michael," I grabbed his arm, "you should sober up before you go. The last thing you need to do is wander the streets. What would Lightman think if he has to bail you out of the drunk tank in the morning?"

"He'd realize I'm a lot of fun." Riley teetered. "Y'know, hanging around for a while doesn't sound like such a bad idea." He let me lead him to the couch. "You've got a lovely place." He stared, wide-eyed, at the room. "I used to have a place like this, except the walls were beige and the couch was brown."

"How about I make you some coffee?" I poured the water and put a dark roast cup into the machine. A minute later, I put the mug on the table in front of him. "Drink this, Detective."

"Michael," he insisted. He picked up the cup and took a long sip before putting it down. "Did I interrupt anything?" He looked around the room, searching for something or someone. When he didn't spot whatever he hoped to find, his gaze settled on me. His fingers found the sleeve of my robe, and he played absently with the silky material.

"Not at all. I was having problems falling asleep," I admitted.

"Insnowmia?" He scrunched his face together, realizing the word didn't come out correctly. "Snomnia."

"Insomnia?"

He pointed a finger at me and smiled. "That's it."

"Drink some more coffee," I insisted, debating if my worries warranted a conversation.

"Then I won't be able to sleep either." He shook his head to clear the cobwebs. "What's keeping you up? Is it the car? Because, damn, that was close. I mean like bug on a windshield close."

"It wasn't a big deal."

"Guess not, since I'm still here. So what's bothering you?"

"Kemper said I'm getting special treatment at the station because I'm female. That *you're* giving me special treatment."

"Kemper's a douche. You're smart and have an excellent record." He drained the mug and put it back on the table. I scooped it up to brew another cup while he sunk deeper into the couch cushions and put his feet on my coffee table. "And you're beautiful."

"See, stupid comments like that undermine everything else you said." Leaning against the kitchen counter, I rubbed my face. "You're not supposed to let that play a role in determining my ability to do the job."

"I don't see how it could. If anything, Hawking would

have been a better choice today. He's bigger. He would have shoved me farther. But when he landed on top of me, that might have hurt, so maybe picking you was a good idea." He smiled. "I think it was."

"Is that why you let me shadow you at work?"

"I let you ride with me because you have a knack for taking care of what needs to be done. The fact that you're easy on the eyes is a bonus."

"Stop it."

"Stop what?"

"The only thing I can say about my looks is that with enough makeup I make a convincing sex worker. And frankly, I'm not sure that's a good thing. But let me make one thing clear, I will not whore myself out for this job or any job. If you're hoping to cash in because you let me ride with you, you can forget it. I don't trade favors, sexual or otherwise."

"I wouldn't do that," he snapped. "Where would you get an idea like that?"

"Kemper."

Riley rolled his eyes. "He's a dick. You need to be careful around him."

"Funny, he said the same thing about you."

"Well, I'm right. He's not." Riley shifted sideways on the couch to look at me. "I bet I could be a damn good gigolo."

"Oh-kay."

"I'm hot and have no problem using that to my advantage." His arrogance was starting to make him less attractive.

"It's different, and you know it." I brought the refilled mug back to the sofa and handed it to him. "When women use their looks, ugly rumors circulate. What makes it worse is when men use their position to force those women into compromising situations. That's just sick. In fact, it's criminal. And you want to guess who gets screwed in the process? The woman. Haven't you heard the things they say about Preston?"

An angry fire burned behind his eyes. "They aren't rumors when they're true." He took another sip of coffee, calming as if the hot liquid had put out his internal blaze.

"You've used your looks for the job. In fact, it was required to do the job. That's precisely how you were able to work as a decoy for vice, so stop being so self-deprecating. You're gorgeous. Own it. Insecurity won't lead to a detective's shield."

"Why are we still talking about this?" I asked.

"Because it's bothering you." He tugged on my sleeve again. "I picked you because you have an exemplary record. Part of the reason for that is because you have looks to go with your brains. That's why you were able to work for vice, and it's how you were able to lure out a predator. But I'm not a predator. I partnered with you because you nearly arrested Frank. Anyone who does that has earned my respect. And tonight, you proved that I chose right. Kemper would have let me go splat."

"You're probably right about that."

"See?"

"Hawking would have done something."

"If he was paying attention," Riley said. "And after he called me sir and saluted."

I gave his arm a playful slap. "Be nice. Hawking tries to be respectful."

"Just the way Jack likes it, which makes them the perfect pair and us the perfect pair."

Stifling my yawn, I studied his relaxed posture. He appeared slightly more sober than when he arrived. "Tell me the truth. Why did you come here tonight?" I asked.

"To return your phone." He looked apologetic. "I should get going. You probably want to go to bed."

I didn't believe him. After all, there was no reason why he couldn't have stuck the phone inside my desk drawer for the morning. "Are you able to get yourself home?"

"Yeah." He got up from the couch and banged into the coffee table on his way to the door and tripped. He rubbed his shin, cursing under his breath. "Maybe not."

"You're in no condition to go anywhere. Sit down and let me take a look at that."

"Now who's taking advantage?" he teased.

"Shut up." I lifted his pant leg, finding his shin had already started to swell. "I'll get you some ice."

"You should see the bruises on my back from slamming into that car. Did you get banged up too?"

"Not really." I tossed the ice pack to him before going to the linen closet and pulling out a spare pillow and blanket. "But I landed on top of you. You landed on the car and then the asphalt."

He smiled. "Next time, I want to be on top."

"Who said there's going to be a next time?"

"How about a first time?"

I ignored him. "Here. Make yourself comfortable. Don't burn my house down, and don't bang into any more of my furniture. I'm going to bed. You can sleep here or stay until you sober up. If you leave, lock the door behind you."

"Are you going to accuse me of something insane if I stay?"

"Only if you try something insane, and keep in mind, I sleep with a gun."

He laughed. "Me too."

# NINE

Despite being slightly hungover, Riley arrived at work before I did and splurged on two drink carriers of lattes and a dozen donuts for our team. "Help yourself." He pointed to the open box of donuts when I joined the detectives in the squad room. Hawking and Kemper hadn't arrived yet, which meant I was early, as usual.

I pulled one of the vanilla lattes out of the carrier and selected a glazed donut from the box. Detective Preston pushed the stack of napkins toward me while Lightman scowled. Nothing I did could ever please that man.

Riley folded his arms over his chest and stared at the board. Nothing had been added since he left last night, which only irritated him. "Did Stuart Stanfield identify Isaac Bertrand or Chris Skilven?"

"He said he didn't recognize them," Preston said. "But the officer who interviewed him said he was being cagey about answering. More than likely, he was threatened too."

"Or his wife told him what happened and passed word along that he should keep his mouth shut," Lightman mumbled.

Riley cursed. "I reached out to Frank, hoping he'd be able to shed some light on whether the Stanfields have any ties to the Street Bishops. He said he'd find out what he could and meet me around lunchtime to discuss it."

"Why does that matter?" I asked. "We know two of Big Bill's men were at the hospital. We also know the Stanfields were targeted by that gang. Even if we can connect them, the Stanfields won't cooperate. They're afraid what will happen if they do."

"Then we give them something else to fear," Lightman said. "Given what we know about how Big Bill runs the MC, he should be picky about selecting targets. The people the Street Bishops go after are almost always crooks. That'll give us leverage against the Stanfields. Criminal charges and hard time scare people more than the possibility of retaliation, at least they should."

"I thought you said innocent people were being robbed," I said. "Now you're saying the victims are guilty too?"

Lightman hated that I pointed that out. "We don't know for sure. But this is an avenue worth exploring, especially since the Stanfields were victimized on two separate occasions."

"But we've run backgrounds on every one of the victims, even the businesses that were robbed. Nothing popped in the system. That's why it took until the shooting at the storage unit for you to put the pieces together and figure out the Street Bishops were behind this. Going back over the same things won't change the outcome. They have no connection, at least none we know about."

"She's right, Jack. That's why I'm hoping Frank can shed some light on this. He's been drifting between the MCs, hoping to figure out who knew what. Now that he knows where to focus his efforts, we should get better results." Riley offered me a smile.

"She doesn't know what she's talking about," Lightman insisted.

Riley snorted. "Maybe not, but without her instincts, I'd be in a hospital bed beside Kathryn Stanfield and eating my donut through a straw."

"What do you think we should be doing instead, Sarconi?" Preston asked.

Her question surprised me. "Finding the driver and vehicle that tried to run us over might be a good place to start."

"I agree." Riley reached for his own cup and took a long sip. "To be honest, that's what I'm most interested in at this point."

"You've made that crystal clear," Lightman grumbled. "Come on, Mike, you know we're doing what we can. Units have been assigned to watch Big Bill's bar and keep tabs on Chris Skilven and Isaac Bertrand. We're also keeping an eye on Skilven's car. But it doesn't have any recent dents or scrapes. Without telltale evidence, a judge won't sign off on a court order. We need more." Lightman turned in my direction, narrowing his eyes. "That's why it's important we find a way to convince one of the victims or witnesses to come clean. As soon as one of them points a finger at Big Bill or a member of the MC, we'll have it made."

Preston uncrossed and recrossed her legs the other way. "That's easier said than done."

After biting into the donut and washing it down with the latte, I put my breakfast down and wiped my sticky fingers on the napkin. "How do we proceed? Do we conduct more interviews? Set up additional surveillance?"

"We don't do anything," Lightman said, cutting off Riley who had just opened his mouth to speak. "We figure out how to convince someone to cooperate, and we go hard at him until we have enough for that court order."

"We can't count on that happening," Riley said. "Lexie's right. We've gone over everyone's background. Big Bill's deviated from his usual routine. That's why we didn't know he was behind this. We found some suspicious merchandise in his apartment, but he knew we didn't have enough to prove it was stolen. He's arrogant like that. Whatever he's up to is different from anything we've seen from him before."

"Do you think he's working with someone?" Preston asked.

Riley shrugged. "Maybe Frank can tell us."

Lightman squinted at the board, the wheels in his head turning. He had a thought, but he wasn't willing to share it.

Frustrated, I ate the rest of my donut, wiped my hands, and threw away the napkin. By the time I returned to my seat, Kemper and Hawking had arrived. Kemper tried to apologize, but I wasn't ready to forgive him. However, we had to work together, so I let the cold shoulder thaw to just above frigid.

"Let's not get into this now," I said. "We have work to do."

Riley glared at Kemper from across the room. His expression said he wanted to kill, but he kept his thoughts to himself.

I hated how helpless I felt. Without evidence or an eyewitness coming forward, we didn't have enough to move on the Street Bishops. That's why, despite my earlier argument, Hawking, Kemper, and I tore through each case file again, performed another set of background checks, and combed through as much intel on the Street Bishops as the computer spit out.

"Sarconi," Riley called from his desk across the bullpen, "can you print another copy of your notes from Tuesday?"

"I'm sending them to the printer now. Do you need anything else, Detective?" He wasn't usually this formal, but I'd done a good job pissing off Lightman. It was best to keep things professional, the way Hawking had suggested.

"No." Riley grabbed the papers off the printer and checked his messages. "Frank wants to meet in twenty minutes. He said he's got something for us." Riley grabbed his jacket off the back of his chair. "Sarconi, let's go."

"Sarconi, stay," Lightman said.

Now I felt like a dog. "Sir?" I asked.

Riley eyed Lightman, just as confused as I was.

"The two of you went into Big Bill's bar last night. Someone might recognize you if you're together again." Lightman glanced back at me. "Not to mention, you're the one who nearly arrested Frank. It's best if you make yourself scarce when it comes to visiting that neighborhood. But I'm sure we'll find plenty for you to do here."

"Yes, sir." I turned back to my computer screen, fighting to keep the disappointment and annoyance at bay.

Hawking caught my eye and gave me an encouraging nod. "Head down, do the work," he whispered.

I nodded, doing my best to grin and bear it.

Riley tugged his arm through his sleeve. "Do you want me to relay a message to Frank?"

Lightman shook his head, but before Riley could leave, Preston handed him a note. “Pass that on to Frank. He’ll understand,” she said.

“Sure, no problem.” Riley tucked the note into his shirt pocket and turned back to me. “Jack’s right. After yesterday, it might be best if you sit this one out.” He looked at Kemper. “Do you want to tag along instead?”

Kemper jumped to his feet. “Absolutely.”

“Wait for me downstairs.” Once Kemper was gone, Riley ran his hand along the back of my chair, sending shivers through me. I didn’t think he even realized he did it. “I’m sorry,” he whispered. “But this way, no one thinks I’m playing favorites. I’m sure you understand. It’s nothing personal.” He must have remembered what I said last night about Kemper’s accusation.

“Not a problem.” I forced my face into a neutral position and busied myself with going over the cataloged items taken from the various home invasions. If I could find the exact combination that we spotted in Big Bill’s apartment, maybe that would lead somewhere. “Be careful.”

“You too.” And with that, he was gone.

“Hey, Hawking, I could use another set of eyes to proof the compiled manifest,” I said.

“You got it.” He slid his chair over to my desk, and we went back over everything.

With Riley and Kemper gone, Hawking and I got a lot done. It was easier to work without any distractions nearby. Based on a few comments we received from victims and witnesses, we had no doubts William “Big Bill” Dempsey and the Street Bishops were behind the recent string of crimes. But we still didn’t know why. This wasn’t their norm. Something was up. Something big.

“Riley said the MC could be looking to expand in preparation for a turf war,” I said.

“Do you think it could be defensive instead?” Hawking asked. “Someone encroached on Big Bill’s territory, so he’s looking to reclaim what was his.”

“Maybe, but the three blocks he controls haven’t changed. We didn’t see anyone flying other colors in his neighborhood.”

"Let me see what I can dig up." Hawking pulled out the file we had on Big Bill. "Do you want to look into his allies or his enemies?"

"Enemies."

Hawking nodded. "I'll see if he was ever part of another MC or if he has any connections that would explain what's been happening with the recruitment and initiation."

After hours of digging, we didn't find much. Gangs had already pulled everything on every potential in the area, so nothing Hawking and I did was ground-breaking. But I kept coming back to one name. Alfred Sigfried.

Gangs didn't have much on him. He had a rap sheet and had done time with Big Bill almost a decade ago. I wrote his name on a sticky note and circled it, drawing three large question marks beside it.

After taping the information to the whiteboard, I turned to Preston, a new thought dawning on me. "Threatening someone is a crime. How come we can't bring Skilven and Bertrand in yet? We may not be able to prove it, but we have every reason to think they were involved."

She glanced at Lightman's empty desk, but he'd disappeared right after Riley. "You're right, Sarconi, but Jack wants to wait until we have something solid. Something with teeth. A catch and release won't get us far. He's worried what will happen once we are forced to cut them loose. It's safer this way for everyone." Her gaze shifted above my head, and I knew without looking that she was checking the clock. "Michael should be back soon. With any luck, Frank gave him something we can use."

"Since Frank's not undercover with the Street Bishops, how close do you think he can get to them?"

"Close enough."

"Can he get inside Big Bill's bar?"

"Why are you asking so many questions?"

"Frank wasn't at the bar last night. If Big Bill called Skilven and warned him Riley was on the way—"

"You hoped Frank would have overheard Big Bill ordering the hit." She sighed. "Wouldn't that have been nice? Not the hit part, but being able to tie Bill Dempsey to such a heinous crime." She looked wistful. "Frank will come through. He always finds a way." She cocked her head, seeing me in a new light. "I'm sure you did plenty of things you regret as a decoy."

I bristled, unsure what thought triggered that comment, but instead of engaging, I turned back to the board and hung the stack of mugshots of the suspected gang initiates. "These are the potential new recruits for the Street Bishops." I glanced at Hawking, who'd compiled the list based on shifts and changes in nearby MCs with which Big Bill had a cordial or symbiotic relationship.

She smiled. "I'm impressed."

"Thank you, ma'am," he said.

She turned back to me. "What about that stack?" She pointed to the mugshots on the table.

"These," I taped the photos in a new row, "are the men Riley and I encountered at the bar. That must mean they're active members, but who knows."

"We do," she said icily. "It's our job." She pushed her chair out and stood. "I'm going to see what's holding Jack up. Text me if Michael returns or if you receive any additional instructions."

"Yes, ma'am," Hawking said.

She nodded to him and left.

"Wow, we don't have any adult supervision," I quipped. "Quick, search their drawers. I bet one of them keeps a stockpile of candy."

"You're funny, Lex." Hawking returned my grin, finally loosening up a little from his usual stiff, by-the-book behavior. "So," he leaned back to assess our handiwork, "we have strong leads on who tried to run you and Riley over and who threatened Kathryn Stanfield."

"Big Bill must have ordered them to do that too."

"Probably." Hawking dialed up the archived surveillance footage from the nearby robberies. "Sixteen places have been knocked over in the last five weeks. That doesn't include the home invasions. I'd think with numbers like this, we'd bring in whoever we could as soon as we could."

"The angles are shit. No one's been identified. The eyewitnesses are hesitant to come forward. It's not like anyone's been caught red-handed. Like the detectives said, what we need is irrefutable proof."

"Do you think that's why Riley went to meet Devereaux? After last night, the stakes were raised. Riley has a vested interest in putting bracelets on someone."

"The hospital footage should be our smoking gun, except we didn't obtain a copy officially, which complicates matters."

Hawking pointed to the wall clock. "Riley and Kemper have been gone for an awfully long time. Do you think he decided to pay Skilven and Bertrand a visit?"

"Lightman would shit himself."

"Kemper's always looking for action. Maybe Riley figured it was about time they shook things up, or he could have taken Kemper there to teach him a lesson."

"What do you mean?"

"Nothing."

I thought about what he said. "You might be right. Even if we don't have proof the Street Bishops paid Kathryn Stanfield a visit, Riley knows how to bluff. He's also got brass ones. Yesterday, he strolled right into their HQ and never even batted an eye."

"That sounds like hero worship," Hawking teased.

"It's not. If anything, it was reckless. We didn't learn much from that experience, but someone tried to kill him because of it."

"Big Bill must have thought you found something since he told his buddies to perform a hit and run."

"You know, you might be on to something."

# TEN

I went over everything from our visit to the bar. Aside from the duffel bag I spotted in Big Bill's apartment, I couldn't come up with anything else of use. Drumming my fingers on the desk, I worked through what we'd observed outside the bar and the rival gang members we'd spoken to. But I didn't see how any of that could explain why Big Bill's goons would have resorted to such rash actions.

Biting my lip, I reached for the business profile for Big Bill's bar. "Maybe the stripper knows something. We didn't speak to her, but she was the only one in there who didn't look like she belonged in a motorcycle gang."

I ran through the tax forms and employee information, but her name wasn't listed anywhere. Scribbling a note, I stuck it to the side of my monitor. How was I going to figure out who she was and if she had something to tell us when Lightman prohibited me from stepping foot on the Street Bishops' turf?

"What do you think is taking Riley and Kemper so long? Shouldn't they be back by now? Do you think something happened to them?" I asked.

"We would have heard the radio call," Hawking said. "I'm sure they're fine. Then again, I never expected Riley to invite Kemper to go with him this afternoon, and I sure as shit didn't expect Kemper to jump at the chance. Last night, they almost came to blows at the bar."

"Really?"

"It looked that way to me. A couple of guys grabbed

Riley before he could do something that would have gotten him tossed into a jail cell. Kemper puffed out his chest and did the whole posturing thing, but he ducked out before Riley could get his hands on him. For a second, I thought it had something to do with you."

"Why would it? I wasn't even there when it happened. I left after Kemper pissed me off."

"I don't know. I thought I heard your name in the midst of their argument. Kemper does a great job of pissing people off when he's drunk. On the bright side, it looks like all's been forgiven. Even you are talking to him today, and I'd think if anyone was going to hold a grudge—"

"Hey!"

Hawking laughed. "See what I mean?"

"I don't hold grudges, not over stupid things."

"What did Kemper do that pissed you off?"

"He said I wasn't good enough."

"No wonder you left. I'd have done the same thing. Don't get me wrong, I don't have a problem with the guy. He's proven himself to be a capable police officer, but he's a lot like a puppy that shits the carpet. You smack him with a newspaper, but he doesn't understand what he did wrong. And he does it over and over again. At least, he did last night."

"You really don't know what he said to Riley?"

"All I know is a couple of guys from homicide had to hold Riley back, and Kemper took off right after that. But whatever that was about, I guess they made up."

"They must have for Kemper to volunteer to go with Riley today. After all, you heard Riley. He doesn't play favorites. He announced that right before he and Kemper went skipping off into the sunset. Perhaps that's why he asked him to go. Maybe it was an apology."

"Or the reason they haven't come back yet is because Riley's disposing of the body."

I snorted. "Frank would have to help him with that. I'm not sure Riley could get away with doing it on his own."

Hawking found that amusing. "I'd believe it since Riley and the dream team of detectives have no clue how to put a stop to this crime spree."

I faked a gasp. "I never thought I'd hear you say that. After all, they are our COs."

"Shut it, Sarconi. I've learned to show respect to my superiors. It ensures things run smoothly. But that doesn't mean I agree with everything they say or do. Honestly, the longer we assist the gangs unit, the more I fear I'll get a reputation like Lightman's."

"That you have a giant stick up your ass?"

"Maybe."

"Keep this up, and I'm sure you'll knock that right out."

"Just because I'm engaging in friendly chit-chat doesn't mean I'm going to turn into a smartass like you."

"No one would want that," I said.

"Definitely not."

"For the record, I respect the detectives in this unit. All of them. But I'm used to breaking the tension by exchanging barbs. That's how the cops in vice operated. From what I hear, that's how a lot of the high-stress units behave. It's a coping mechanism. I didn't mean any disrespect by it, at least not intentionally."

"Good to know."

I narrowed my eyes. "Have you ever done anything besides patrol?"

Hawking shook his head. "I was assigned a particularly dangerous beat at another station. We saw a lot of action. But my TO was super-buttoned up. That's why I'm like this."

"What happened to him?"

Hawking focused on the board, keeping his attention there. "He was killed in the line of duty. After witnessing that, I got transferred out. That's how I ended up here."

"I'm sorry."

He nodded and changed the subject. "What were you doing at the bar with Kemper last night?"

"He dragged me there, so he could use me to get free drinks. Instead of shutting up and saying thank you, he pissed me off by saying the only reason I get to ride with Riley is because I'm female. Maybe Riley overheard the conversation and wanted to put a stop to the allegations before they turned into something."

"Sure. That makes sense."

"Yeah." My mind flashed to Michael Riley showing up drunk at my apartment. Was that why he came over? Did he want to tell me what happened with Kemper? "Do you think we should call Kemper and see what's keeping them?"

"No," Lightman snapped, striding into the room. He assessed the board. "Riley's on his way back with additional intel, and Preston's at the crime lab, talking to the forensic teams. The two of you will stay here and update the board as new intel comes in. And I'll take it from there."

"Yes, sir," Hawking and I replied simultaneously.

"Don't be cute," Lightman said as if we planned to choreograph our response.

"No, sir," we said again, and I thought Lightman's head might explode. Instead, he stormed out of the room, barking at an officer he passed to get eyes on Big Bill until we could get an arrest warrant issued. I had no idea if that was wishful thinking or if Frank provided a lead. But I was hoping for the latter.

# ELEVEN

When Riley and Kemper returned, they split apart like shrapnel. Hawking and I exchanged a look. Apparently, they still weren't getting along.

After checking his messages and surveying the changes to the board, Riley approached my desk. "It looks like you two have been busy."

"Yes, sir," Hawking said.

"You don't have to sir me." Riley rested one hand on the desk and the other on the back of my chair while he leaned over to read my computer screen. "It looks like you've made a lot of progress. Has Jack seen this yet?"

"Yep." Hawking dropped the sir.

I tilted my head back, trying to make eye contact. "What about Frank? Did he deliver a smoking gun?"

Riley looked like he had a secret. "Maybe. He heard Big Bill wanted to unload some hot merchandise. Since we paid him a visit last night and things have been heating up, he thought it'd be best to get rid of the damning evidence pronto. We're hoping to catch him or one of the Street Bishops in the act."

"In the act?" Hawking asked.

"Selling off the stolen items," Riley said. "More than likely, he'll take them to a pawn shop or some black market dealer."

"Whoever we catch with the goods, we can squeeze," I said.

"Exactly." Riley tapped the back of my chair and straightened. "I already told Jack about it."

"That's why he said units were monitoring Big Bill," Hawking said.

"His bar," Kemper grumbled from his spot beside the copy machine, where he was unsuccessfully trying to clear a paper jam and replace the toner cartridge.

Riley ignored him and flicked the sticky note on the side of my monitor. "What's this?"

"A possible lead." I rested my elbow on the desk and turned sideways so I could see him without hurting my neck. "Big Bill freaked out after our visit. There must have been a reason. Maybe she knows something. If we can find her, she might talk. But I don't know how we'd go about doing that. I didn't find her listed on any tax forms or employee information. If she works in the bar, she'd have to be registered, like the rest of the waitresses and bartenders."

"Big Bill operates that bar, but he wouldn't count the entertainment as hired help," Riley said. "He'd pay her under the table."

"How do you suggest we identify her?"

"Did you check social media?" Riley reached for the mouse, minimizing the window I had open and starting a new search. "The Street Bishops aren't the brightest crayons in the box. If she works there, she must have dated at least one of the guys, maybe more."

"Maybe all of them," I said.

"Riley would know something about that," Kemper muttered.

That time, Riley turned. "What the fuck is your problem?"

Hawking straightened, his muscles tensing as if preparing to intervene if violence broke out.

Kemper held up his palms and backed away from the copy machine. "Nothing. Nothing at all." Letting out a frustrated grunt, he rubbed his brow. "I'll see if Lightman needs anything." He turned a corner, knocked on the door to the conference room, and pushed it open.

"Do I want to know?" I asked.

Riley gave a barely perceptible headshake while he leaned over my keyboard to enter the search parameters. Dozens of photos featuring the bar and various Street Bishops filled the screen. He scrolled down, pausing on each one that featured the stripper.

"She's not tagged," I said.

"What about facial recognition?" Hawking suggested.

Riley continued scrolling and clicking. "I can put in a request, but it's a long shot."

"It's your call," I said.

Riley thought for a moment before stepping away from my desk. "Yeah, all right. It's worth a shot. Send me the link to that photo." He pointed to the one where she was facing the camera head-on.

While Riley filled out the form, Preston burst through the double doors. "Jack?" She looked around the squad room. "Where's Lightman?"

Hawking pointed to the conference room door, and Preston knocked on it, just like Kemper had a few minutes earlier.

"What's going on?" Lightman asked, following Preston out of the room with Kemper at his heels.

"Big Bill's been arrested," she said. "A couple of unis pulled him over on a routine traffic stop, spotted hot merchandise on his bike, and arrested him. It went off just like Frank said it would."

"That saved us time from having to wait for a warrant." Lightman looked relieved. "Have they brought him in yet?"

"The officers just radioed in the arrest. Big Bill should be here any minute."

"Why didn't they wait until he tried to hock the merch before stopping him?" Riley asked.

"He tried to make a deal, but whoever he met in the parking lot got spooked when the patrol car pulled up. The other party took off, and the officers stayed to question Big Bill. By then, he'd already opened his saddlebags. Everything was in plain view."

"How is that a routine traffic stop?" Riley asked.

"Jesus," Lightman sighed, "why are you looking a gift-horse in the mouth?"

Preston glanced from Lightman to Riley. "Big Bill turned illegally, drove the wrong way through a parking garage, and gave them every reason to pull him over. It's not their fault if they weren't immediately behind him since they couldn't dart through the parking garage exit like he did."

"Excellent." Lightman went to the board and drew a large red rectangle around Big Bill. "How big of a bust did they make?"

"The initial search revealed several thousand in stolen jewelry stashed in the saddlebags. They aren't sure what may be in the locked box behind the seat, but there could be more. The officers didn't open it. They'll wait until his bike is impounded and he's been booked. Once we get a court order, we'll check every nook and cranny."

"Any legality issues?" Riley asked.

Preston swiveled in her chair. "We're in the clear."

"And the way they did it means Frank isn't compromised." Riley exhaled.

"As soon as Big Bill's booked, I want him moved into an interrogation room. Let's see if we can convince him to talk before the bastard cries for his lawyer," Lightman said. "Sam, why don't you take a crack at him first? Turn up the charm. He should respond to that."

"I'll do whatever I can to keep him from shutting us down." She shifted her gaze to the man beside me. "Hawking, have you ever sat in on an interrogation?"

"No, ma'am."

"You're about to. Follow me. And don't say a word. This is a learning experience, got it?"

"Yes, ma'am."

"And if you call me ma'am again, I'll have you cleaning the women's locker room with your personal toothbrush. Do you understand?" She smiled sweetly at him, and I decided Detective Samantha Preston was my new role model. It didn't matter if she'd been brusque with me earlier or had a string of torrid affairs. She was a badass.

"You two can call it a night," Lightman said to Kemper and me. "Sam will work her magic, but when that runs out, Big Bill's gonna be begging for his lawyer. His attorney won't be here until the morning, so you might as well get home at a decent hour for once. I want you rested for tomorrow." He jerked his head at the door. "Take off."

Kemper didn't need to be told twice and was out the door before I even shut down my computer. I hung around as long as I could, hoping Riley would tell me if his request was approved, but with Lightman strutting around the squad room like he was on cloud nine, I didn't dare ask and Riley didn't offer.

After forty-five minutes, I decided to call it a night. On my way out, I passed the observation room connected to the interrogation room. On the other side of the two-way mirror, Preston asked Big Bill questions while Hawking meticulously jotted down the suspect's responses.

I watched the interrogation for a few minutes, curious to see what was happening. I'd been on the other side of the glass before, but I had never observed one being conducted like this. The volume on the audio equipment was turned down too low for me to hear, but Big Bill had a lot to say. I couldn't believe the biker was cooperating. Maybe he was full of shit.

I turned the dial on the speaker. But it didn't help. The speaker was broken, but from the blinking red light on the camera, I knew the audio and video were being recorded elsewhere.

Was it possible Lightman's prediction was wrong? Maybe Big Bill wouldn't lawyer up. Maybe he'd give up his accomplices and sell out his new recruits and biker brothers. I didn't want to drive home to have to turn around and come back if the situation changed and I was called in to work another double.

"Lexie," Riley asked, confused why I was watching the interrogation, "are you taking notes?"

"No. Hawking is." I jerked my chin at the glass.

Riley squinted, rubbing his ear like there was something wrong with his hearing.

"The speaker's busted," I said.

He fiddled with the dial before giving up. "They should have put him in interrogation room two. At least the equipment works in there."

"The camera's working. That's all that matters."

"I can't believe Big Bill went to make the sale himself." Riley watched the action for a few more moments. "Frank said Bill wasn't trusting his guys with this. I don't know why."

"Did Frank have any guesses?"

"Not really. He thinks there might be some dissension among the ranks, but he's not clear why."

"Speaking of, how was your outing with Kemper?"

Riley tore his eyes away from the glass to look at me. "We should talk about last night."

"What about last night, Detective?"

"Michael. My name is Michael." He stepped in front of me, blocking my view of the interrogation and closing the door behind him. "Are you mad at me?"

"Why would I be mad?"

"I can think of two reasons."

"Two?"

"I'm sorry I showed up at your doorstep drunk. And I'm sorry I took off this morning when I heard you get up. I didn't know what to say to you, so I left."

"There was nothing to say. You needed somewhere to sober up. That was it. It was no big deal. Yesterday was rough."

"Yeah."

"Okay." I turned to leave, but Riley grabbed my arm, pulling me backward. I stumbled, falling into his chest. My heart raced, and I flashed back to the previous night on the pavement. The air sizzled. "If we keep doing this, someone's gonna get hurt."

His Adam's apple bobbed. Once he made sure I was stable on my feet, he let go. "Last night, you mentioned a few things Kemper said. That's why I let him shadow me today, to prove him wrong, to make the point I don't pick partners based on if I want to sleep with them. But you haven't said much to me since we got back. I was afraid you may have let some of that crap he was spewing about why I chose you fester. You know none of that is true, right? What I said last night," he rubbed his head, "well, the parts I remember, I teased you a bit about being attractive and I wanted to make sure you knew that wasn't it. I mean, you are, but that's not why I wanted to work with you."

"You can't help yourself, can you? Are compliments how bad boys like you get all the ladies?"

"You think I'm a bad boy?"

"Actually, I think you're a badass."

He smiled. "Thanks."

"So why do I get the feeling you and Kemper want to go another round?"

"You heard about the bar?"

"Of course, I heard. Everyone saw it happen."

"Do you know why?"

"Enlighten me. Hawking thought it had something to do with me. I'm really hoping that isn't true."

"It's not entirely untrue." He focused on my eyes. "Correct me if I'm wrong, but didn't you tell me Kemper was making accusations about your job performance and my motivation for picking you?"

"Yes."

"Right, so I had to set the record straight and put him in his place."

"So you knew what he said before you came over, and you still showed up at my door."

"I wanted to make sure he wasn't there."

"Where?"

Riley rubbed his eyes. "At your apartment."

"Why would he be at my apartment?"

"If I answer that, you're going to get mad."

"Tell me."

"Seriously, Lexie, you don't know? Maybe you shouldn't take the detective's exam, after all."

"Hey." I shoved him. "Tell me."

"Kemper has a thing for you. That's why he was saying shit. He wants to poison the waters to make sure he doesn't have any competition."

"That's ridiculous."

"No, it's not." Riley ran a hand through his hair. "That crap he was spouting could hurt your reputation. So I made sure he wouldn't run his mouth again."

"Great," I said sarcastically.

"I owed you for saving me."

"I didn't save you."

"Really? I thought that was you who put all these bruises on my back."

"Don't complain. The alternative would have been worse. But anyone would have done it. It was nothing."

"Maybe, but you're something special. Kemper sees it, and he knows that I see it too."

Butterflies fluttered in my stomach, but I shook it off. "Stop."

"I will on one condition. Pay me back for taking care of the Kemper situation by treating me to a slice or a sandwich. After all, it's dinnertime, and I'm starving."

"I'm not taking you out to dinner. If anything, you should be offering to buy me dinner." As soon as the words left my mouth, I realized that had been his plan. Michael Riley was a world-class manipulator. Just another negative quality to add to his list of attributes, right above gorgeous eyes and sexy body.

"Fine. Twist my arm. I hope you have a hankering for Chinese takeout, but we're eating it at your place."

# TWELVE

I drove home, changed out of my work clothes, pulled on a sweatshirt and jeans, ran a brush through my hair, and forced myself to leave the bathroom before I did something stupid, like put on makeup or curl my hair. This was not a date. I didn't know what it was, but it wasn't a date.

I dug through the kitchen drawers for plastic utensils, grabbed a few beers from the fridge, found some condiments, and put everything out on the counter. Unsure what else to do, I settled on the couch and waited for him. Maybe I should change or fix my hair. Would he want to eat out of the containers or off actual dishes? Maybe we should use real silverware? Or was he a chopstick guy?

A few minutes later, he knocked.

"It's open," I called, doing my best to appear less neurotic than I felt.

"You're a cop. You should know better than to leave your door unlocked," Riley scolded, carrying a plastic bag that smelled of Asian spices. He cocked an eyebrow at me. "You look comfortable."

"I am."

"Good." He put the bag on the coffee table and pulled out a couple of cartons. My stomach growled, and he laughed. "Someone's hungry. It's a good thing I suggested dinner. You would have starved."

I grabbed a container of egg drop soup and nestled against the corner of the couch, pulling my legs up and sitting sideways to face him. We ate our soup in silence before moving on to the main course.

"Do you want my egg roll?" I held out the fried object.

"You don't want it?"

"I despise egg rolls. Now if it were a cream cheese wonton, I wouldn't have even offered. I would have just inhaled." I let him take the offered snack.

"How do you feel about shrimp toast?"

"I've never had shrimp toast."

His eyes went wide. "Next time, we're getting shrimp toast."

"Next time? Why would there be a next time?"

He pinned me in place with his gaze. "You think this is case closed? That we're done working together?"

I hadn't thought about it or the possibility of what would happen when I was no longer assigned to assist gangs. "It depends on what Big Bill says, but stopping the crime spree is a good thing. It'd be nice if it was case closed."

"You won't miss me?" He snagged a piece of broccoli from the container and popped it into his mouth, chewed, and swallowed. "Has working together been so terrible that you're counting the seconds until you're free of me?"

"No. I like working with you."

"And I like working with you, but regardless, we still have to eat. There's no reason we can't do that together if you get reassigned."

Since the day we met, he'd been flirting. He'd come close to crossing a line, but he'd back off before things got too serious. Admittedly, I'd been playing the same game.

"You still haven't answered my question. Why did you really come over last night? I don't believe for one second you thought Kemper was stupid enough to show up here," I said.

"I wasn't sure." He bit into the egg roll to buy time. "You wouldn't join me for drinks, but I ran into you going to the bar with Kemper. You said you weren't seeing anyone, but he was carrying your purse. I am a detective. I do notice these things." He buried his chopsticks into the carton of beef and broccoli. "After Kemper left the bar, I wondered if he came to see you. I didn't know what had transpired. I thought you might be together. That you were flying below the radar."

"Why would I date someone who treats me like that?"

"I wouldn't treat you like that." Riley went back to eating, not looking in my direction.

"Care to explain that one?"

"Nothing to explain. I enjoy spending time with you. I'd like to do it personally and not just professionally. Kemper realized he had competition and hoped to turn you away from the idea before I brought it up."

"We work together. The department frowns upon personal relationships, especially within the same chain of command. Lightman would send me back to vice in a heartbeat. And frankly, I barely know you, but I'm guessing someone like you knows all the hazards of dating at work. You must realize it's a bad idea."

"Someone like me? You don't know anything about my history, and you haven't even bothered to ask. That's not fair."

"I think it is."

"No. You can't say that until you get to know me." His blue eyes shone with determination. "I like kung pao chicken, beef and broccoli, and hot and sour soup. My place is too messy for houseguests, and I made an ass of myself today by taking that putz with me instead of you." He put the carton on the table and scooted closer. "What more do you need to know?"

I stared into my carton, hoping to come up with a witty response.

"I'm also a wonderful kisser and a great lay," he said.

"Can Detective Preston vouch for that?" I saw the look on his face. "Y'know what," I climbed off the couch to get another beer, "don't answer that. Maybe you're right about Kemper, but that doesn't mean he was wrong about you. You and Kemper can find something else to fight over because I'm not a prize that can be won."

"I didn't—"

"But that's how it feels."

"Are you sure about that?" His fingers brushed against mine as I reached for a napkin. A shock went through me.

"We have amazing chemistry, Lexie. I see it on your face. You feel it too. That first time we touched and every time since. That's why the idea that I could be using you has you twisted inside out, but I'm not that kind of guy. I'll prove it to you. At work, at home, anywhere. I want to get to know you better. I want you to know me. To learn that you can trust me. I'm not sure how else to make that happen. Most people go out. They go on dates. They have fun. Work's hectic right now, which makes that difficult for us, but I'll take whatever I can get. Chinese on your couch seems like a good starting point."

"I worked vice for over a year with the sleaziest men in the city drooling all over me. I'm not looking for a physical relationship with anyone right now. You shouldn't waste your time. The answer is no."

"Fine, let's be friends. Once you get to know me, you'll see that I'm not a bad guy. Maybe you'll even change your mind."

"Don't count on it."

"I won't." He held out his hand. "So friends?"

"Friends."

# THIRTEEN

By the next morning, everything was back to normal. Riley and I were friends. Kemper had toned down his attitude, and gangs was abuzz as new details emerged.

Big Bill wanted to negotiate a deal. His lawyer and someone from the district attorney's office were hashing out the details. From the constant in and out taking place inside the interview room, whatever Big Bill had to say was big. Who knew his nickname would be so apropos?

Lightman didn't like that Big Bill was getting offered some sweetheart deal. Bill ran a motorcycle club which was just a fancy way to say gang. Normally, taking down the leader was the objective. That put this entire situation off kilter. And Lightman liked things to follow normal patterns and run smoothly. Maybe he and Hawking weren't that different after all.

Lightman paced the squad room, throwing nervous glances down the hallway and bitching quietly to himself. Preston's eyes never left the corridor as she watched the ADA talk on his phone. Riley, unlike the other two detectives, pecked away at the keyboard, oblivious to everything.

"Okay, what's going on?" Kemper finally asked. "What did Big Bill say?"

"He hasn't officially said anything yet," Lightman replied, surprising us by answering. "Unofficially, his crew's been stealing this stuff to pay off a debt they owe to a rival MC."

"What MC?" I asked.

Lightman looked at me like I was a buzzing gnat. "The V-7s."

"How did they earn that debt?" Hawking asked.

"Big Bill's crew is tiny. According to him, the Street Bishops paid protection money to the V-7s to avoid hassles and any trouble that might ride their way. Originally, they held the V-7s at bay by giving them a cut of their profits, but when sales slowed, the Street Bishops had to get creative to keep up with the weekly tribute."

"That's why they've been stealing from everyone and anyone they can find," I said.

"It gets worse," Preston said. "The V-7s caught wind of what Big Bill was doing and added a few targets and locations to the list. Instead of using the Street Bishops as a source of passive income, the leader of the V-7s turned them into his private army."

"Did they perform hits?" Kemper asked.

"We'll see once they finish signing the damn paperwork. But I'd say things are gonna get dark, real fast." Lightman sipped his coffee. "The V-7s' leader, Alfred Sigfried, has been assimilating members of the Street Bishops into his MC. Once they prove themselves via the thefts and miscellaneous missions, Sigfried takes them under his wing."

I knew Sigfried had something to do with this.

"Which put Big Bill and the Street Bishops at an ever-increasing disadvantage," Preston said. "Big Bill needed more men and more money to make up what he was losing, all the while still having to pay off Sigfried."

"Like a loan shark," I said. "The Street Bishops could never get out from under the V-7s' control."

"That's why Big Bill makes so many deals." Riley glanced in my direction before turning back to his computer screen.

"Hence all the break-ins," Kemper said. "But which MC initiation is it? The Bishops', or the V-7s'?"

"Hard to tell at this point," Lightman said. "However, Big Bill must have figured if he got enough guys behind him, he could tell Sigfried to shove it. That's why he's cooperating. He wants us to take care of his problem for him."

"How?" Kemper asked. "If he rolls on the V-7s, he'll be rolling on a bunch of his former guys."

"Do you think he cares? They betrayed him first," Lightman said. "Once Bill rolls on the V-7s and we make sweeping arrests, he'll take over the entire area. No more protection money. No more thefts. He gets what he wants. He's hoping we'll play along since that'll mean the break-ins stop and we get credit for pulling a bunch of violent criminals off the streets."

"Only to replace them with a different set of violent criminals." Hawking sighed.

"That's police work, boys and girls," Lightman said.

"How do we stop that from happening?" I asked, my mind running through the possibilities but not coming up with much of anything. "Yes, we want the crime wave to end, but how do we stop the Street Bishops from taking over?"

"We can't," Lightman said.

Preston looked torn. "Actually, maybe we can, Jack. It depends on Big Bill. He may not offer up a list of his current crew. But they have more stolen property stockpiled they'll want to convert to cash. As long as we're paying attention, we could get them that way."

"That's the long game," Lightman said. "And that's assuming they don't unload it before we are in a position to arrest them."

"Frank said Bill has a lot more stashed somewhere, more than what he told Sigfried about. Bill called it his rainy day fund," Riley said.

"How did Frank hear about that?" I asked.

"The same way he heard about Bill selling off his stash."

"Which was?"

"He overheard the bartender talking on the phone. The bartender's not technically part of the Street Bishops since he doesn't ride, but he runs the bar and watches over Big Bill's apartment."

"Can we turn him?" Lightman asked.

Riley shook his head. "Frank said no, and if we try, we'll compromise our UC. Frank pretended to be passed out at the bar when he overheard those things. He was the only one there besides the bartender and Big Bill. We can't do that to him."

Lightman considered it for longer than he should have before agreeing. "Big Bill may be untouchable, but he can't negotiate a deal for his entire crew. We'll build a case against each individual separately if we have to."

"Before this case, we rarely heard about the V-7s," Riley piped up. "They aren't in the database. Only Sigfried is. He was Big Bill's cellmate. Are we certain Big Bill isn't full of shit? He knows he needs to serve up some valuable intel or else he's going down for the crime spree."

"If his intel's sound, he gets the deal. And if it isn't, we throw the book at him. It's as simple as that." Lightman dropped into a chair. "I hate waiting for these legal eagles to come to a decision. It's holding us back from doing actual police work."

The ADA poked his head into the room. "Hey, Jack, we need to talk."

Lightman groaned. "Yep."

I went to the coffeemaker, only to find it empty. "Who finished the coffee?" I asked, but everyone ignored me. Rolling my eyes, I brewed a fresh pot.

Preston joined me to refill her mug and took a sip. "We ought to keep you around, Sarconi. You make great coffee."

"Thanks," I said, wondering why she was being so friendly. Maybe she drank the last cup.

She looked a little sheepish. "Riley and I will compile as much information as we can on the V-7s in case Big Bill's story pans out. I thought, since you're great at organization and research, you could go to the records room and sift through the old case files. Like Riley said, there's very little about the V-7s in the database. Even though almost everything is digitized, every once in a while a file is corrupted or something gets missed. I like to be thorough. And everything's easier when we have hard copies on hand to review."

"No problem." I concealed my dread behind a smile. "I'll

see what I can find."

Taking my coffee, I went upstairs, signed in, and began the arduous task of searching for anything relevant. The V-7s only came into existence eighteen months ago, so I focused on Alfred Sigfried instead.

He'd spent half a decade behind bars. His laundry list of crimes included operating a prostitution ring. Idly, I wondered if I'd ever encountered him or his working girls when I was in vice.

After copying the relevant files, I returned downstairs, placed the papers on the corner of Preston's desk, and looked around the room. Only Kemper remained.

"Where'd everyone go?" I asked.

"Preston and Riley went to check something. Lightman's in the interrogation room with Big Bill and the lawyers. And Hawking didn't feel well, so he went home."

"Okay." I put the files on top of Preston's desk. "I found something interesting, so I'm going to check with vice to see if they have anything on Alfred Sigfried or the V-7s. If Preston gets back before I do, tell her where I went and why."

"All righty." Kemper tossed a look in my direction. "Hey, Lexie, about the other night, I wasn't trying to say you were incompetent or anything."

"No sweat."

"Really? You've barely spoken to me since. I was afraid you were holding a grudge."

Apparently, I exuded grudge-holder vibes. "Life's too short, but if you want to make it up to me, don't do it again." I returned to the stairwell and went down the steps to vice.

Returning to my old stomping grounds was anticlimactic. I expected to see a few familiar faces or hear someone call out my name, but neither happened. Knocking on the lieutenant's door, I waited to gain admittance and asked if he knew if the V-7s were involved in prostitution. He looked through a few files but didn't find anything worth mentioning, so he passed my question off to the closest detective.

Again, I waited for answers, but none came. After

almost two hours of digging, I gave up and returned to the gangs unit. This time, I found myself alone. Even Kemper had left.

Perhaps Lightman was still inside the interrogation room. Deciding I should check, I headed down the hallway and entered the attached observation room.

# FOURTEEN

My jaw dropped. From what I could tell, Big Bill had been shot. He was slumped over the table. Blood dripped down the sides and onto the floor. Where were my fellow police officers? Where were the attorneys? Why wasn't anyone responding to this?

I burst into the interrogation room to check his pulse. Suspects weren't supposed to die in police custody, particularly from a gunshot wound inside an interrogation room. How could this have happened? Who fired the shot? How come no one heard it?

I searched for his pulse but didn't find it. I yelled for help. Officers and paramedics were on the way. Until they arrived, I had to secure the area. This was a police station. Help was fifty feet down the hall and would be here any second.

The door to the interrogation room slammed shut behind me. Spinning around, I came face to face with a scrawny guy in a dark hood. He held a gun in his hand, which he aimed at me.

"Remove your firearm, real slow," he said.

The hood obscured his face. He pressed his back against the rear wall. He was standing in the only blind spot inside the room. That's why I hadn't noticed him through the two-way mirror. He must have snuck in to perform the hit and got trapped when the door closed and locked. The gun in his hand had a suppressor, which explained why no one heard the shot.

"Sir," I used the calm authoritarian voice we were taught in the academy, "I need you to lower your weapon."

"Do what I say." Footsteps sounded outside the room. "Now."

"I can't do that." I reached for my gun, pulling the strap free and letting my fingers caress the handle. "You need to relax. Why don't you tell me who you are and what happened here?"

"Bitch, don't try anything. Move your hand away from your gun, and keep it away. If I see you go for it, I'll kill you. If anyone else enters this room, I shoot you first. Now tell them to stay back."

The door swung open, but I blocked the other officers from entering. "Stay back. We have a situation here."

"What kind of situation, Sarconi?" one of them asked, unholstering his gun and holding it down at his thigh.

I nodded at the weapon in his hand. "Yeah, it's that kind."

"Shit."

The group split up. A few radioed in the code while the others tried to determine the best angle to take out the shooter. Too bad he wasn't cooperating with their efforts. He remained pressed against the wall, protected from the armed officers in the adjacent room and the hallway. His gun remained trained on me. One misstep, and he'd fire.

Even though my colleagues were only a few feet away, I was alone. It was just the shooter, a dead Big Bill, and me.

At this distance, he wouldn't miss. But he was too far away for me to rush him. He'd fire, and I'd die. Until I came up with a better plan or the cavalry saved the day, I'd do as he asked.

The shooter leveled his gun at my face. "Good girl. Now I need you to get me out of here."

Fear and adrenaline coursed through my veins, and I tried to recall my training. Help was five feet away. I needed to control the situation while they devised a plan.

"What do you want?" I asked, attempting to distract him with a negotiation. "You're inside a police station. Getting out of this alive might be tricky. You have to help yourself here. Lower your weapon."

He didn't fidget or show fear. He kept the barrel of his gun trained on me. "Come here."

I didn't move.

"I will kill you if you don't listen," he said. My hand moved to my gun. "Don't do that. Get your hands up."

"Okay." I raised my hands to hip height, keeping the tips of my fingers near the handle.

"All the way."

I did as he said.

"Put them on top of your head and lace your fingers together." He waited until I complied. "Now get your ass over here. I won't say it again."

Hand-to-hand combat training was mandatory, so moving in closer might increase my chances of subduing him or distracting him long enough for my fellow officers to take him down. It was my best bet and my only choice. He had a gun and wouldn't take no for an answer.

Slowly, I stepped toward him. He reached for my belt, yanking at my holstered weapon. He pulled it free from the leather, and I spun, elbowing him in the face. My gun crashed to the floor and skittered underneath the table.

He shoved me into the wall and fired a shot. The bullet whizzed past my head. Even silenced, it deafened me in one ear before striking the cinderblock. The discharge caused four police officers to race inside with their weapons drawn.

The shooter grabbed my arm, spun me in front of him, ducked behind me, and held his gun to my head. He made sure to keep me between him and his impending death.

"You kill me, and I'll make sure she dies too," he said.

He concealed his identity beneath a mask, but his eyes spoke volumes. He was serious. He held my arm so tightly, his fingers left bruises.

"You're gonna get me out of here," he hissed.

"There's nowhere to go," someone said.

The shooter sounded as panicked and vicious as a cornered animal. "I'll make sure you die before I do if you don't get me the hell out of here, right now." His trigger finger itched and flexed. I believed he'd do it.

"Okay," I said.

Yanking on my braid, he pulled me flush against his body. The barrel of his weapon pressed into the side of my neck, and I bit my lip to keep from crying out as the hot metal burned my skin.

"Everyone keep cool," I said, mustering more calm than I thought I possessed.

I didn't struggle as he edged along the wall, toward the exit. He rounded the doorway, keeping his back against the wall and slamming my side into the doorknob as we turned. I grunted in pain, and for a second, I thought a couple of the officers were going to open fire.

"Just keep cool," I said as he inched us along the corridor. He made sure to stay sandwiched between the wall and me, forcing the responding officers to make room as we headed toward the exit.

The tension was thick. Radio calls sounded in the background. SWAT was on the way.

Lightman skittered to the edge of the squad room with Riley by his side. I didn't know where they came from, but I was relieved to see two familiar faces. Another call went out over the radio, announcing a lockdown due to a hostage situation.

Somehow, the fact that this was a hostage situation and I was the hostage had eluded me. But the thought sent a ball of dread into the pit of my stomach. I felt dizzy and inhaled a deep breath.

I was going to die. The gunman already killed one man. Surely, he wouldn't hesitate to kill me once he realized he wasn't going to make it out of this alive.

"Move it." The shooter yanked me along at a faster rate. I stumbled, and he swore, pulling me so tightly against him, I could feel the cell phone in his pocket pressing into my leg.

"There's nowhere left to go," someone said to our left. "You're not stepping foot outside of this police station."

"Then neither will she." He flattened further into the wall, pressing his back against it and keeping me in front of him. He'd been edging toward the exit, but with the latest announcement, he was afraid someone would try to take him from behind. The angles hadn't been great before, but they were worse now.

Why did I ever step foot inside that interrogation room? A sob tried to escape my lips, but I swallowed it back down. I needed to hold it together. This was the job. I knew the risks, even if I never imagined something like this would happen.

I had to do something to help myself, but between his grip and the gun, I'd be dead before I could do anything. On the bright side, he would never see the light of day again either.

"Lexie," Riley's voice cut through the radio squawks and whispers, "you're going to be okay. Trust me. Everything's fine. Just look at me."

I locked onto his blue eyes, seeing an inferno erupting in their deep pools. He stepped out of the squad room and into the hallway. The other officers sought protection from doorways and furniture, but Riley remained out in the open, completely exposed to the lunatic with the gun.

"Don't speak to her," my captor said. "I'm in charge. Now clear the way so we can pass."

"Listen, buddy, you have three seconds to do the right thing and let the lady go," Riley said, and I shuddered, frantically searching for SWAT's laser sight. "Lexie, look at me." Even if my captor didn't know what was about to happen, I did. "Keep your eyes on me. I'm right here. I'm not going anywhere. You're going to be fine. Nothing's going to happen to you. I won't let it."

"Bullshit." The guy dragged me another few feet, his back still against the wall as he used me as a human shield. But armed officers at the other end of the hallway made him reconsider, and he froze in place, trapped and unsure where to go.

"Two," Riley whispered, his eyes on mine. "One."

The force of the impact propelled my captor forward, knocking us both to the ground. He landed on top of me, and I screamed. It wasn't professional, but I couldn't help it.

The cops swarmed, pushing the assailant off me, confiscating his weapon, and cuffing him, even though he was dead from the blast that had gone through the cinderblock and into the back of his skull. SWAT had the most powerful weapons outside the military, including rounds that could penetrate layers of steel and concrete. So they shot him through the wall.

Riley raced to me, kneeling on the ground and pulling me into his arms. He held me close. "Are you okay?" His focus kept shifting between what was happening with the shooter and with me. "Lexie, look at me. Let me see those pretty eyes of yours. Are you okay? Were you hit?"

He grasped my face in his hands, quickly assessing my head and neck for any injuries. No matter how hard I tried, I couldn't stop trembling. It was the adrenaline surge and the shock of what just happened.

"He killed Big Bill," I managed. "He was in the interrogation room when I went inside. I didn't see him. He was hiding next to the glass."

"It's okay. You're okay." Riley hoisted me to my feet. But the world spun, and I clung to his strong arms which were around me again, hugging me to his chest. "You did good. It's over now. You're safe."

"Give her some room to breathe." Preston tugged one of Riley's arms loose. "Apparently, our gofer has to make sure this place runs smoothly. Where was Lightman and the officer assigned to keep watch over the suspect? Who the hell let this jackass into the station in the first place?" She jerked her head at what remained of the assailant, and my gaze followed the movement.

Seeing the pool of dark red blood, the pieces of skull and brain matter, and the look of sheer shock on what was left of my captor's face, I was hit by a strong wave of nausea and ran to the nearest bathroom. I wretched until my body couldn't take it anymore, and I collapsed, my cheek dropping against the cold porcelain toilet seat. Randomly, I considered the number of germs that must be on it. Luckily, there was nothing left in my stomach to expel, or that thought would have made me sick.

Riley followed me into the bathroom and pressed a cold, damp cloth against the back of my neck. He stroked my back and made sure my hair didn't fall in front of my face.

He didn't say anything.

"This is the ladies' room, Michael," Preston said from behind. "Unless you're planning to cut something off, I'll take it from here."

"Sam," he growled, but she made a tsk sound. "Fine." His lips brushed against my ear. "I'll be right outside if you need me."

I nodded, and he left.

"It's okay, Sarconi." Preston knelt in the spot Riley had vacated, pulled my hair out of my face, and wiped the remaining blood spatter off me. "We all react like this when something that traumatic happens. At least you made it into the bathroom rather than vomiting all over our DB." She smiled, attempting to crack a joke. "Come on, let's get you cleaned up. Once you go back out there, a few detectives will want to take your statement and ask you a dozen questions. You're entitled to have your union rep present if you want, but they aren't looking to blame you for anything. They just want to know what happened. You weren't at fault. In fact, you're the only one in this whole damn place who was paying attention today. If it hadn't been for you, that creep would have snuck out, and who knows who else he might have killed."

"Who was he?"

"We're working on it. I'm sure Michael's tasked half the department and everyone in homicide to do some digging. We'll get to the bottom of this." She narrowed her eyes, seeing the burn on my neck. "Does anything hurt? Do you need medical attention?"

"I'm okay. I just want this shift to be over."

"The sooner we get off this disgusting floor, the sooner you can go home."

# FIFTEEN

I remained at my desk, sipping a soda and jittery as hell. I'd written my statement and recounted the event a dozen times. From the intelligence that had been collected so far, the shooter, Stryker King, ran with Alfred Sigfried's crew. Sigfried must have suspected Big Bill was going to rat on him and sent King to take care of the problem. It was ballsy to send someone into a police station to kill a guy, and clearly, King was stupid enough to think he could shoot his way out.

Det. Michael Riley had been hovering since the shooting, and now that I was finally free to call it a night, he drove me home, even though my car was right outside. But after what happened, my body was numb and buzzing at the same time. That was probably a bad sign.

"I never should have let that guy get the jump on me," I said. "I should have paid more attention. Checked the room."

"You couldn't have known," Riley said. "You kept your wits about you. You did what you had to."

"I didn't do anything. I should have fought."

"He would have killed you."

I blinked. "This feels like a bad dream. I'm not sure any of it is real."

He parked outside my apartment building and studied my eyes. "It's just the shock of today. You'll feel better in the morning. All you need is a stiff drink and a good night's sleep."

"I can't feel anything."

He lifted my hand in his and pressed my palm against my chest. "Do you feel your heart beating?"

"I guess, but it seems disconnected, somehow."

He frowned but didn't say anything else. Instead, he came around to my side of the car, opened the door, and took my hand. My fingers held a slight tremble. I didn't know if that was from his touch or the earlier ordeal. He took my keys, unlocked my apartment, and stepped inside.

"I'll make you a drink. Where do you keep the booze?"

"I don't think I can stomach that right now. But help yourself." I pointed at one of the cabinets and went into the bedroom. "Can I ask you a favor?"

"Anything."

"Will you stay for a little while? I don't want to be alone."

Something teasing crossed behind his eyes, but he didn't say whatever was on his mind. "Sure. Why don't you take a shower and get cleaned up? It'll make you feel better."

"Yeah, I guess."

He poured some bourbon into a glass, took a seat on my couch, and flipped on the television. "I'll be right here."

After the horrors of the day washed down the drain, I dried my hair and went into the living room to find a glass waiting for me. Michael was watching a baseball game, but from the way his jaw muscles clenched and his fingers drummed a beat against the side of his glass, he wasn't seeing what was happening on the screen.

"Thanks for staying." I took a seat next to him and downed the liquor, cringing as it burned my throat. The only thing I wanted was to feel his arms around me again. I tried to shake it off.

"Are you feeling better? Two close calls in one week are never a good thing." He turned off the TV and brushed his fingers against the burn on my neck. "Does that sting? Do you want some ice or aloe?"

"I don't know. All I can think about is how it could have ended in the blink of an eye. If SWAT had been an inch off,

I'd be on that floor too."

"They're professional shooters, trained for tactical resolutions. You were safe."

I flashed to the look on his face before the shot was fired. "Every day, I wake up knowing this could be a possibility. I've had close calls, but they never get easier. At times like this, I wonder if I should even be a cop."

"Lex, you're safe. It's normal to be rattled. The department has a shrink on the payroll. Maybe you should think about talking to him."

"Did you talk to him after you almost got hit by a car?"

Riley sipped the last of his drink. "I took my aggression out on Kemper instead."

"That's not healthy."

"Especially for Kemper." Riley snickered. "But I have talked to the shrink before, when I've found myself in worse jams. It's something to think about."

"I'm pretty sure Lt. Peterson's insisting on it. But that's not going to help me right now. All I want is to get the feel of his hands and the sound of his voice out of my head."

"I know something that might help." Riley took my face in his hands, searched my eyes for permission, and kissed me.

To both our surprise and his delight, I kissed him back. And then it turned into a frenzy. Nothing but raw emotion and physical desire.

"Lexie," he whispered, breaking the kiss, "I don't want to take advantage. You're vulnerable right now."

"I'm not vulnerable." My hands had a mind of their own and had unbuttoned his shirt and were working on his belt buckle. "Sorry, I wasn't thinking. It's been a long day. I guess I just wanted something to take my mind off of it."

"Yeah, well, that was the point." He studied his partially unhooked belt for a moment. "We're just friends, no benefits, right?"

"I don't know anything right now. I just want it to stop. When I close my eyes, all I see is his gun in my face, and when there's nothing but silence, I hear that shot ring out and the wet sound of the bullet piercing his skull."

I shuddered again, and Michael lifted me onto his lap.

"Then let's not think about anything for the next few minutes." He grasped my face in his hands and kissed me again, encouraged by my earlier actions. His eyes burned with lust, and the look caused my stomach to flip. Even though we had done nothing but kiss, I could feel the heat rising between us. "For the record, this has nothing to do with our dynamic at work. But I'll stop if you tell me to. This is your call."

His words set off warning bells in my brain. "We shouldn't. We work together."

"No one has to know." He looked sincere, at least sincere enough for my revved up libido, and I kissed him again, desperate to lose myself in something besides the images of blood and brain matter that surfaced behind my eyes.

We broke apart long enough for me to take my sweatshirt off. He smiled at the lace-trimmed camisole I wore underneath.

"Always full of surprises," he said.

I moaned as he caressed my left breast and suckled the right through the thin material. I arched into him, wanting him to remove the cloth barrier in our way.

"Michael." My voice was ragged, filled with desire and need.

He stopped momentarily, shedding his unbuttoned shirt and letting it drop to the couch beside us. His eyes held a question. "Stay with me, Lex. Stay here in this moment. Nothing else exists. Be here with me."

Then he found my mouth and kissed me. Our lips did battle. He pushed me back on the couch and alternated between nipping and licking along my collarbone. I squirmed underneath him. While my body screamed out yes, my mind couldn't get on the same page.

When he gently bit down, I jerked upright from the sudden jolt of pain, and he grinned evilly. "You still with me?"

"Michael–"

"Do you expect me to do all the work?"

He wanted to play, but concern was beneath the surface. I could see it in his eyes and hear it in his voice. Was he worried about me or afraid I'd come to my senses?

Pushing him backward, I straddled his lap, aware of the thick denim on denim. He let out a pleasurable groan, expecting things to progress further.

Rational thought flickered on inside my brain. "We have to stop." I pressed my palms into my eyes in order to think without seeing the need behind his blue irises. "I can't do this."

"Oh-kay." He sucked in a breath, the corner of his lip curled upward. "What can't you do?"

"Have sex. Mess around. Whatever it is we're about to do. We can't. I can't." I extricated myself from his lap on shaky legs. "I'm sorry."

He reached for me, but I stepped backward. "This is on me. I shouldn't have come on to you. I thought it's what you wanted. I thought it'd help." He adjusted himself and put his shirt back on.

"Michael," I began, not sure if I wanted to apologize for changing my mind or berate him for letting things escalate.

"Don't worry. It's okay. It never happened." His phone buzzed, and I jumped, gasping and reaching for my weapon which wasn't on my hip. He held up his palms. "Take it easy. It's just a text message."

"Yeah."

He grabbed his phone off the coffee table and read the waiting text. "That's the station. Hopefully, they've made some progress figuring out what happened this afternoon."

I looked down at my discarded top layer. "I'm really sorry about this."

"There's nothing to be sorry about. This was fun." He pressed his lips to my forehead as I took a deep breath, my heart rate slowly returning to normal. "I wanted to take your mind off things, but this wasn't exactly my A-game since we're just friends. No benefits." He winked. "You should stay home tomorrow. Call in and tell them you're taking the day off. It'll give you time to get your head on straight."

"No. I want to know what happened."

"You need to get some rest. And I need to know you're safe. But if you insist on going to work, call me. I'll pick you up since your car is at the station."

"Thanks."

"Anytime."

~*~

When I woke up, it was noon and my clock radio was playing a pop song. The music must have been on for the last five hours, but it wasn't enough to wake me.

Briefly, I wondered if I sustained hearing damage. But more than likely, I was exhausted, emotionally and physically.

Did I almost have sex with Michael Riley last night? I hid my face in my hands and tried to justify the insanity that had overtaken my life. What had I been thinking? We'd just gotten back on an even keel too.

Pulling myself out of bed, I trudged into the kitchen to make some coffee. I was starving, but there was nothing to eat. I was searching the pantry when a knock sounded at the door. Opening it, I was surprised to find Riley holding a paper sack from a nearby burger joint.

"Hey," he looked unsure of himself, a look I hadn't seen the cocky detective exhibit before, "how are you?"

"Embarrassed." I gestured for him to come inside. "I'm sorry about last night. And I'm starting to sound like a broken record."

"There's no reason to be embarrassed. Yesterday was crazy. I get it. We don't need to talk about it. Your nymphomaniac side is one secret I promise to protect." He smiled, and I slapped his arm. "When you didn't call this morning, I got worried. I also happened to remember how lacking your fridge and pantry were and thought you could use something to eat." He put the bag on the table, an amused glint in his eyes as I rifled through the contents, unwrapped the burger, and took a huge bite. "Obviously, I was right."

"It was bound to happen at some point."

"I'm also wondering how you managed not to starve before you met me."

"I used to be more responsible. You've made me

reckless."

He frowned. "You weren't reckless. King would have gotten the drop on anyone."

"Maybe one of these days I'll believe that." I took another bite of the burger. "Is Lightman pissed I didn't show up this morning? I forgot to call in sick."

"I covered and told him you said you'd be late. The people investigating yesterday's incident have a few more questions. So whenever you're ready, I'll drive you to work."

# SIXTEEN

When we arrived at the station, I was ushered into an office and had to recount what happened yesterday. Now that I had time to process, the investigator wanted to make sure my story hadn't changed and I didn't leave anything out. I hadn't.

After that, I returned to the squad room.

Preston smiled at me. "You look better today, Sarconi. Is everything okay?"

"Yeah, I just had to go through another recount of yesterday's events. By now, I'm pretty desensitized to the whole thing."

"That's good," Lightman said, "because I need to have a word with you." I followed him into the lieutenant's vacant office, and he closed the door behind us. "What were you doing checking on the interrogation?"

"I was looking for you." Did Lightman think I was telling internal affairs he was at fault? Was he at fault?

"I'm glad. We wouldn't have the leads we do if we didn't discover Stryker King inside that interrogation room. Even though Big Bill can no longer testify, he gave us a lot of dirt on Alfred Sigfried and the V-7s. We're going after Sigfried. As we speak, units are keeping tabs on his associates. Everything that happened yesterday is the break we've been waiting for. Good job, Sarconi. There might be a permanent place for you here." The way he said those words made me think he wanted to ensure my loyalty to him, but I didn't say anything. I simply thanked him and returned to the squad room.

"Hey," Riley met me at my desk, "Frank identified the stripper. Her stage name's Jezabelle, but her real name is Jessalyn Belknap. She's twenty-eight and lives three blocks east of the bar. I got her address." He waggled his eyebrows at me. "Want to take a ride?"

"Am I allowed?"

"Why wouldn't you be?"

"You heard what Lightman said. He didn't want me going near that neighborhood."

Riley held up the scribbled address in both hands. "It's three blocks east. That's an entirely different neighborhood. The Street Bishops and V-7s have nothing to do with that area."

"Are you sure?" This sounded like an excuse to get me out of the station, not that I minded.

He reached down and lifted his badge, carefully assessing it. "Gangs detectives should know those kinds of things. And this says I'm a gangs detective." I fought to keep from smiling, which made him smile. "I got you, Lexie. No more close calls today. I promise."

"You can't promise that."

"Sure, I can."

I looked around the room. Everyone was working on something. Unlike most days, the station was quiet. A nervous energy permeated the various levels. The cops inside were on edge after what happened yesterday. And that collective anxiety was bound to make me more anxious. "Yeah, okay."

He tucked the address slip into his pocket, announced where we were headed, and left before Lightman had time to process the words and object. I hurried to keep up as we went down the stairs and out the front door.

"Why do I feel like I'm ditching math class?" I asked.

"Did you ever ditch math class?"

"Maybe."

He unlocked the doors to the unmarked car and climbed behind the wheel. "Oh really?" He waited for me to buckle up before he put the car in gear.

"Did you ever skip school?"

"Sure. Everyone did. That's why they invented senior ditch day. I may have even organized it."

"You seem more star quarterback than slacker to me."

"Huh." He considered my words while he drove toward Jessalyn Belknap's apartment. "What makes you think I played football?"

"I don't know. Maybe it wasn't football. Maybe you were just big man on campus. Whatever got all the cheerleaders."

"Were you a cheerleader?"

I snorted, finding the notion ludicrous. "I ran track and cross-country."

"Damn, I should have guessed that." He found a too-small parking space and squeezed in, nearly taking off the nose of the car in the process. But somehow, he avoided a collision. "And you were right. I did quarterback in high school, but I wasn't good enough to play in college, aside from some pick-up games and intramural flag football."

"Shit."

"What?" He checked the mirrors, afraid he had dinged another car.

"You're a sports guy."

"You say that like it's a bad thing."

"It is."

"But you're athletic. You ran track and cross-country."

"I know, but you're one of those guys who watches sports. I bet you go to the bar to watch the games."

"What's wrong with that?"

I opened the car door and stepped out, scanning the area for gang colors and motorcycles. "Nothing."

He didn't believe me, but he dropped the subject as we headed up the walkway to Ms. Belknap's apartment. After getting buzzed into the building, we knocked on her apartment door, but she didn't answer. On our way out, I spotted her walking down the sidewalk.

"Michael," I pointed to the woman, "that's her."

We jogged to catch up, falling into step beside her. She had an oversized, reusable grocery bag slung over her shoulder. She wore skinny jeans and a white blouse with rhinestone-encrusted sunglasses. The stones matched the ones on her nails. This was definitely the same woman.

"Ms. Belknap," Riley said, "may we have a word?"

She turned to look at him, and he discreetly pointed to his badge. "What is this about?"

"You work at Bishop's Bar."

"I dance. That's not illegal."

"No, ma'am," Riley said. "But we have a few questions about the establishment that we hoped you could answer."

She glanced from Riley to me. "I remember you. It took guts to walk into that bar. You're either stupid or damn confident."

"I'd like to think it's the latter," Riley said. "I don't know if you heard, but Big Bill bought it yesterday afternoon. The bar's under new management."

I studied her carefully while Riley spoke. "You didn't know?" I asked.

She shook her head. "I knew he'd been arrested. I didn't know he got popped."

"Any idea who might have been behind it?" Riley asked.

She didn't slow as she approached the nearby market. "It wasn't me."

"But you know who wanted him dead," I said.

"I know enough to keep my mouth shut."

I met Riley's eyes. Whatever Ms. Belknap knew was what almost got us killed. "Do you think the person who killed Big Bill knows you'll keep your mouth shut?"

She picked up the pace, pushing her way into the supermarket and heading for the produce section. But we stuck to her like fresh gum on a shoe. She grabbed a few apples and tossed them into her bag before giving a cantaloupe a sniff.

"Ms. Belknap," I said, "your life could be in danger. We wanted to warn you to be careful." I glanced at Riley, making sure it was okay to reveal what had happened over the last few days. He nodded, so I continued. "After we left the bar, we were almost run over in a parking lot. A witness was threatened to keep silent, but that didn't stop us from building our case against Big Bill. However, once we took him into custody, he told us a lot. We can keep you safe."

"Alfred Sigfried wanted Big Bill dead," she said.

Riley turned, leaning against the display stand while he made sure we hadn't been followed. "What can you tell us about him?"

"He showed up at Bishop's Bar last night. He tore the place apart. He's taking over."

"Did he find Big Bill's hidden stash?" Riley asked.

Her eyes darted to him. "How do you know about that?"

"Big Bill told us a lot. He said he hid it so no one could find it."

"Sigfried found it. It took him a while, but he found it. I don't know how he knew it was in the bar or even that Big Bill had it. If I had to guess, I'd say a former Street Bishop shifted allegiances."

"Any idea what Sigfried plans to do with his newfound fortune?" Riley asked.

"Pawn it. He knows several shops that don't ask a lot of questions."

"The same places Big Bill used?"

"No. He doesn't trust any of those. Sigfried's a paranoid psychopath. He'd assume you'd already have people waiting for him there. He has his own list of places."

Riley clicked his pen. "I'll need names."

"No way. You have no idea how dangerous he is. I'm not telling you shit."

"Sigfried will come after you whether you talk to us or not. He has no reason to trust you. Big Bill didn't trust you. That's why he tried to have us killed. Sigfried's already proven he's far more effective at killing. It's only a matter of time before he comes for you."

She went down the next aisle, stocked up on several pantry items, and made her way to the checkout. "I'm not saying another damn word until you promise to protect me."

"You have my word," Riley said. "Unless you'd rather take your chances that the remaining Street Bishops will keep you safe."

"As soon as Big Bill died, so did his MC. Sigfried claimed the bar and the Bishops as his own. There are no more Street Bishops. He stripped them of their colors and patched them into the V-7s. Whatever Big Bill had belongs to Sigfried now." She swallowed. "Including me."

"We'll get you out," I said. I didn't know how, but Riley gave her his word. She may not have believed him, but I did.

# SEVENTEEN

Jessalyn Belknap agreed to give us details on the Street Bishops, including several of her former boyfriends, their hangouts, their contacts, and everything she had heard about Alfred Sigfried and the V-7s. We had narrowed down the most likely places Sigfried would go to fence the stolen jewelry Big Bill had stockpiled. Since we had eyes on the pawn shops and eyes on Sigfried, Lightman and the rest of the gangs unit were confident we would catch Sigfried in the act.

"I don't understand this," Kemper muttered. "Sigfried hired Styker King to kill Big Bill. Why can't we nail his ass now? What the hell are we waiting for?"

"We don't have proof," Hawking said. "There's no paper trail linking Sigfried to King. And Big Bill never said King would be sent to kill him. It's another one of those things we know, but without evidence, we can't prove it. So we have to wait and see."

"This is such bullshit." Kemper put his hands on his head and spun in a circle. "There should be easier ways to do things."

"Not if you want to stay on the right side of the law."

Annoyed, Kemper walked off. Whether he was calling it quits or taking a break was anyone's guess.

Jessalyn Belknap had been moved into protective custody. An officer was currently occupying her apartment in case Sigfried sent someone to tie up that loose end. So far, there had been no movement on that front. It was possible Sigfried hadn't known enough about the stripper to consider her a threat. But Big Bill knew. However, he didn't send someone to silence her. Instead, he sent someone to take care of us. Big Bill may have been a lot of things, but he never hurt his people unless they hurt him first.

"She's safe, right?" I asked when Riley went past my desk.

"Yeah."

"Okay."

He continued on his way, and I went back to researching the pawn shops where Sigfried liked to do business. After compiling business profiles for each of them and running background checks on the owners. I pulled up a list of their known associates, checking for overlap. Ms. Belknap never mentioned Sigfried using a middleman, but I wanted to make sure we didn't miss anything.

Detective Lightman tapped on my desk. "Call it a night, Sarconi. Shift's over."

I looked around the room, bleary-eyed. I didn't remember anyone saying good night to me, but I had been too focused on what I was doing. I glanced toward Riley's desk, but I didn't see him either. Surely, he would have told me he was leaving.

"Go home." Lightman picked up the legal pad I'd been scribbling on and flipped through the pages. "This looks promising. I'll make sure it gets passed along to the right people. We'll get this guy."

I returned home from work, made dinner, and went to bed early. From the long hours and tedium of being behind a desk, I was tired. Maybe I was still shell-shocked. The department psychologist told me having difficulty sleeping or sleeping too much was normal, but I hoped tonight I'd get a good night's sleep without any interruptions or horror-filled dreams and that I wouldn't sleep through my alarm again.

What woke me this time was the sound of my phone ringing. By the time I found the bothersome device, the noise had stopped, but I had a waiting message. The station was swamped. All available officers were to report for duty.

Feeling as if I'd just left, I jumped in the shower, pulled on the closest thing, and went to work. If they wanted us in uniform, I had one waiting in my locker. But I didn't want to end up out on patrol in the middle of the night after everything that had happened this week.

"Lexie," Kemper said when I arrived at the station, "we've got reports of a hold-up at Tenth and Albemarle. A bystander said a bunch of motorcycle guys showed up with sawed-off shotguns and demanded the money from the drawer. Lightman and Preston are on the scene, but two more calls came in right after that."

"Let me guess. These other two calls relate to the V-7s?"

"Yep. One apartment the Street Bishops hit was targeted again. Hawking is on his way there. The other call was to an address a few blocks from their territory. An officer was assigned to keep watch on the place."

"You mean Jessalyn Belknap's place?"

"That'd be the one."

Dread filled my belly. "Where's the officer now?"

"She scared off the intruder and pursued on foot, but he jumped on a bike and escaped. Lightman wants her to go through the mug books and work with a sketch artist, so we have to secure the apartment until Lightman's dream team can tear themselves away from the hold-up."

"Okay."

"You can ride with me, but you need to change first." Kemper fingered his uniform shirt.

Dammit. "Give me two minutes." After a quick trip to the locker room, I followed Kemper to the cruiser.

"What were you doing when you got the call? You look way too awake for four a.m.," he said.

"I might have been dreaming. I'm not sure. But the wide awake thing happens when the super fails to fix the hot water in your shower."

"Oh, that sucks."

"Tell me about it."

Kemper gave me a sideways look. "Are you sure you're

ready to be out in the shit again?"

"Why wouldn't I be?"

"C'mon, Lex, don't make me say it."

"I appreciate your concern, but I'm fine. If I wasn't, I wouldn't have been cleared for active duty."

We made it to the scene in ten minutes. A few cruisers were already out front. As we went up the stairs, I offered to secure the apartment if Kemper kept watch outside. The officer assigned to guard the scene gave me a rundown of what had happened and when it happened, signed off, and left.

Since there wasn't much for me to do, I remained in the hallway. Whoever came here didn't plan to rob the place. They came to kill Jessalyn Belknap. While I waited, I wondered if whoever Sigfried sent to do the job had been one of the former Street Bishops or one of Sigfried's own people.

Looking around, I hoped to find a surveillance camera in the hallway, but I didn't see one. This wasn't the kind of apartment building that valued security.

Curious, I went to the door and peered inside. From what I could see of the studio apartment, Ms. Belknap didn't have a lot of places to hide things. And while she had a nice TV, a total body workout machine, and an open closet with what I imagined were items she wore on stage, I didn't see much else of value. This definitely didn't fit the prior M.O.

"Does anyone have a twenty on Riley?" Lightman asked over the radio.

"I haven't seen him. I don't think he showed up," an unfamiliar voice replied.

I pulled out my phone, wondering if I should call him. Surely, Lightman had tried that. Still, I dialed and waited. But the call went straight to voicemail. Riley's phone was off, or he didn't want to talk to me.

Since it was Friday night, Riley might have been inebriated. He'd proven he liked going out for drinks after shift. Maybe he went home to sober up or had other matters to handle. Maybe he was on a date.

My stomach clenched, and I recognized that feeling as

jealousy. How stupid was that? I listened for a response to confirm Riley's location, but no one had any idea where he was.

Could he be in trouble? The thought came to mind, but I did my best to squelch it.

After spending the next thirty minutes keeping watch outside Belknap's apartment while my mind ran through all sorts of terrible scenarios, a man in a dark blue jumpsuit approached. He tugged on the lanyard around his neck, pulling it free from his coveralls. He was with the crime lab.

"Officer Sarconi?" he asked.

"That would be me. How can I help you?"

"I'm Ian Davies. Detective Lightman requested I print the place." He showed me his identification and badge. "May I begin?"

I radioed for verification before letting him into the apartment. He started working, and we talked as he spread black powder and placed tape over the fingerprints.

"Any idea what happened here?" he asked. "I heard something about a crook busting in on a cop."

"We were keeping watch on this place. I guess he didn't realize it."

"I guess not." He continued to dust for prints. "The number of break-ins lately has been insane. Is it true this is part of some gang's initiation?"

"That's the current working theory."

"Well, if it is, I'm glad they aren't randomly popping people. But still, home invasions are the worst. It destroys a person's sense of privacy and safety."

"You sound like you have some experience." I omitted the part about how this had probably been an intended hit and not a break-in.

"A few years ago, someone broke into my place. After that, I had to move. I never felt safe there again."

"That sucks."

"Yep." He sighed "Shouldn't America's youth have better things to do with their time than screw with people? What happened to playing gory, zombie-killing video games and smoking pot behind the school gym? At least that's what we did as kids."

"And you became a police officer?"

"Crime tech," he clarified. "Completely different. I can be a video game loving dork, and as long as I lay off the prohibited substances, the department's happy with my work."

"Nice."

He finished up a few seconds before Detective Preston arrived. She nodded to the tech as he packed his belongings and left the building.

"Sarconi, I'll take it from here. Do you have anything to report?"

"You know as much as I do about the situation." I made sure we were alone in the hallway before I asked, "Is Jessalyn Belknap safe?"

"Michael went to check on her. I'm sure she's fine. A little freaked out, but fine nonetheless. He would have told us if she wasn't."

"Riley's there?"

She arched an eyebrow. "Why do you seem surprised?"

"Lightman was looking for him."

"Yeah, Jack gets like that when he doesn't know where his people are. Since our source is being kept at a safehouse, Michael turned off his phone. He always takes witness safety seriously. That's why no one knew where he was."

"If he turned off his phone, how do you know this?"

She laughed, her eyes crinkling in the corners. "Because I know Michael." She jerked her chin toward the stairs. "Go back to the station. Jack's already on his way there. By now, I'm sure he's devised a plan of attack. But he probably needs someone who knows how to use the copier and make coffee to keep things running smoothly."

"I'm on it."

"Hey, once Michael knows Jessalyn is safe and briefs the officers keeping watch over her, he'll head back to the station. Make sure you tell him to pop in and see Jack before he sneaks away again."

"Sure thing." I continued down the hallway to see if Kemper had been relieved. If not, I'd take his car, and he could bum a ride with Preston. But just like me, Kemper was free to go.

# EIGHTEEN

Once we were back inside the police station, I found Riley and passed Preston's message along. He looked busy. His desk was covered in case files, and he was on the phone. He held up a finger for me to wait. "Right. That's what I said." He paused. "Okay. I wanted to make sure we were taking every precaution." He put the phone down. "Did you hear what happened at Belknap's place?"

"I was assigned to guard it until Preston took over."

"You could have worked the scene yourself. You would have had a better idea of what to look for than Sam." His desk phone rang, and he rocked forward to pick it up. "Go for Riley."

Quietly excusing myself, I took a seat at my desk and hoped no one would ask me to do anything for the rest of the night. I was tired and wanted nothing more than to go back to bed. Five minutes later, Lightman appeared, and we worked nonstop through the rest of my scheduled shift. Even though Big Bill was dead and the Street Bishops were no more, the crime spree hadn't stopped. If anything, the V-7s were escalating.

The hold-up resulted in one dead. Kemper hadn't mentioned it, but I didn't think he knew. I ran the shop owner's profile, but he had no known criminal ties. He simply hadn't handed the money over fast enough. The murder was senseless.

"I'd say it was a distraction," Lightman muttered.

"That's why they did it. They wanted us to be so focused over there that we'd miss what they were doing to Belknap."

"Maybe," Preston said. "Or maybe Sigfried decided to pick up where Big Bill's crew left off. At least we have security footage this time from the shop."

"Some good it does," Lightman said. "The asshole shooter was covered head to toe, and they all wear the same damn cuts and jackets, anyway."

"What about the bike?" Riley asked. "They customize the shit out of their rides."

"Get on that," Lightman ordered. "I'd like to have this guy in the box by start of next shift."

"Lexie, can you do me a favor?" Kemper asked, interrupting my eavesdropping.

"What is it?" I wished I could tell him no. I was nearly through working another double.

"Can you copy your notes from Lightman's debrief? Since this thing keeps getting bigger, I was asked to liaise between this unit and homicide. They want copies of everything we got."

I hit print and pointed to the community printer across the room. "Help yourself. But fair warning, my notes are pointless. They contain the same things we've seen and heard a million times. I'm sure if Lightman assigned you to work with homicide, he's already updated them on his findings."

"Someone's in a bitch of a mood."

"It happens. Deal with it."

"Chicks," he muttered.

"Are you complaining about something, Sarconi?" Riley asked, his eyes teasing. It was easier for him to give me a hard time than it was for him to contain his annoyance with Kemper. Luckily, Kemper took the notes and ducked out. "Did you hear what Jack said? We have work to do on identifying the bike."

"We? I thought he assigned you to do it."

"I need to check on something else. Help a guy out? Lend a hand? Please." He pushed out his bottom lip. "I'll make it up to you at a later date. Maybe with a later date."

"I'm off the clock."

"You're a cop. There is no clock."

I caught the slightest amused glint in his sparkling blue eyes that immediately brought a smile to my face. He looked like a little boy with a secret, and I raised a questioning eyebrow. "What?"

"I pulled everything from records already. The box is on my desk. You should get started." He winked and sauntered away.

"Asshole," I said to his retreating back, hoping he heard the playful tone in my voice.

I pulled the chair out from under his desk and opened the file box. As promised, there was a stack of files, but there was one other item inside the box. I plucked the sticky note off the smaller box.

*Thought you could use a little something to brighten your day. They matched your eyes, so I couldn't resist* was scrawled on the paper that had been attached to a velvet box. Inside was a pair of earrings.

I shoved the lid back on the file box and dragged it over to my desk. Once there, I opened my bottom drawer, took out my purse, and tossed the jewelry inside. Apparently, Riley hadn't given up on the idea of our friendship turning into more.

Unfortunately, he hadn't been lying about the files. Resigned to doing more work before calling it a day, I recruited Kemper and Hawking to help as soon as they returned to the squad room.

Two hours later, we identified the bike from the surveillance footage as one belonging to Deacon Reynolds. This wasn't the first time he'd knocked over a place. He served a nickel for another armed robbery, but no one had been seriously injured that time. He'd also been in more than his fair share of bar fights. Deacon Reynolds wasn't a good guy, which explained why the V-7s were happy to welcome him with open arms.

I texted Riley, but he told me to share my findings with Jack. So that's what I did. Lightman phoned for an arrest warrant. Now that Lightman had his wish of having the suspect in custody, he sent the rest of us home.

Safely inside my apartment, I called Riley to thank him for the earrings and tell him what Lightman had planned. Assuming we couldn't flip Reynolds, Lightman would get Reyolds to warn Sigfried the cops were on to their operation and force him to move up the timetable on selling off Big Bill's stolen stash. If we arrested the V-7s or Sigfried while in possession of that, it'd be a lot easier for us to draw a line between Sigfried and the contracted hit.

"That might work," Riley said. "Jack usually knows what he's doing. If nothing else, it should shift Sigfried's focus away from Jessalyn Belknap and back to keeping tabs on his own crew. Thanks for going through those files and comparing photos. We wouldn't have the ID without you."

"Yeah, no problem. Where did you run off to?"

"I had something to take care of."

"Like what? Jewelry shopping?"

He laughed. "What do you think of the earrings? Do you like them?"

"Yes, but you shouldn't have. Didn't anyone tell you it's illegal to bribe a police officer?"

"It wasn't a bribe."

"Yes, it was. You tricked me into doing your work."

"I did not. The earrings are a gift. A little something to cheer you up. You've seemed off these last few days since all that shit went down. Are you okay? I wanted to ask, but we've been busy."

"I haven't been sleeping well. Nightmares," I admitted.

"Do you want to talk about it?"

"Not really. I've already poured my heart out to the department shrink. Plus, you were there. You know what happened."

"I also know what happened afterward." He inhaled deeply. "Not to further complicate things, but what would you say to going out sometime? I owe you a real date after rounding second and trying to steal third."

Memories of his mouth and hands flooded my mind, and I sighed.

"Is that a yes?" he asked.

"Can I think about it?"

"What's to think about? Haven't you gotten to know me

yet? This is because we work together, isn't it?"

"That's part of it."

"If I were some guy you met at a bar, would you go out with me?"

"I don't pick up men at bars. That stopped when I left vice," I retorted, and he laughed at the joke. "It's also because I haven't dated anyone in a long time. My last boyfriend didn't like that I wanted to be a cop. It was too butch of a profession for him to accept."

"That's because he was an insecure prick. I'm neither of those things, and I love that you're a cop. I wouldn't be here without you, and I wouldn't know you otherwise."

"Let me think about it."

"That means yes."

"It means maybe."

"Which means yes."

I grinned. "Shut up. We have to finish this case first. Once I'm back walking a beat or finding my footing with another unit, there won't be any work issues. It'll make things easier. Less complicated."

"Easy's overrated, but I'm not giving up." He let out a deep, contented sound. "And I know where you live, so don't even think about ducking me."

"Ducking? Oh, don't worry, Michael, I'm not thinking about ducking you. But I might be thinking about doing something else to you."

"I sure as hell hope so."

# NINETEEN

Detective Lightman got his wish. Deacon Reynolds was in the box. The tough guy act lasted through the first five minutes of questioning before he lawyered up. That was to be expected. Reynolds had been through the system. He knew how it worked, and we had him dead to rights.

Unfortunately, the fingerprints taken from Jessalyn Belknap's apartment weren't a match to any of our suspects. Most of the latents belonged to her and the officer who'd been watching the place. The man who came to kill Jessalyn had worn leather gloves that matched his leather jacket. According to the officer, he also had on motorcycle boots, a motorcycle helmet, relaxed jeans, and drove a bike with shiny blue paint accented by flame decals.

I went back through the records I'd perused the previous night, but I didn't find the bike. "Could it be new?" I asked.

"Maybe." Riley flipped through the pages again. "Then again, it could have a fresh paint job. These guys work on their bikes all the time. They are constantly adding mods and changing things."

"You sound like you know bikes."

"I have to with this job."

"Is that all it is? You exude badass. And a lot of badasses ride bikes."

"I may have had one at one point. They handle well in traffic, but that's the beginning and end of it."

I wondered if there was more to the story, but now wasn't the time to push.

"I'll see if the officer can give the sketch artist a more thorough description of the getaway vehicle. Some of these custom parts are pretty unique. Even if we can't trace the color or decal, we may be able to identify the assailant based on something else," Riley said.

"Like the mirrors?"

"Who knows? But I'm out of ideas, unless Reynolds knows who Sigfried sent to perform a second hit."

"It's not like he's talking."

"That's why Jack bluffed and fed him all that misinformation. Now we just have to hope Reynolds is smart enough to get word back to Sigfried that we're moving in on the V-7s. I'm keeping my fingers crossed Sigfried will panic and try to unload the stash." Riley squinted. "Frank's gonna make sure the V-7s know we're getting closer. That a bust is imminent."

"The more pressure, the better," I said.

"I'll try to remember that."

I gave him the evil eye. "Do you think you're funny?"

"Sometimes."

"Whatever, Detective." I clicked a few keys, bringing up Alfred Sigfried's rap sheet. Maybe there was some clue in here on what he'd do now, but all I saw was violent offense after violent offense. "The more I learn about Alfred Sigfried, the more I'm starting to think he could be a serial killer. First, Big Bill. Then that failed attempt on Jessalyn. If he thinks Reynolds talked to us, that would be number three."

"That would only apply if he performed the kills himself."

"Are you sure?" I asked. "That seems like a technicality."

Riley's brows scrunched together while he considered it, but when he didn't come up with an answer, he shrugged. "Let's hope Reynolds is smart enough to figure out how to get word back to Sigfried from his new home at central booking and that Sigfried will take Reynolds' warning as a sign of his continued loyalty and not send a hit squad after him."

"Do you ask Santa for these things? Or do you have a magic lamp you like to rub?"

He gave me a devilish grin. "I could go so many places with that, but I won't." He picked up the folder. "We have too much work to do." And then he walked away.

For the rest of the day, we reviewed what we knew about the three crimes that occurred the previous shift. The repeat apartment break-in fit perfectly with what we'd seen previously. The robbery turned homicide was more extreme but still fell in line with what we'd come to expect from the gang. The only crime that stood out was Belknap's apartment, and we knew exactly why that was.

The units that had been assigned to monitor Alfred Sigfried reported he was at Bishop's Bar during the liquor store hold-up. He hadn't been part of the crew that had circled the liquor store, and he hadn't gone to silence Belknap. After Reynolds was arrested, Sigfried had gone to ground, along with whoever remained in the V-7s. Hopefully, Detective Frank Devereaux would be able to tell us more.

I briefly saw Riley the next day, but that was it. Over the course of the week, we failed to identify the bike or biker who'd been sent to silence Belknap. Instead, we sorted out the mess left in the aftermath of Big Bill's demise.

The Street Bishops had been absorbed by the V-7s. It wasn't a violent affair. It was more like a corporate merger, where all employees were retained. We brought in every member of the gang we could find for questioning, but no one would squeal on Alfred Sigfried. Whatever loyalty the Street Bishops had to Big Bill died with him. But something told me that had more to do with fear than anything else.

Friday, Detective Frank Devereaux entered the squad room looking rough around the edges. His eye was black, and his nose had been broken. He'd been in a fight.

"What happened?" Preston asked, surprised to see him.

Frank shook his head. "Where's Jack?"

She pointed to Lt. Peterson's office, and Frank continued on his way.

"Are you okay?" Riley asked.

"Yeah, but my cover's been blown. The V-7s are gonna be moving on this soon." Frank barged into the office. Even from my spot across the squad room, I could hear him laying everything out for Lightman.

An hour later, the entire unit was called to the conference room for another briefing.

"The V-7s have doubled in size over the last month," Lightman said. "But their newest members are still on the hook for previously owed protection money, so they've ramped up their game and have escalated to knocking over convenience stores, liquor stores, and ransacking every apartment they can in the hopes of hitting a big score. The bigger their score, the more Sigfried expects from them. They'll never get out from owing him. He's behaving like a loan shark. It's exactly like Big Bill told us, but we don't have enough hard evidence to arrest Sigfried since he's careful and hasn't been on the front lines, committing these crimes. However, Sigfried knows we're on to him. Reynolds got word back to him, and after Frank's identity got leaked, Sigfried thinks we're closer than we actually are."

"At least the beating was good for something," Frank muttered.

"Sigfried wants to liquidate everything. He still has what Big Bill kept as part of his rainy day fund and whatever hot property the V-7s have snatched in the last week or two," Lightman said.

"Is he planning to run?" Riley asked. "He runs an MC. I don't think he'd ride off into the sunset. They usually rally. Stay and fight, and all that."

"He's not running," Frank said. "He wants to ditch anything we can use as evidence against him before we serve a warrant or raid his place."

Lightman drummed his fingers impatiently on the table. "I ordered the units assigned to watch him to give him some breathing room. We want him to make a move, so we can catch him in the act. Unfortunately, as soon as they pulled back, he took off. And we lost sight of him."

"Shit." Riley squeezed the bridge of his nose. "This is fucking unbelievable. Can't we drag one of his biker buddies in and force him to tell us where Sigfried went?"

"No one in the MC will help us," Frank said from the corner. "They know Sigfried would put a hit out on anyone who snitches. That's how he ensured their loyalty so quickly."

Preston sighed. "He's terrorizing his own crew. Why won't they turn on him? They outnumber him. Why haven't they tried to take him? How scary can one guy be?"

*Serial killer*, I mouthed to Riley, when he looked in my direction.

Frank cleared his throat. "It's a weird dynamic. The way things work on the inside is more like a dictatorship than anything else. He calls the shots, provides for them, and they reap the benefits. He also doles out punishments. However, ever since he heard Big Bill ratted him out, he's been on tilt. He doesn't trust anyone. It's only a matter of time before he kills one of his own for something stupid. When that happens, the tables might turn, but not until."

"We need to stop him before someone else dies," Riley said.

Preston nodded.

"Why didn't he kill you, Detective Devereaux?" Kemper asked.

I stared at Kemper, wondering where he got the balls to ask the question.

Riley bristled, and Hawking gave Kemper a sharp look. "Don't put shit like that out there," Hawking warned.

"It's okay," Frank said. "I know what you meant. Honestly, I got lucky. After they realized I was a cop, they took me out back. But there must have been a nearby patrol car responding to a call. The two assholes thought the sirens were for them, so they ran. That's when I got the hell out of there. I might have also suggested I was wired and killing me would guarantee they never saw another sunrise."

"They probably wouldn't have," Kemper muttered.

"Regardless," Lightman said, getting the conversation back on track, "we know Sigfried's preferred pawn shops. He has a lot of hot items to move, so he might spread the stash out among different shops to bring in the most cash and avoid extra scrutiny, or he'll dump it all at one location if he needs money fast. Either way, we cover all the shops and wait for him to show." He pointed to Preston. "You can break down the rest."

"We'll divide into teams. One detective will be assigned an officer to ride along. We'll use unmarked cars and monitor the three pawn shops Sigfried is most likely to use. Additional units will cover the remaining shops."

"What happens if this doesn't pan?" I asked. "Sigfried could send someone else to fence the stolen items."

"If he does, we arrest them," Lightman said.

"Worst case, we put all the V-7s behind bars, and Sigfried will have no choice but to come out of his hidey-hole." Preston pointed to the blown-up mugshots of the V-7s' roster. "Any one of these men could be potential targets. We'll use them to get to Sigfried, but Sigfried is the priority. Don't forget that. However, familiarize yourselves with what everyone looks like, if you haven't already."

"We've been staring at their ugly faces for weeks now," Kemper said. "I'd recognize them in my sleep."

"Good. Are there any questions?" Preston looked around the room, her gaze stopping on the three of us huddled near the back wall. Unlike the detectives, we remained standing. "Kemper, you'll ride with me."

He nearly grinned, but Hawking elbowed him.

"That leaves us," Lightman said, pointing at Hawking. "We'll take the pawn shop in the southeast." He pointed to a red circle on the map displayed behind him.

That left Detective Riley with only one option. He got up and moved between me and Hawking to grab a printout of the mugshots. "I guess you're stuck with me," he whispered. "I don't understand how I always end up drawing the short straw."

"All right, you've got your assignments. Keep your eyes peeled. Let's get to it," Lightman said.

# TWENTY

I grabbed my copy of the photos and followed Riley out the door.

"The short straw? Is that what you call it?"

"No, I call it the jackhammer. Actually, a very lovely lady called it that, and the name stuck."

I tried not to laugh. "You need to censor what comes out of your mouth. I didn't need to know that." I climbed inside the unmarked Mustang and fidgeted with the seat belt. "What is wrong with you? God, what is wrong with me for finding that funny? I don't think there's any way she could have meant that as a compliment."

"It was definitely a compliment. You should try it out sometime. See for yourself."

"Detective Riley—"

"Yeah, I know. I'm creating an unsafe work environment." He shot a glance in my direction as he pulled out of the lot and headed to our assigned location. "For the record, I was only joking around."

"I know. I'm just busting your balls."

"You do enjoy doing that."

"Girl's gotta have a hobby."

"Maybe you're creating the unsafe work environment."

"I'm pretty sure I didn't proposition you."

"Not today, but there's still time. Speaking of, have you worn the earrings yet?"

"How is that a speaking of?"

"You'd have to be in my head. On second thought, that's not a safe place for you."

"I haven't worn them yet. They aren't appropriate for work, which seems like the theme of this conversation."

"You don't like them?" he asked.

"No, I do."

"But?"

"While thoughtful and sweet, I worry they came with strings attached."

"No strings."

"Really? You bribed me into doing your work by hiding them in a box of files."

"Technically, we're partnered together. So it was our work, not mine. If anything, asking you to do it proves I'm not giving you special treatment." He took his eyes off the road to look at me. "But those aren't the strings you're talking about. This is about what happened in your apartment." He drove one-handed with his left hand on the wheel, making the muscles in his forearm bunch as he turned the car right, heading down another street. "Joking aside, I don't play like that. I asked you out, but no pressure. You can say or do whatever you want. I won't let it interfere with how we do our jobs."

"I didn't mean—"

"I know," he said. "I just wanted to be clear on that." He turned back to face the road. "Is this because you haven't been able to stop thinking about me since that night?"

"I never said—"

"You didn't have to."

I found him infuriating. Charismatic, but infuriating. "Listen to me. I know I've been hot and cold with you. I've got plenty of baggage that I bring to the table, which you don't deserve. And it's complicated by other things, like our jobs. As you pointed out, you outrank me. At the moment, you're in my chain of command. Fraternizing is a huge no-no."

"We aren't in the military."

"You know what I mean."

"Is that why you're holding off on saying yes to that

date?"

"If it was just a date, it wouldn't be such a big deal. It wouldn't matter."

"That's all it is, Lex. It's a date."

"And then what?" I knew it was way too soon to think one date would turn into a second or third, let alone a relationship. "I'm not sure I want anything more than that. But unless you're just looking for a one night stand, in which case, I don't want to go out with you, then where does that one date leave us? We already know we get along. That we have chemistry."

"At this point, I'd call it sizzle." He made a hissing sound, like steam rising.

"Yeah, so what do we do with that?"

"I could tell you."

I gave his arm a shove.

"We have fun, Lex, and we see where it goes." He glanced at me. "And that's the problem." He wiped a hand over his mouth, his jaw clenched. "Your ex-boyfriend screwed you over," he gripped the steering wheel even harder, "and you don't want to get burned again. I get it. It's difficult to get past. I know it is. I've been there myself. God, I'd love to teach that guy some manners, but I'm not him. I want you to know I haven't been with anyone since the night I showed up at your door, drunk on tequila."

"Oh, wow, look who's having a dry spell." I couldn't help the sarcasm.

"You can trust me. I won't hurt you, Lexie. If you give me a chance, I'll prove it."

"Just not at work."

"Right." He looked conflicted. "I'm not everyone's favorite person, and I don't want our fun to hurt your reputation. When I said you had detective chops, I meant it. I won't let our association hurt your chances at a promotion, so I can wait as long as I have to. Something tells me you're worth it. You're different from most women I know. You're not afraid to show your vulnerable side or point out your own flaws."

"Maybe I'm nuts."

"You know what they say about the crazy ones. Best sex

ever."

"Is that all you're waiting for?"

"Not all, but I'd be lying if I said I wasn't looking forward to it. And I never want to lie to you."

I rubbed my eyes with my free hand. "If that desire is based on the lewd and sexist things that get whispered behind my back, you should know those are remnants from my days working vice. I've never dated a cop. I've never been involved with anyone in the department. And those things they say about me aren't true."

"I haven't heard anything, but I'll knock out some teeth if I hear someone saying shit about you." He shot me a look. "However, since we're on the subject, you might have heard some things about me. Unfortunately, I can't say they aren't true. You should know, Sam and I used to be a thing."

"What happened?"

"It doesn't matter. It's in the past, but I have no desire to rub her face in any of my new..." He faltered.

"Conquests?"

"I don't think of you like that. I don't know how to think of you. But I do think about you." His voice sounded deep and sexy when he said that.

My mind flashed to an image of him in the shower, steam rising around his toned, naked body. *Stop*, I scolded myself.

"Would you," he stuttered slightly, "like to go out on an actual date sooner than we planned? Like, say tonight, just to see if all this worry and talk is even worth it?"

For someone as attractive as he was, Riley lacked finesse. But a detective who looked like him didn't have to ask girls out, at least not more than once. But I found the way he fumbled around the question endearing.

"But you just listed all the reasons why we should wait. Now who's acting insane?"

"C'mon, Lex, I don't know what to do here. You obviously like me, but you have doubts, and the longer we drag this out, the more excuses you'll come up with as far as why we shouldn't give this a try. You can't deny that. I know how you think. And I'm crazy about you. Give me a chance. It's the only way I'll ever be able to prove that I'm a good guy."

A truer sentiment had never been uttered, and I caved. My stomach flew into my throat as a million butterflies took flight inside of me. "Okay, but I'm warning you, I don't have sex on a first date."

"Okay, we'll have sex and then go on a date. And before you change your mind, that was a joke. I was kidding."

There was a one in a million chance this wouldn't end horribly wrong. Michael Riley was a bad boy, unbelievably sexy, a little wild, and a professional badass. This was the exact type of guy mothers warned their daughters about, and yet, I was drawn to him, knowing he'd probably break my heart. But the small voice inside my head held out hope. Michael was kind, generous, and fearless. Things between us could be phenomenal. And despite my dislike for unnecessary risks, something we were always cautioned against in the academy, Michael Riley was one risk I had to take.

"Where are you taking me tonight?" I asked as he parked the car near the pawn shop and we began our surveillance.

"It's a surprise."

"In other words, you have no idea."

"That's the surprise." He brushed his hand against my leg as he reached for the MDT. "We might as well get comfortable. We're gonna be here all day." He entered some data and adjusted his seat. Then he dug through his pocket for a pen and paper and scribbled down some notes that he hid from me. "Pay attention, Officer." He jerked his chin at the windshield. "We're here to scout this location for signs of gang activity. And our suspects look nothing like me."

I focused out the windshield, glancing at him occasionally as he diverted his focus from the paper to the surrounding area and back again. "What are you doing?" I finally asked.

"Prep work for this evening." He put the list into his pocket. "And now we wait."

The only problem with stakeouts was they tended to last

forever. Riley and I played twenty questions for a while as he attempted to get to know me better. Unfortunately, I wasn't that exciting. I told him about my family, the pets I had growing up, where I went to school, my best friend Amber, and my uncertainty about taking the detective's exam.

He spoke about his brothers. One was a detective in Philadelphia and the other was working metro. They had dreams of leadership and were hoping to land a lieutenant or captain position one day. "I don't know. I've never been as driven as they are. Sometimes, I think I must be adopted. When I was a kid, I wanted to be a painter, and then I wanted to be a race car driver. And I think, before it was all said and done, I had come up with the worst possibility of all."

"Which was?"

"Firefighter." He chuckled. "My dad still holds a grudge over the fire department's hockey win over the police department from fifteen years ago. To him, that idea was worse than saying I was going to become an assassin for hire, which I proudly announced when I was ten after watching the movie, *The Jackal.*"

"But let me guess, you watched *Die Hard* afterward and decided to be the next John McClane which is what led to that shiny detective's shield of yours."

"Nice Bruce Willis reference." He reached out and gently brushed a lock of my hair out of my face that had come loose from my ponytail. I shut my eyes as his thumb caressed my temple, my cheek, and my jaw. "You're breathtaking."

"You're not so bad yourself."

He gave me a bittersweet look. "Then give me a real shot at this."

"I said I would."

"No, you agreed to a date. But you have doubts. I can see them right there." He pointed at my face, circling his finger around.

I grabbed his hand to stop him from pointing at me and he pulled me closer and kissed me. It was electric, and I sighed into his mouth.

"You're really good at that," I whispered. "But this is work. Professional boundaries, remember?"

"Promise me, no matter what happens between us, you won't let it get in the way of work. That you won't deny yourself the opportunity to move up, become a detective, join gangs or intelligence, or whatever, and do whatever it is you want."

"Okay. I promise."

# TWENTY-ONE

After ten minutes of sitting in silence, I tore my gaze away from the pawn shop and glanced at Riley, who'd been watching me watch the area. "What?"

He met my eyes, looking sincere in his admiration. "Lex, I think I could–"

A car parked, and a man got out. At first, I didn't recognize him. He wore a hooded jacket. But when he turned to look around before pulling something out of the trunk, I saw his face. "Isn't that Alfred Sigfried?"

Riley reached for the radio, calling it in while we watched from our vantage point. "I never thought we'd get eyes on Sigfried. Frank must have lit some dynamite underneath him when he got made."

"What do you think he's got in that bag?" It looked like a gym bag but half the size.

"Hopefully, the stolen shit he took from Big Bill."

We watched as Sigfried made his way down the street and entered the pawn shop. Riley opened the car door, checking to make sure his gun was holstered underneath his jacket and his cuffs were concealed from passersby.

"Wait here. We don't want to spook him. If he makes a run for it and gets back to his car before I grab him, follow him."

I slid across the front seat and got behind the wheel. "Are you sure you don't want me to go with you? This isn't exactly protocol."

"He's already leery. If he sees both of us, he'll take off or worse. For all we know, he has half a dozen loaded firearms in that bag. Backup is on the way. But if I need your help, I'll call. Until then, keep watch from here. Let me know if any of his pals show up. I don't want to walk into an ambush."

Anxiously, I waited for backup to arrive. The last place Riley needed to be was alone with an armed assailant. Several cars drove by, but no one stopped. I didn't recognize the vehicles, but I didn't hear or see a single motorcycle. Alfred Sigfried was alone.

Riley remained outside the pawn shop, window shopping while he kept his eyes on Sigfried. At least he was taking a few precautions before entering an unknown situation.

Two minutes later, Lightman and Hawking pulled up beside me. Lightman got out of the car, signaling for me to roll down the window.

"What's going on?" he asked.

I filled him in, nodding to where Riley was positioned.

"Okay, stay here and maintain eyes on the area. At the first sign of trouble, you let us know." Lightman marched off in the direction of the pawn shop.

Hawking got out of the car and stood beside it. "Sigfried might recognize us from the canvassing and follow-ups we've conducted. That's what Lightman told me before we got here."

"Do you think Sigfried saw us? As far as I know, we never got near him."

"I don't know." Hawking stared at the pawn shop. "I only see the one door. Do you think there's a back entrance?"

"Just the side door. It opens into that alley. Riley and I debated whether it was a dead end when we first arrived, but we don't know for sure."

Hawking looked up and down the street before taking in the entire neighborhood. "It probably is. The way the roads run, I don't think it cuts through. There could be a gate or something." He tucked his thumb into his belt and tapped his fingers against the leather, something a lot of uniformed officers did. "Lightman should have asked us to check it out, though."

I agreed, but I kept the thought to myself. With four of us, two could watch the front and two could watch the back, or, in this case, the side. "They think Sigfried will try to escape in his car."

"Does Sigfried own a car?" Hawking asked. "I don't remember a mention of one."

"Maybe he stole it."

"Then he wouldn't care if he left it behind."

I didn't like this. "Riley mentioned the possibility of an ambush. But I'm hoping the V-7s' loyalty doesn't run as deep as Sigfried hopes."

"They could be planning to run another distraction event, like they did last time. That way, the cops will be looking over there while Sigfried is here."

"Maybe." I didn't like Hawking's suggestion. It made me nervous.

The waiting was interminable. My leg bounced against the seat cushion, and I turned the volume up on my radio for fear I would miss something. But still, we waited. A minute later, Riley and Lightman entered the pawn shop. This was it.

My radio squawked. It was Riley. "Suspect on the move. He's wearing a navy blue hooded jacket and jeans. He went out the side door."

"Shit." I burst out of the car and raced after Hawking who'd taken off for the alleyway beside the pawn shop.

"He's heading east on foot and should be considered armed and dangerous. Two plainclothes detectives are in pursuit," Riley said through the radio.

Hawking hit his radio. "Be advised, two more officers are joining the pursuit."

Two patrol cars pulled up, just as I reached the mouth of the alley. "Go around." I gestured with my hand. "Head him off." And then I ran after Hawking.

It didn't take long before I caught up to him. The alleyway had a gate bisecting it. A hole had been cut in the chain-link. A piece of navy material had gotten snagged.

It was a tight squeeze, but we pushed through. We emerged on the other side, listening for radio calls. The last message we received said Lightman and Riley had split up. The radio squawked again, and Hawking slowed his pace. I practically slammed into his back.

"Where are they?" He checked his radio to make sure it was functioning and asked for a twenty on the suspect.

"We lost him," a very frustrated Lightman responded. "Rendezvous at the pawn shop. We'll bring the owner in for questioning."

"Copy that." Hawking looked at me. "Race you back?"

"Not on your life." We headed back the way we came at a brisk pace. I turned around a few times, wondering where Riley and Lightman were. They should be behind us, but there was no sign of either of them. "Do you think we went the wrong way? They said they split up, east and west, right?"

"They could have detoured down a side street or alleyway. We were too far behind to have seen what happened," Hawking said. "I don't see how they lost the suspect. It should have been a straight shot."

"Maybe they tried to box him in, but he slipped through somehow. For all we know, he had a car waiting on the other side." I hated this. I hated not knowing what happened.

"On the bright side, at least we don't have to explain how Alfred Sigfried eluded us."

"We might. We were sitting outside the shop, doing nothing but twiddling our thumbs."

"Shit, that's what Lightman's going to make it sound like." Hawking made a humph sound. "We'll get all the blame."

"Do you think it was our fault?"

"We followed orders."

But I knew better. We should have been guarding the only other exit. If we had, Sigfried wouldn't have escaped. I couldn't help but think Riley had told me to stay with the car because he wanted to keep me safe. He'd practically said as much on previous occasions. Maybe after that shit with Stryker King, he reassessed his position on having me watch his back in the field.

"Once we get promotions, we can call the shots," I said,

my mind going in two different directions.

"I'll second that," Hawking said.

"You'll second what?" Lightman asked, surprising us from behind. "What are you two talking about?"

"Other things we could have done to assist in apprehending Sigfried," Hawking replied smoothly. "How long were you in pursuit, sir?"

"Long enough." Lightman studied my gaze, which was focused on the alleyway he had emerged from, just off to our left. "Are you looking for Riley?"

I nodded. But he didn't offer an explanation, and I didn't ask any questions. Instead, the three of us returned to the pawn shop to question the owner and secure the scene until a search warrant could be obtained.

The shop contained a ton of electronics, everything from smart phones to home entertainment centers. This had to be Sigfried's primary cash exchange location. As I browsed the cases, I wondered how much of the merchandise was hot.

Lightman asked questions while Hawking meticulously took notes. I leaned against the back wall and felt something give. Furrowing my brow, I knocked against the paneling, listening for a hollow echo.

"Detective," I called, waiting for Lightman to turn before I repeated my knocking, "there's something back here."

He spun to face the owner. "Open it."

"What? She's crazy," John Wolfe, the store owner, said. Wolfe had priors for selling illegal weapons and stolen merchandise. "That's a freaking wall."

"I'm not asking you again," Lightman said, his voice low and even. "You open it, or I'll put your head through it. Either way, I'm gonna find out what's inside."

Hawking glanced at me. Neither of us had spent enough time with Lightman to know if he'd follow through on the threat. But Mr. Wolfe believed him. He swallowed audibly and came around the counter. He hit a button and the panel slid to the side, exposing a dozen handguns, a few grenades, and a couple assault rifles.

"I have no idea how those got there," Wolfe said, and Lightman rolled his eyes.

"Mr. Wolfe, you have the right to remain silent," Lightman clicked a pair of handcuffs around Wolfe's wrists, "but the more you cooperate, the more likely I am to overlook whatever else we find in your shop. I don't particularly care what you're doing. I just want Alfred Sigfried. So I'll give you a minute to think about it. And if you don't want to cooperate, then I'll have no choice but to arrest you."

While the three of us waited for Wolfe to decide, the patrol cars returned. Riley climbed out of one of them and said something to the officers inside. They drove away, but the officers from the other vehicle exited and the three of them joined us inside the shop.

Riley stood near the door, his arms folded over his chest. He was bleeding. A deep cut ran from his ripped sleeve down the length of his arm, and his cheek was bruised and swollen. He looked angry.

"Are you okay?" I asked.

His eyes flicked to mine, seeing the worry there. He nodded before returning his attention to Lightman. The other detective glanced in his direction but didn't say anything. I didn't know what transpired, but something happened during the pursuit.

More police vehicles arrived on the scene, and Lightman dismissed Riley and me.

"You drive." Riley went around to the passenger's seat. Before I even started the car, he pulled out the first aid kit and pressed a piece of gauze against the cut on his arm.

I gave him a worried look, but he played it off with a rugged smile. "Should I take you to the ER?" I asked.

"No, I'm fine. I just don't want to get bloodstains on the new upholstery. The department's cars don't stay nice very long."

"What the hell happened?"

"Sigfried got away."

"I know that, but what about your arm? And your face?" I stopped at a red light and gingerly touched his cheek.

"Chain-link fence and a brick wall. I'm okay. Really." He focused out the windshield. "The light's green."

"Are you sure? You might need stitches."

"Lexie, I'm fine. Stop being so dramatic. Getting banged up is par for the course." He snorted. "So is getting banged." I knew he said it to distract me from worrying about his injuries, and I gave him a withering glare and continued to the station.

Once we arrived, Riley disappeared inside the locker room to clean and bandage his wounds, and I went to my desk to start on the paperwork. My involvement in the botched apprehension was minimal, so it didn't take long to write my report. By the time I was finished, Riley was back at his desk.

"Can I see what you wrote?" he asked, so I showed him. "Thanks."

An hour and a half later, Lightman, Hawking, and the responding officers returned from the pawn shop. Mr. Wolfe was arrested for trafficking stolen goods. More severe charges could come to light in the next day or two, but we had enough to detain him for now.

"Sarconi, I need a word," Lightman said.

Automatically, I gulped, feeling like I'd been called into the principal's office. Out of the corner of my eye, I saw Riley tense, the muscles in his arm bunching. He threw an intense look at Lightman.

"Now, Sarconi," Lightman said.

"Yes, sir." I followed him down the corridor and into the stairwell. "What's wrong?"

"Nothing." He towered over me, stepping closer. "Nice work back at the pawn shop. You really made the owner sweat when you happened upon that hidden panel. How'd you know it was there?"

"It was luck."

"Luck, huh?" He eyed me. "If you say so." He fell silent as a pair of officers went down the steps, passing us with respectful nods at the detective. "Riley said he told you to wait in the car. That you didn't know the pawn shop had any other exits."

"We saw the side door but thought it might lead to a dead end. We weren't sure. As soon as Hawking and I heard the call, we joined the pursuit on foot, but we were too far behind. We never got eyes on Sigfried. If you radioed sooner, we might have been able to circle around and cut him off."

"Did you write that in your report?"

"No, sir." Why would he even think I'd include that in my report? "I can't attest to what occurred in an area where I was not present."

"Very good. I'm glad you have the lingo down. After that scuffle with Stryker King, internal affairs has been keeping tabs on everyone in this unit. They may have questions about what happened today, about how we botched such an easy takedown. I'm guessing they'll want to talk to you about it. It's good to know you can remain professional."

"What does any of that have to do with what happened today?" Immediately, I regretted asking the question.

"It's the same gang. Same types of people. Sigfried ordered the hit. He was responsible for sending King into the station." He scooted unbearably close, disregarding my personal space. "Let me ask you something. Do you blame me for what happened to you the other day?"

"No."

"Do you believe I'd intentionally let a perp like Sigfried get away?"

"No, sir."

"Then we don't have a problem here." He patted my shoulder. "Normally, I have a feel for what my team is thinking, but you're new to this unit. It's nice to know we're on the same page." He looked at his watch. "Finish your paperwork and check out at shift change. You've been working too damn hard lately."

# TWENTY-TWO

That strange encounter with Detective Lightman left me baffled. The rest of my shift was nothing but a blur. When I made it home and unlocked my apartment door, I couldn't help but think of everything that had happened today. Most of it made no sense. Even if Riley had been hesitant to put me in another dangerous situation, I doubted Lightman would have had the same qualms, especially when I had Hawking to back me up.

A headache formed behind my eyes, and I squeezed the bridge of my nose, grabbing a pen and paper to detail the few facts I knew. This was a puzzle that didn't make sense. At least, it didn't make sense to me.

The knock at my door made me gasp, and I reached for my Glock. This case was making me jumpy. And I thought this unit would be safer than vice. Snorting at my own idiotic thought, I checked the peephole and opened the door.

"Shit."

Riley held a slightly wilted bouquet of wildflowers. "Are you allergic?" He pulled the flowers away.

"No. It's not that." I reached to take them from him, but he put them behind his back, forcing me to reach around and hug him as I tried to grab them. He put his free hand against the small of my back and pulled me close as both of my arms encompassed his waist.

"Hi," he said quietly.

"Hi." I lifted onto my tiptoes and brushed my lips against his, an impulsive act I immediately regretted. "Don't hate me, but I forgot."

"You forgot that you like flowers?"

"No." I grabbed the bouquet from his hand and led the way into my apartment. "I didn't forget that I like flowers. I forgot that we had a date. After what happened this afternoon, I wasn't sure you'd remember either."

"I made a note." He held up the list he had scribbled earlier in the car.

"Why didn't I think to do that?" I dug through the cabinet beneath the sink for a vase, getting a little dizzy in the process. When was the last time I ate?

"It seems you've been making other lists." He frowned at the information I'd been trying to piece together. "What did Jack say to you after we got back?"

"He said I did a good job." I filled the vase with water and put it on the counter. "That guy gives me the creeps. I know he's the detective in charge, but the things he does don't add up."

"I'm sure everything's fine. You worry too much."

"God, look at you." I focused on the bandages peeking out from beneath his short sleeve shirt. "Where was Lightman when that happened?"

"I don't know. We got separated during the pursuit."

"That does not instill within me a vast amount of confidence in Detective Lightman's abilities."

"Look at you and the big words." He circled his arms around my waist. "Are you going to let me take you somewhere nice, or would you rather stay here and talk shop all night?"

"Will you be honest with me for a minute?"

"I told you I never want to lie to you." His brow furrowed. "What's up?" He stepped back, resting his hips against my kitchen table.

"Why didn't you ask me to watch the side door? That's proper procedure."

"I thought it was a dead end."

"Why didn't we check?"

"Jeez, Lex," he rubbed his forehead, "I made a mistake.

Are you going to rake me over the coals because of it?"

That wasn't what I meant. "Even if you made a mistake, why didn't Lightman send Hawking and me to the side door?"

"How would I know? Why don't you ask Jack that question?"

"Michael—"

He held up his palms and backed away from me. "What is this?"

"Were you trying to protect me?"

"Protect you? Protect you from what?"

"Sigfried."

He rubbed his eyes, clearly annoyed. "I told you how I feel won't interfere with the job. We haven't even gone out yet, and already you're accusing me of stupid shit."

"Michael," my tone took on an edge, "I want to understand how he got away. Tell me what happened out there today."

"Fine. I watched Sigfried through the window. When he presented what I'm certain was stolen contraband to Wolfe, Jack and I entered the pawn shop. We approached the counter while Wolfe handed Sigfried what I can only imagine was several thousand dollars. Before we could get close enough to get hands on Sigfried, he turned, grabbed the cash, and ran for the side door."

"Why did he turn?"

"The bell above the door gave us away," Riley said. "That's why he ran out the side since we were still too close to the front for him to get past us. I radioed about the pursuit, and we took off. I chased that son of a bitch for three blocks before he jumped into a car. I didn't get the plate. Patrol picked me up, and we circled. But we never spotted that damn car."

"You didn't radio after he got into the car. I didn't know what happened to you."

"My radio got snagged at the same time my shirt got caught on one of the jagged wires at that gate. I didn't realize it wasn't working until I needed to use it."

"And the bruises on your cheek?"

"I face-planted against a brick wall." He exhaled. "Why

do you need to know that?"

"I just want to understand what happened. Hawking and I never saw any of the pursuit. We thought it was our fault."

"It wasn't."

"Where was Lightman while all this was happening? Shouldn't he have been behind you?"

"One would think." Riley shrugged. "I don't know what happened to Jack. He probably got caught in the gate, same as me. Maybe he took a wrong turn or tried to cut Sigfried off by going down another alley. Most of those side streets are blocked by fences or dead ends. That's why I thought there was no point in you guarding the door."

"Yeah." The pounding in my skull was getting worse. "The car Sigfried arrived in was stolen. We should have run the plate. We should have done something."

Anger and frustration filled his eyes. "I know."

"Lightman said the two of you pursued the suspect, but he wasn't winded or banged up when we found him. Given everything, I don't think he tried very hard to catch Sigfried."

"Now I know you've lost your damn mind. Did IA put you up to this? Are you reporting to them? Did they want you to ask me these things? Is that why you've been so hot and cold after declaring we were nothing more than friends? Is that why you agreed to go out with me? Are you using me to get dirt on Jack or my unit?"

"No one put me up to anything. I'm just confused why things went down the way they did. And now you're looking at me like I'm crazy or a snitch. I'm not manipulating you. If anything, I'd say you're the one manipulating me."

"Look, I've had a tough day. The last thing I want to do is talk about work." He returned to my living room. "I should go. We can reschedule for another night when you haven't forgotten we've made plans."

"Michael, I'm sorry."

"Yeah. Me too." He slammed my front door behind him.

I was stunned. We weren't even dating yet, but already, the sting of rejection burned through my entire body. The empty, painful hollow began in my stomach and erupted in a strangled gasp. This was stupid. I was stupid for even considering dating someone from work.

I plucked the bouquet from the vase, tossed the ugly flowers into the trash, poured the morning's coffee grounds on top, and slammed the lid shut. Yes, it was childish, but it made me feel better. I would not wallow in self-doubt or pity. Riley was being defensive, which set off my spidey-sense. He screwed up, and he knew it.

My head hurt, but the last thing I wanted to do was stay home and think about Riley or work. So I touched up my makeup, grabbed my purse, and went down the stairs to find a cab. With my cell phone in hand, I scanned my address book for a friend who might want to get mildly drunk in the middle of the work week. Just when Amber answered, someone cleared his throat. I turned, spotting Riley waiting in the lobby.

"What's up, girl?" Amber asked.

"Hey, Am. I hit the wrong number. Let me call you back." I disconnected before she could say another word. "I thought you left," I said icily. Riley had never seen me angry, but he was about to. "That was what the parting words and slamming door indicated. I might not be a detective, but those clues seemed pretty obvious even to a lowly officer like me."

"I fucked up."

"Yeah. You fucked up. And I fucked up for forgetting. That doesn't mean you can storm out when I ask you a question."

"No, Lex," he shook his head, as if I didn't get it, "at work. I fucked up at work."

"Yeah, I know." My headache was on the cusp of full-blown migraine. "I don't care. All I wanted to know was why. Was it because of me, because of what happened with Stryker King or the car that tried to run us down in the hospital parking lot, or because you can't separate work from whatever the hell this was that we thought we'd try? But you didn't want to talk about it or explain. Instead, you left. So leave." I pointed to the door. "Go. I don't want you here." My chin trembled, and tears stung my eyes. I wouldn't cry. Not in front of him. Not over something this stupid.

"Hey, listen," he took a step closer, reaching for me, but I batted his hand away, "today had nothing to do with you. You would have gotten Sigfried. You would have caught him, and that would have been it. What happened is on me and maybe Jack. But mostly me." Riley took a breath. "Before Jack arrived, Sigfried made me. He may have spotted the badge or the gun before I even entered the shop. I don't know. But he was antsy. He was out the door before we had a chance to announce. It happened so fast. By going through the alley and me getting stuck at that damn gate, that's how he got such a lead. I should have had you wait at the side door. But I honestly thought the car was a better bet. I thought the alley was a dead end. But you're right, we should have checked."

"Yeah."

"I'm guessing Jack branched off and ran up on a dead end. He must have. That's the only thing that makes sense. I didn't see it happen, but that doesn't mean it didn't." It sounded more like a question than an explanation. "We should have realized the thing about the car sooner or figured Sigfried would have a contingency. This guy's been out of prison long enough to know he doesn't want to go back and will do anything to make sure it doesn't happen."

"Besides following the straight and narrow."

"Yeah." Riley reached for me again, but I stepped back.

"You accused me of working with IA. That makes me wonder how much you trust me. Whatever your deal is, it's not my problem. All I wanted to know was what happened. That was it. And I wouldn't have even cared if you had just told me, but you didn't." I put my palm against the wall and used my other hand to shield my eyes from the bright overhead lights which were making my headache worse. Now was not the time for a migraine.

Riley moved against me, pinning me against the wall. His hands were gentle against my sides even as I slapped at his wrists.

"Stop," I warned.

"No." He pressed his lips to my temple, and I turned

further into the wall, trying to get away from him. I thought I could do this, but this was a bad idea. The scene upstairs proved it. "It scared me to see your suspicions written down in black and white and to hear those accusations coming out of your mouth."

"I didn't accuse you of anything." My resolve weakened as his warm hands continued to rub my ribcage. "I asked you a question."

"But I couldn't answer because I don't know what happened. I don't know why I didn't send you to guard the other exit. Maybe I was worried what would happen to you. But I honestly think the reason I told you to wait was because I thought that alley was a dead end and Sigfried would drive away, which for the record he did."

"Different car," I said.

"How was I supposed to know that?"

"I don't want to fight. I'm going upstairs. I'll see you tomorrow." I pushed past him.

"Lexie, wait."

Against my better judgment, I stopped. "What is it?"

He swallowed, tugging my chin up until our eyes met. "There have been whispers that Jack left Big Bill unattended intentionally. It means nothing. People say shit all the time. But..."

"You think it's true."

"I don't know." He looked to be in utter agony. "But if your suspicions are correct, it makes me wonder if Jack could be working for Sigfried. We've been trying to stop these crimes for months and never made enough progress or collected enough evidence to make an arrest, even though we suspected Big Bill was behind it."

I wasn't sure if Riley was thinking clearly. "Are you sure you're not jumping to conclusions, like you did with me upstairs?"

"I hope I am. All I know is, whoever let King into the station to eliminate Big Bill is the same person responsible for nearly killing you. And god help him if I ever find out who that is." Riley's hands tangled in my hair, and he pressed his forehead against mine and shuddered. "I couldn't stand in your apartment for another second, thinking I might be responsible for every horrible thing you've been through since your temporary reassignment. So I called Sam and asked her to pull Jack's report. I was curious to see what it said."

"You didn't have to do that. I doubt Lightman's to blame. He's been a cop too long to do something like this. You were first on scene, so he deferred to you. And you made a mistake. Unfortunately, we all did." And standing here right now was mine.

"You're the only thing that matters to me outside of work. I have to keep you safe."

"That's not your job. If you think it is, then we're done before we even get started. You can't protect me. By now, you ought to know that's not how this works."

"Are you sure I can't apply for the position of white knight?"

"That's not funny." I pushed away from him. "Goodbye, Michael."

Riley saw the hurt and betrayal on my face for the first time. "Lexie, please. It was a joke."

"I don't think—" I grimaced at the sudden sharp pain in my temples.

He grabbed me before I stumbled. "Are you okay?"

"I'm fine. I haven't eaten all day, and the stress isn't helping. When my blood sugar gets wonky, I get these headaches. But I'm sure you'll use that as another excuse to think I can't do this job."

"I don't think that. Do not put words in my mouth." He slipped an arm around my waist. "Now I'm taking you upstairs and ordering dinner."

"No, you're not."

"Watch me." When we made it to my front door, he let go. "I order a mean pepperoni. Or are you a mushroom girl? Pineapple and anchovies?" He smirked. "I bet you can't get enough of the meat lover's special."

"I kind of hate you."

"I don't really care." He stood behind me, waiting for me to unlock the door. When I looked back at him, he had his phone out and was halfway through placing an order. "Speak now or I'm choosing the toppings."

"Plain cheese. I hope that's not too boring for you."

"It's not. It's perfect." He massaged my neck, and I leaned my head back, finding it helped ease the pounding in my temples.

I climbed onto the couch, too spent to argue anymore. This was the first time Riley had worn me down enough to get his way. And I didn't like it.

While we waited for the pizza, Riley placed a pillow on his lap so I could lie down. He rubbed my shoulders and back, and I closed my eyes, worried I was making a mistake by letting him stay.

"I don't want to fight like this," I said. "Not now. Not ever."

"We won't."

"Are you sure? Something tells me you're gonna break my heart."

"I won't. But next time we have a date planned, don't start the evening by breaking my balls."

# TWENTY-THREE

I awoke the next morning to a warm body and strong arms wrapped around me. My head rested on Michael's chest. The steady, reassuring beat of his heart echoed in my ear. Apparently, Michael Riley wasn't a heartless playboy after all.

Closing my eyes, I didn't want to start a new day. The last thing I wanted was to go to work or go another round. Inside my apartment, we were safe from the stresses of the job. And in this perfect moment, there was no more back and forth. My mind didn't fill in worst case scenarios that involved Michael discovering he couldn't stand me, or cheating on me, or one of us getting hurt or killed in the line of duty. Right now, everything was as close to perfect as it could be. And then the phone rang.

Michael shifted, reaching toward the nightstand. He grabbed the object, hitting answer without looking or thinking.

"Riley," he said, his voice thick with sleep.

"Who the hell is Riley?" Amber's voice came through the earpiece. "What are you doing with Lexie's phone? Where is Lexie? Have you done something to her? I'll call the police if you don't tell me where she is right now. You should know she's a cop. They'll find you and kill you."

"Huh?" Michael opened his eyes and blinked a few times. He pulled the phone away from his ear, realizing it wasn't his. "Sorry." He handed it to me.

"Morning, Amber," I said reluctantly, knowing exactly what was about to happen.

"What's going on? Are you okay? Who answered your phone?"

"That was Detective Riley. We work together, remember?"

"You're at work? It's six a.m. When are you supposed to get your beauty sleep?"

"If it's that early, why are you calling?"

"Because you didn't call me back last night, and I have an early shift at the hospital. They don't give us a break either. I guess we're just supposed to make googly eyes at plastic surgeons, so they'll work on us for free."

"Don't you make the schedules?" I asked.

"Not the point."

"Amber, it's six a.m. Can we please talk about this later?"

"That depends. Is Detective Riley going to answer your phone the next time I call?"

"I don't think so."

"Uh-huh." She didn't sound convinced. "You never said you were at work. And he sounds like he's half-asleep."

"Goodbye, Amber."

"Oh my god, did you get back on the horse?"

"Goodbye," I repeated, hitting the disconnect button. So much for my perfect tranquil moment.

"I'm a horse," Riley murmured into my hair. "Am I a stud?"

"I don't know. How did we end up in my bedroom?"

"You fell asleep on the couch. And when I carried you to bed, you insisted I stay."

"Really? I insisted? That doesn't sound like me. I'm pretty sure I wanted to kill you."

"Nope, you changed your mind after the pizza and back rub."

"I think I'd remember that."

"Guess not." He turned to look at the clock. "I have to go home, so I can get ready for work."

I didn't know how I felt about any of this, but Riley slept beside me all night with no expectation of sex. That had to count for something. "How do you think our first date went?"

"You think this was our first date?"

"It was our first fight. It might as well be considered our first date."

He laughed. "Makeup sex would have been better than apology pizza."

"I don't have sex on a first date."

"So it was our first date." He smiled, planting a few wet kisses on the side of my face. "After the pizza, you fell asleep and cuddled with me all night. That's a pretty amazing first date, minus the fireworks at the start of the night."

"Did you cop a feel?" I asked, cognizant of my bra digging into me. The stupid contraption must have been invented by a man and most definitely wasn't intended to be slept in. Then again, sleeping in my clothes wasn't comfortable either, and I was sure I'd have red indentions from my belt buckle pressed into my stomach. Either that, or Michael would since I used his body as a pillow. A very firm pillow.

"I am a gentleman." He slid out from beneath me, so he could climb out of bed. "And gentlemen never tell."

"Jerk."

He leaned down for a kiss, but I turned away, not wanting to assault him with morning breath after eating garlicky pizza. "Not until I brush my teeth."

"I'll settle for your cheek in the meantime." He gave me a quick peck. "We'll call that the goodnight kiss since I didn't get to kiss you goodnight on account of your unconscious state."

"I'm sorry. I don't entertain much. Somehow, the fact that I'm not supposed to fall asleep when I have company must have slipped my mind."

"And you said you didn't sleep with someone on a first date." He winked. "Liar."

"I never said that. Obviously, I'm totally cool with it."

"I am too." He waited a beat. "Are we cool? We both said some things. I'm not sure where we landed on everything."

"Yeah, we're cool."

"So we'll do this again sometime?"

"Not the fighting. If we do that again, I'm out."

"Noted." He went into the bathroom.

I climbed out of bed, ran my fingers through my hair, and went into the kitchen to brew some coffee. I found a few travel mugs and filled one for him to take.

He met me in the kitchen, gladly accepting the coffee. Then he detoured into the living room and collected his belongings. "Were the flowers a casualty of our fight? Or do you really hate flowers?"

"The first," I admitted, sipping my coffee.

"Okay. I just wanted to make sure before I splurged on another floral arrangement. If flowers don't do it for you, speak up now because I'm also great at buying candy and lingerie."

"I wouldn't say no to candy, but lingerie's pushing it." I looked at him. "After everything that happened, you still want a second date?"

"And a third. And a fourth. And a lot more after that." He went to my door. "We'll talk about this tonight. I'll call you."

"Won't you see me at work?"

"Yes, but that's work, so I'm going to call you."

"You might need to negotiate the phone schedule with Amber."

"What are you going to tell her about the stud?"

"That after being a total asshole and almost sabotaging the entire evening, the frog turned into a low-rent prince."

"I got demoted from a horse to a frog." He lifted one eyebrow. "Maybe you should wait until date number two before you tell her anything. That way, her first impression won't make her think you're dating another horrible jackass." He opened the door. "Next time, we'll start things the right way. I promise."

"Don't make another promise you can't keep," I warned.

"I'll see you soon." He started to pull the door closed behind him. "And just so you know, you're adorable when you sleep."

# TWENTY-FOUR

When I arrived at work, Detective Lightman was inside the lieutenant's office. The door was closed, but angry words echoed throughout the squad room. This wasn't good. Another man entered the office without knocking, and the conversation continued. When a call came in, I volunteered to ride with Kemper. The station was the last place I wanted to be right now.

On my way out, I noticed Riley speaking to Preston. Putting two and two together, I had a feeling the reason Lightman was getting reamed was because of the questions Riley raised last night. He had done that on account of me and my suspicions.

Lightman was going to be on the warpath today, and I had no intention of getting caught in the line of fire. Hopefully, Riley would duck and cover too, at least until this mess blew over.

"Earth to Lexie." Kemper snapped his fingers in front of my face. "What planet are you on? Mars? Saturn? Uranus?" He laughed at the juvenile joke.

"I'm here. I just zoned out."

"Well, try to pay more attention. We have another home invasion, and even though it's in a different neighborhood and unlikely to be connected with the V-7s, we need to make sure."

"Wow, look at you, taking police work seriously."

"I have to. Lightman's fit to be tied. Did you see the

internal affairs investigator this morning? He arrived in the squad room with a truckload of files. While they were looking into Big Bill's murder, something else pinged."

"What?"

"Lightman's personal spending is off the charts. Word is he could be on the take."

"He could have inherited the money, or he moonlights on the side. It's none of our business."

"Fine, but I thought you'd want to know."

Kemper remained silent for the rest of the drive. When we arrived at the latest crime scene, the elderly woman who reported the break-in answered the door. She appeared distraught. It took ten minutes to calm her down.

"Did you see the intruder, ma'am?" I asked.

She shook her head. "They must have been here while I was sleeping."

"Did they hurt you? Touch you?"

"No, nothing like that. But look at this place." She waved her arm at her living room. "It's been ransacked."

The room looked pristine. I could even make out fresh vacuum lines on the carpet. "Did you straighten up after they left?"

"No." She pointed emphatically at her entertainment center. "Don't you see the problem?"

I looked at Kemper, hoping he'd take over. He went to the entertainment center and studied the shelves. "What's missing?"

"Nothing, but the whole thing's been moved."

"Moved?" Kemper asked, eyeing me. Bogus calls weren't uncommon.

"Where did they move it?" I asked, playing along as Kemper walked through the rest of her apartment to make sure nothing was amiss.

"Not far, just a few inches in the other direction." She dropped into a rocker and furrowed her brow. "Maybe two inches that way." She pointed to the left.

"I see." Kneeling down, I scooted the coffee table slightly to the left, noticing the deep indentions in the carpet. The furniture hadn't been moved.

"Not that," she squawked, and I slid the table back to its

original place. “The television and entertainment center.” She pointed across the room. “It was centered on the wall before. Now, it’s not.”

“Someone broke in, decided to steal your television, but changed his mind, and put it back in the wrong place?” Kemper asked.

“That’s what I think happened,” the woman said, sounding ridiculously sincere.

“Okay, how about I put it back where it was, and we’ll call it a day?” I asked, realizing the only reason she called us was to move her furniture.

“That sounds fair.”

Sighing, I spent the next twenty minutes adjusting the shelves on her entertainment center so the glare from the window wouldn’t reflect on the screen. Kemper had taken a seat beside her and was making helpful suggestions as I went. If there wasn’t a witness, I would have shot him.

Once she was satisfied with the placement of her TV, I reminded her making false reports was a crime and wished her a good day. “The next time we’re tasked with moving furniture, you do it,” I said, laughing. Calls like this were pointless and could cause problems if more serious calls came in, but things were quiet today. So the bogus call lightened my mood. Not everything had to be dire. “In fact, the next time I need my furniture moved, I’m calling you.”

“Hey,” Kemper protested.

“You owe me. You could have helped. That stupid entertainment center had twelve different shelves and four settings for each shelf position. We could have been finished in half the time if you didn’t sit on your ass and suggest she might like the TV a little more to the left.”

“There was a glare if she sat on the couch. It needed to be moved to the left.” He chuckled. “I was just doing my job to the best of my ability. Protect and serve, Sarconi. That’s exactly what I was doing, protecting her television from a glare to better serve her needs.”

“Well, I think you should do something to serve my needs.”

“Oh yeah?” His eyes twinkled. “What needs would those be?”

"Lunch. And you're buying." I narrowed my eyes at him. "What did you think I was going to ask you?"

"I don't know. But I would have been up for it or down for it. Whichever you prefer."

"Ugh."

"Ease up, Lex. You're always so uptight. I'd expect that from Hawking, but not you." He parked outside a sandwich joint. "Turkey breast and Swiss?"

"Yep." I was surprised he knew my standard lunch order. "Thanks."

He opened the car door. "No problem, milady."

# TWENTY-FIVE

When we returned to the station, an angsty gloom had settled over the gangs unit. Since our blunder yesterday, Alfred Sigfried and the V-7s had vanished from our radar.

"Bishop's Bar is closed," Preston said, hanging up the phone. "No one's inside."

"They're never closed." Riley swore, rubbing a hand over his face. "Patrol's been sitting on their other favorite haunts, but there's been no activity."

"And nothing at Sigfried's apartment either," Lightman said. "He's in the wind. We should have gotten him yesterday. That was supposed to be our slam dunk. We take him, and then we take down his crew. Now, we have nothing."

"It's a motorcycle gang," Kemper said, again proving he couldn't read the room. "They can't disappear. They drive those loud ass bikes with the vroom vroom engines."

Hawking rolled his eyes. Even he couldn't save Kemper from himself this time.

Lightman looked like his head might explode. "If you think they're so easy to find, why don't you go find them? In fact, why don't you and Sarconi go back out on patrol and see what you can dig up? Call me when you find some motorcycles that belong to the V-7s."

"Jack," Riley's voice took on an edge, "you know that's—"

"What?" Lightman spun on him. "You want to drive

around and help them look? As far as I'm concerned, the reason we've got nothing is because you didn't do your damn job yesterday." He addressed the entire unit. "From here on out, when we move on a suspect, we cover the back door, the side door, the fucking windows. We cover every known exit, and anything that looks like an exit. If you see a chimney, I want someone watching to make sure our suspect doesn't pop out the top."

"We've issued a department wide BOLO. Every cop in this city will be on the lookout. The DA's office is working on getting us arrest warrants for every single member of the V-7s and every former member of Big Bill's crew. We'll get them. Like Kemper said, they can't stay hidden that long. They're bikers. They like to make a ruckus," Preston said.

Lightman worked his jaw for a moment, turning back to Kemper and me. "I wasn't kidding. You and Sarconi get your asses back out on patrol and see what you can dig up. You hear any calls come in regarding home invasions or hold-ups, I want you there. Report back whatever you find."

Again, I saw the protest on Riley's lips, but I shook my head and grabbed my things. "Yes, sir," I said.

"Head down," Hawking mumbled as we went past him. Truer words had never been said.

"At least we get away from Detective Sourpuss," Kemper said once we were back in a squad car. "I didn't mean to get you in trouble too. You didn't do anything."

"It's okay." But I knew this was payback for yesterday. "Lightman's right. We screwed up. We should have apprehended Sigfried, and we didn't."

"So let's see if we can find him."

Of course, we had no such luck.

The rest of the day flew by with unrelated calls. It was nice to get out of the station and back on a beat. None of the robberies or break-ins were that serious. A few kids had shoplifted. Someone came home to a broken window, which was vandalism and not a break-in. A store had been robbed, but the surveillance cameras had caught the guy in the act. Considering Lightman was on the warpath, working patrol made for an easy day.

While I changed back into normal clothes, Riley came into the locker room. "Lexie?"

"Hey."

"I'm really sorry."

"It's no big deal. Lightman's right. We need Sigfried."

"Are you okay?"

"Uh-huh."

Riley gave me a questioning look before making sure we were alone. "Are we okay? Last night was bad enough, but now with Jack being...well...Jack, I just wanted to make sure you hadn't changed your mind about things."

"You mean you wondered if I came to my senses yet."

"Lex," he sighed, "it won't always be like this. I made a mistake. I won't do it again. I hate that he's taking my mistakes out on you. I was going to say something."

"Don't," I said. "Please don't. It will make it worse. I know it will, and I don't want that."

"Yeah, okay." He scratched the back of his head and looked around. "Is there anything I can do to make it up to you?"

"Not really." I checked my phone to see I had a message from Amber. She wanted to meet for dinner. "Can we pick this up another time?"

"Hot date?"

"Dinner." I enjoyed watching him squirm. "With Amber."

"All right," he said. "But I still plan to call you later."

I moved closer, running my hand up his chest. "Stop trying so hard."

He stared into my eyes for a moment, the question obvious on his face. *Were we done?*

Truthfully, I didn't know. But I'd worry about that later. Right now, I needed to hash things out with my sounding board and see what she had to say. If anyone could help me see things from all angles, it was my best friend.

We decided on our usual haunt, a bar and grill situated almost equidistant between our two apartments. It was closer to the hospital than the station, which meant she was tasked with getting a table and ordering a pitcher of beer and an appetizer while she waited for me to arrive.

I found her in a corner booth. A tall, blond guy with a dragon tattoo on his bicep was chatting her up. Shaking my head, I joined them.

"Should I find somewhere else to sit?" I asked. She squealed, shoving him out of the way so she could get up and hug me. "I'll take that as a no."

"Sit your ass down. Chad's just leaving."

"But I thought—" Chad stuttered, confused why she no longer had any interest in him. "I paid for the pitcher of beer."

"And we appreciate it." I poured a glass and toasted in his direction. "Better luck next time."

"Bitch," he muttered.

I took out my badge. "Officer Bitch," I corrected. He held up his hands and backed away from the table. I looked at Amber. "Poor, Chad. You need to stop tricking men into buying us beer."

"He was a player." Amber twirled her ponytail around her finger. "From the moment I came in, he's been gaming me and staring at the girls. Someone needed to teach him a lesson." She sighed. "You didn't seem quite this offended when you were working vice. Back then, you despised being hit on. For a while, I thought you were going to decide to play for the other team."

"I wasn't that bad."

"Taking a celibacy vow is pretty bad." She raised an eyebrow at me. "But that had more to do with the pinhead you dated. I swear, you should have let me castrate him."

"Why are you bringing all this up? Vice is old news, and my ex is ancient."

"You didn't think so the last time we went out." She picked up a cheese fry and chewed thoughtfully. "That was less than two months ago." Her smile brightened. "In two months, little Lexie found another man. So tell me about this mysterious Riley."

"He's a detective."

"I need a bit more than that. Is he good in the sack?"

"I don't know. We haven't gotten that far yet. I'm not sure we will."

"Uh-huh," she narrowed her eyes as if she didn't believe me, "but you guys had a sleepover. He was there last night when you called, wasn't he?"

"Yes and no."

I proceeded to fill her in on our fight and our attempt at a first date. As usual, she was enthralled with the details of my dating life. Good or bad, she had been there for all of it. We'd been friends since kindergarten and had stayed close through high school, college, and numerous crushes and break-ups.

"It sounds like he messed up, but I don't think he ever meant for it to hurt you."

"I'm sure he didn't."

"So I don't see what the problem is. Your issues are work issues. Once you figure out where you want to transfer, you won't have these obstacles anymore. So don't waste your time worrying about them now." She refilled her glass with beer. "Go bang his brains out."

"I have to be sure."

"Sure that he's a good lay? You said he has great hands and a nice-sized package."

"And he's a really good kisser." I remembered our make-out session.

"Then he'll get you there." She turned serious, knowing I wasn't the slutty one out of our group of friends. "But this isn't about that. This is about the fight. Do you think he's one of those controlling assholes? Because you don't need to waste your time on one of those."

I played with the straw wrapper. "I don't think so, but work makes things weird. And with the way this case has gone, it could be weeks or months before I get back on patrol. The smart decision would be to pump the brakes until this is over."

"What he's looking to pump has nothing to do with brakes," Amber retorted, and I scowled at her. "But it's more than that. What aren't you telling me?"

"What if he made that bad call because he can't separate our work life from our private life, assuming we ever even get that far? How is that going to work? Won't that make him just as bad as my ex?"

"No one could be as bad as your ex."

I opened my mouth to provide examples of men I'd arrested who were clearly worse, but she waved it away.

"It sounds like you're missing the point, Lex. No one wants you to marry this guy. Go bonk his brains out, and then if you decide he's good enough for a repeat performance, you see where that goes. It doesn't have to be more than that."

"I know, but he says we have chemistry. He's already talking more dates, even after the date from hell."

She nodded the same way the department psychologist had. "So what you're saying is Detective Riley is a masochist."

"Amber." I shushed her, but she didn't take the hint.

"Has he exhibited any other sadomasochistic tendencies? Do you think he's into bondage and pain?"

I rolled my eyes, but my first encounter with Frank played through my mind. "I have no idea if he has any kinks. But that's not the point."

"So what is?"

"I don't want to go through another messy relationship and an even messier break-up. Riley's reputation suggests he's a player."

"And Kevin was an asshole." Amber knew not to mention my ex-boyfriend's name. I didn't like to hear it. As far as I was concerned, he didn't deserve to be called a word that wouldn't be bleeped on broadcast television. "I get it. He was your first real love. Your first real adult relationship. But you're twenty-six years old. You have your entire life ahead of you. Why can't you have fun instead of wondering if this thing with Riley is going to turn into something? Casual dating is great. You screw who you want. And you go on. You don't have to worry about cheating because there is no commitment. And if he can't handle it at work, that's his problem. You're not going to be sticking around long enough to have to put up with his toxic machismo beyond this case, right?"

"I can't do it that way. I've seen and experienced too much."

"Y'know, life would be far less complicated if you had

gone to work in your parents' store and got your masters instead of becoming a cop."

"Too late," I said.

"Fine, then I'm gonna have to meet this Michael Riley and have a friendly chat with him." She grabbed my phone before I could stop her and dialed his number.

"Amber," I lunged across the table, but she turned to the side so I couldn't reach the phone, "this isn't funny. Don't do it."

"Hey, Riley," she said, and I knew he must have answered, "this is Lexie's friend. We spoke this morning. I'm not quite clear on why you thought you should answer her phone at six a.m., but I'm willing to let that one slide if you agree to meet us. We're at McGinty's Bar and Grill. Do you know where it is?" She paused. "Great. I look forward to meeting you too."

"Tell me you didn't do that. Tell me it was a joke and that you reached his voicemail or called my house phone or something."

"I love you. And you like this guy. So we need to see if he passes my test because I'm not going to stand by and let someone else break your heart. He needs to know what's what." She refilled my glass. "Drink. You look like you need it."

I put my face in my hands. Sometimes, I really didn't understand why we were friends.

Thirty minutes later, Riley showed up. I wanted to sink into an invisible puddle underneath the booth. Unfortunately, my body didn't cooperate with my wishes, and he spotted us easily. He sauntered over, dazzling us with a smile.

"I am so sorry for what's about to happen," I said. But he held the smile and slid into the booth beside me. "You have the right to remain silent. You should wait for counsel to arrive before saying a word."

He laughed, a deep, amused sound, before extending his hand across the table. "Amber?"

"Riley," she said it like it was a foreign word as she shook his hand.

"Michael, actually," he corrected. "Michael Riley."

"Can you spell that for me? I'm also going to need your badge number, three references, and closest living relative."

"You can have my card," Riley said, removing one from his pocket like this was a business meeting or job interview. "Will you also be needing a urine or blood sample before the end of the night?"

"That would be lovely. We'll pop over to the hospital and get that taken care of after we have a chance to chat."

"Amber thinks she runs the place," I said, "so you shouldn't joke about that. She might just take you up on the offer."

"It depends on how he plays his cards." She stared at him like a predator preparing to pounce.

"We've known each other since we were little, and although she appears to be a functioning adult, she lacks basic social skills and the ability to mind her own damn business."

She stuck her tongue out at me, and I kicked her underneath the table.

"Ladies," Riley said, "thanks for asking me to join you. I wasn't expecting this." He motioned to the waitress for another pitcher of beer and leaned back in the seat. "Shall we get started with the inquisition?" He was being a good sport, but I wanted to push him out the door and tell him to run far and fast. If he didn't give up on the idea of dating me after dealing with Amber, there was a good chance he never would.

"How many people have you slept with?" she asked.

"Don't answer that," I hissed. "I don't want to know."

"Fine." She looked smug. "How many relationships have you been in since high school?"

"Six," he replied.

"How old are you?" she asked, already calculating the estimated lengths of these relationships.

"Twenty-nine."

Amber continued asking rapid-fire questions while I buried my face in my hands, occasionally intervening if the question was too personal. None of the things she asked were any of her business. I didn't even know the answer to most of the questions, like how many times he'd moved in the last five years.

When the interrogation ended, he shifted in the booth, rubbing circles on my back. Pulling my head out of my hands, I gazed across the table, mouthing to Amber that I would kill her. She waved it away and excused herself.

"Did I pass?" Riley asked.

"I don't know. You're still here. Don't you think now's the perfect time to make a break for it?"

"I'm having fun. Are you?"

"Michael—"

"Does this count as a second date? Because I had something a little nicer planned, but hey, getting to meet your best friend is an honor."

"I didn't know she was going to call you. She grabbed my phone. I'm sorry. You can leave. I won't blame you. She had no right. I should have stopped her."

"She's looking out for you." His fingers grazed my cheek, and his blue eyes bore into mine. "She cares about you. I care about you too." He moved to kiss me.

"Ahem," Amber cleared her throat, holding an order of buffalo wings, "enough with the kissy face. I brought a peace offering." She studied me. "Lex, your mascara's all over the place. Go freshen up."

"Amber," I warned.

"It's okay." Riley slid out of the booth so I could get out. "I'm not going anywhere."

I went into the bathroom and checked my reflection in the mirror. "Dammit. I'm not even wearing mascara." She had me so flustered about this awkward impromptu meet and greet that I didn't know if I was coming or going. Storming out of the bathroom, I slowed as I approached the table.

"While you were having six different relationships and however many one-night stands, Lexie was dating the only man she ever loved. And the entire time she was in the police academy, he was screwing someone else. I've tried to tell her to play the field, but she isn't wired that way. And dealing with perverts who've asked her to do all kinds of nasty things has only made this worse. She thinks you're looking for something serious, but if you aren't, walk away. Don't hurt her. She can't go through that again. I can't watch her go through that again. And you work together. Is dating even allowed?" She stopped speaking when she spotted me, but I felt betrayed.

The butterflies were back, and my heart was racing. I had to know what Riley was going to say.

"I'd never do anything to hurt her or jeopardize her career. She's stronger than you think. She needs to trust herself enough to take risks. She second-guesses a lot of things and changes her mind often when it comes to dating, but at least now I understand why."

Inhaling a breath, I tried to hide the hurt and betrayal as I returned to the table. They fell silent, and Riley scooted in so I could sit.

"Are you okay?" he asked.

"Yeah." I stared at Amber. She knew without a doubt that I had heard enough of their conversation to be reeling from the one, two punch that I never expected her to deliver.

"Lexie—" she began.

I held up my hand. "I want to call it a night, but you're leaving first before you stick your nose someplace else where it doesn't belong. I don't want or need you to fight my battles. I'm a big girl. I can take care of myself."

"I know that." At least she had the decency not to defend herself.

"Then go. And don't you ever do anything like this again."

She picked up her purse. "I want you to know that I did this for your own good. I'll call you tomorrow." She hugged me, even though I didn't make a move to reciprocate it, and then she was gone.

"For the record, I really don't understand women," Riley said. "Your friend's a handful, isn't she?"

"I'm sorry she called. I'm sorry you showed up. And I'm sorry that she aired the unedited version of my dirty laundry all over the place. My baggage comes in a nice matching set, doesn't it?" I laughed, a bitter sound emanating from the painful void in my chest. "My parents own a luggage store which makes this whole thing poetic in a sick and twisted way."

"Lexie?"

"I can't be with someone who wants me to be timid and meek or has some kind of notion that he's the protector and I'm the damsel in distress. I appreciate someone watching my back. That's tantamount to the work we do, but it's a two-way street."

"You saved me, Lex."

"I pushed you out of the way, and you stayed with me in the hallway with King. That made us even. I need you to look me in the eye and tell me you didn't ask me to wait in the car because you had to keep me safe."

"I don't know why I did that."

"Dammit, Michael. Can you promise me you won't do that again?"

"I promise."

I let the words sink in while I thought about everything else. "What kind of cop doesn't know the man she's living with is banging the next door neighbor? Not once or twice. But three times, I found her slutty thongs in our laundry. Three times. The first time, I dismissed it as something left in the washing machine by another resident. The second time, I started to get curious. But deep down, I knew, and I didn't do anything until I came home and found them together in the shower."

"If it makes you feel any better, I found my ex-girlfriend sucking off my best friend." He kissed my temple. "Amber was only telling this story because she doesn't want you to end up with another asshole. Regardless of what happens between us, trust your instincts. Don't let this one hiccup define you. What he did had nothing to do with you."

I licked my lips. "You're the only person, besides Amber, who knows all the gory details of my past. And you haven't left yet, even though you get how uptight, jealous, and neurotic this makes me."

"You, neurotic? No way."

I pushed away from him. "I really am ready to call it a night. I need to go home and hide under the covers, eat some ice cream, and wallow. But pretend I didn't tell you that."

"Okay." He paid the tab, which I protested but he ignored, and walked me to my car. "Are you okay to drive?"

"I'm not drunk. Do you want me to walk a straight line or lean back and touch my nose?"

"No." He kissed me, a long, lingering kiss that made my heart ache. "But I'm going to call you in two hours. Is that enough time for you to get home and do all those things I'm not supposed to know about?"

"Probably. I only have a pint of fudge swirl in the freezer. The container's small enough that it won't take long to hit carton."

"Well, if you need someone to make an ice cream run for you, let me know." He looked like he wanted to say something else but didn't. Instead, he held my car door open while I slid inside.

# TWENTY-SIX

Over the course of the next few days, Riley was attentive but not smothering. We spoke regularly on the phone. He even brought takeout and ice cream to my apartment two nights after the fiasco at the bar but was called back to work on account of a department store robbery. Gangs didn't think it was connected to Sigfried or his crew, but Riley wanted to make sure. Too many days had passed without a single sighting.

After Sigfried's close call at the pawn shop, he had yet to surface, so we were exploring every and any option. John Wolfe, the pawn shop owner, didn't have the same hang-ups as the V-7s and former Street Bishops when it came to protecting Alfred Sigfried. Wolfe only looked out for number one. And we were grateful because he gave us everything Sigfried had attempted to pawn.

Among the items were two handguns registered to the owner of one of the earliest known home invasions, which we had linked to the Street Bishops. The other items included dozens of engagement rings, some gold jewelry, and three high-end gaming laptops. Almost all of the items had come from Big Bill's hidden stash. Unfortunately, Wolfe didn't know where Sigfried was hiding, and the contact information he had on file was the same as what we had for his last known address. But he wasn't there.

However, every single cop was determined to find him. We had all the evidence we needed to arrest him for the thefts. Surely, once we took him into custody, it wouldn't take long to connect him to the assaults, murders, and other associated offenses. But we didn't have him, and we didn't know where he went. Units hunted him in droves, but he had vanished. And every moment he remained on the loose was a personal affront to Michael Riley and the rest of the gangs unit.

Detective Riley smiled when I walked into the squad room the next morning. His eyes were always so expressive, and right now, they were screaming *I have a secret*. Before we had a chance to speak, Lightman entered the room.

"We received a tip on a Sigfried sighting. We're moving on this now," he said, not giving anyone a chance to ask a question before he was out the door.

"You heard the man," Preston said as Kemper, Hawking, and I exchanged confused looks. "Move your asses."

By the time we made it downstairs, Lightman had assembled dozens of patrol officers inside the roll-call room. Lt. Peterson stood before the group, handing out assignments.

"The judge granted sweeping arrest warrants for everyone in the motorcycle club. We've finally figured out where they've been hanging out since Bishop's Bar closed, so we're going to move on them too. Remember, these bikers are unpredictable, so be prepared for anything," Peterson said.

"Consider them armed and dangerous. Many of them have a known history of violence." Lightman pointed to Alfred Sigfried's blown-up photo ID. "If you see this man, apprehend him immediately."

Peterson resumed the briefing. "Our objective is to bring everyone in at once, so no one escapes. You've each been assigned a location and suspect. I don't want to see you again until that man or woman is handcuffed in the back of your squad car. Do you understand me?"

A round of nods and 'yes, sir's echoed throughout the room.

"Move out, people. Time is of the essence. Once they see

us coming, they will attempt to go to ground again. We have to be smart about this and fast. Stay safe out there," Peterson said.

The patrol officers hurried out of the room and to their waiting squad cars.

Lightman herded the rest of us into a small circle near the lieutenant's podium. "Patrol is handling the V-7s. That leaves us with finding and apprehending Sigfried." He pointed to a spot on the map. "A tip came in that Sigfried was holed up at this address. Several surveillance units are already on the scene. They haven't spotted him, but our tipster said he was last seen going into this house." He showed us a photo. The house was small with a fenced in yard.

"Whose house is it?" Riley asked.

"It belongs to Sigfried's aunt. However, we've verified she's out of town on business."

"Is she covering for Sigfried?" Detective Frank Devereaux asked.

"We don't believe so." Lightman looked around. "But the windows are covered. We have no way of knowing who or what is inside that house. We should expect the worst."

"Maybe we should call in SWAT," Kemper joked.

"If necessary, we will. However, I'd prefer our unit handles this. Sigfried's made us laughingstocks and turned our team upside-down." Lightman grabbed a pen and drew on the map. "Unlike last time, we're going to make sure this place is surrounded and we cut off all escape routes." He marked a spot on the map. "Frank and Hawking, you cover the back. Sam and Kemper, you take the east. Watch the sides in case he jumps a fence or tries to escape through the neighbor's property. Mike, you take the west." He pointed a finger at Riley. "Don't screw this up again."

Riley kept his eyes on the map and the blueprint of the house just beneath it. "I got it," he said.

"You better." Lightman pointed to the front door. "I'm going through the front. If he rabbits, I trust you'll grab him." Lightman looked at Peterson. "I'm hoping for a smooth takedown, but keep area units advised in case we need them."

"Will do. Good luck," the lieutenant said.

We headed to the garage. I was a few steps behind Riley when Lightman called out, "Sarconi, where are you going? You're with me."

"Sir?" I hadn't expected that.

"Did I stutter?" Lightman asked. "You have shitty luck. Last time, the two of you missed the mark. I'm not risking that again. You're with me. Mike's on his own, unless he can't handle it."

"I can handle it," Riley said. "But nothing better go sideways this time." He gave me one last look before Preston pushed him toward an unmarked cruiser.

I followed Lightman to his car and climbed into the passenger's seat. I didn't like this, and neither did Riley. But it was for the best. I didn't want any feelings to cloud Riley's judgment or mine. This was better.

"Now you're gonna see what real police work looks like," Lightman said in that condescending way as we left the station. "You've earned it. After all, how many officers can keep their cool when a gun's pointed at their head?"

"All of us," I said brazenly.

"No. That's what they want you to think. I've seen men twice your size shit themselves in situations like that." He glanced at me. "You've got a pair of brass ones dangling between those shapely legs of yours."

I remained silent, not mentioning the inappropriate nature of his comment. It was sexist on so many levels. But we were about to make a bust, so now wasn't the time.

"What's the plan? Knock on the door and see if Sigfried answers?" I asked.

"Pretty much." Lightman looked at me. "I see no reason to complicate things. If he runs, we grab him. But if he's smart, he'll surrender."

"And if he puts up a fight?"

"That should be no sweat for someone as brave as you. You've been in several scrapes under my tutelage. It's time one of them results in something positive. My team could use a win. Are you gonna help us get that win today, Sarconi?"

"Yes, sir," I said, but saying that had probably jinxed us.

Too bad my great aunt wasn't here to tell me to turn around three times, throw salt over my left shoulder, and spit. I didn't think most Italians were superstitious, but she was. And based on her beliefs, this conversation would result in a lot of bad juju.

We were halfway there when Lightman spoke again. "You don't worry about anything, do you? Not chain of command. Not common decency. Nothing."

"Sir?"

"You talked to the detectives from internal affairs after the shooting. Then you spoke to Riley and Preston about what you thought might have happened at the pawn shop. But for some reason, it slipped your mind to talk to me about it."

My stomach clenched, but I did my best to remain calm.

"Is there any particular reason why you want to jam me up?" he asked. "I thought we had an understanding. Weren't we on the same page?"

"I'm not trying to jam you up, sir. I simply didn't understand how someone as experienced as you could let a perp escape."

"Let him escape? You think I wanted him to get away? That I had nothing better to do for these last few days than live and breathe intel on where this asshole might be hiding?"

"No, I—"

"Are you afraid of me, Sarconi?"

"Should I be?" Even as the words left my mouth, the voice in my head screamed yes.

"Of course not. We're on the same side. That would be stupid." Lightman parked the car and turned to face me. "Don't pretend you have any idea how easy it is to chase down a suspect. You've never had to do that before. Those jerk-offs you used to collar for vice had their pants around their ankles by the time you announced, so they were easy pickings. Fish in a barrel. Shit like that. But this is trench warfare. Stay on my six. Do what I say, and do not question me. It's about time someone reminded you of your training." After making sure the rest of the team was in position, Lightman looked at me. "Are you ready?"

"Yes, sir." But he was wrong about a lot of things. Mostly, me. However, we had a job to do, so I followed Lightman down a long, narrow walkway, through the wooden gate, and to the front door of the tiny house.

Lightman stood to the side, gesturing that I stand on the other while he knocked. He waited a beat, but when we didn't hear movement inside, he knocked again. Before he could say or do anything else, a shotgun blast tore through the door.

My hand went to my firearm, and I aimed at the splintered door. He kicked what remained of it down and went in high. I knelt next to the door, scanning for the shooter. Once I was positive it was clear, I followed him inside.

Lightman was fifteen feet ahead of me as we cleared the house. Once we determined there was only one hiding place left and no one had fled the building, Lightman announced our presence. "This is the police. Throw down your weapon, and open the door."

My radio went off. The teams outside had been advised of the situation but were holding position for now. We didn't want this to be another one of Sigfried's misdirects or distractions.

"I won't ask you again," Lightman said.

"Whoa. Hold up. Don't shoot, dude." A teenager, probably fifteen or sixteen, cracked open the bathroom door and attempted to slide the shotgun out.

Lightman stepped forward and grabbed the barrel, yanking the shotgun out of the kid's hand before he could comply. "What are you doing shooting at police officers?"

"My cousin told me to fire at the first person who rang the doorbell," the kid said. Lightman pushed him onto the ground, frisked him, and gestured for my handcuffs. "How was I supposed to know it was gonna be a couple of cops?"

"What if it was the mailman or one of your neighbors wanting to borrow a cup of sugar?"

"I don't know." The kid trembled.

"I bet you don't know much," Lightman muttered.

"Who did you think would be at the door?" I asked.

"I thought it'd be some biker from a rival MC," the kid

said. "Al knows a bunch of scary dudes."

"Who's Al?" Lightman asked.

"My cousin."

"Alfred Sigfried?" I asked.

The kid nodded. "He showed up a few days ago and said he needed somewhere safe to crash until he could get some things together."

"Where is he now?" Lightman asked.

"I don't know. He left yesterday. He hasn't been back since."

"Did he leave anything behind?" I asked.

The kid shook his head. "He took everything with him, except some cash. He left me a few hundreds."

"What was he getting together?" I asked.

"He didn't say. And I have nothing else to say either." The kid suddenly sounded tough, probably because guns were no longer pointed at him.

"I'll make you say something," Lightman threatened.

"He's a kid," I said, hoping Lightman would realize we couldn't question him without a guardian or someone from child services present.

"They all are at one point. That doesn't mean they won't blow our fucking heads off." He dragged the kid to his feet. "What's your name?"

"Jacob Miller, and that's all I'm telling you. I'm remaining silent from here on out."

"The hell you are." Lightman keyed his radio. "No sign of Sigfried, but we have one suspect in custody." Lightman hauled Jacob to the car, shoved him into the back seat, and closed the door. "Let's tear this place apart. Sigfried may have left a clue behind."

# TWENTY-SEVEN

"Did you find anything?" I asked Detective Preston.

"Sigfried didn't leave anything damning or valuable behind. He's too smart for that."

I closed the refrigerator door. We searched the house, high and low, but the biker hadn't left a trace behind.

"Maybe the kid can shed some light on things," Preston said, steering me away from the cabinets which I'd already searched. "Sigfried left him with instructions and gave him cash. They must be close for the kid to pull the trigger on someone."

"He pulled the trigger on the front door. I'm not sure he had any idea what would happen when he did."

She pointed to a few shoot 'em up video games in the den. "He may have had some idea. I'm guessing Jacob Miller idolizes his older cousin to risk doing something that insane. Even if Sigfried didn't give the kid any details, Miller might have seen or heard something we can use. I'm going to head back to the station and get started on that."

"You mean Lightman's not conducting the interrogation?" I asked.

"Jack's not the best with kids, but he may sit in. Did you want in on the interrogation, too?"

"That's not why I was asking."

"Doesn't mean you can't pick up a thing or two on questioning persons of interest." She hitched her eyebrows. "Yay or nay?"

"I'll do whatever Detective Lightman wants."

She gave me an odd look. "You must have had one hell of a ride here."

We went outside to find Lightman waiting outside the car. He was on the phone with someone, discussing the case and the kid we'd taken into custody. Riley and Devereaux were searching the shed with Kemper and Hawking.

"Find anything, gentlemen?" Preston called.

Devereaux stuck his head out. "We've got a ton of the usual crap, and that's about it."

"I'm going to head back. Crime techs already pulled whatever they could," she said. "Kemper, let's go."

"I'm heading back too. This is a waste of our time. Maybe patrol found something we can use." Devereaux tapped Riley on the shoulder. "You coming, bro?"

Riley sounded distracted. "Yeah, in a minute."

I glanced back at the car, but Lightman wasn't going anywhere yet. Instead of seeing what he was doing, I stepped into the shed to see what had caught Riley's attention. On the floor were several pairs of gardening gloves, hoes, trowels, fertilizer, and plant food.

"What is it?" I asked.

"I'm not sure." Riley wiped his hands on his pants and stood. "But nothing in here is dusty. No cobwebs. And despite all this, I'm not seeing any fresh dirt. Everything looks brand new."

"Is that important?"

"I don't see how, but it strikes me oddly." He stepped out of the shed. "The garden is in desperate need of weeding and maintenance, so why do the Millers have landscaping gear when they don't use it? I didn't see a single potted plant inside the house either."

"Maybe it's a new project Ms. Miller wants to take on after she returns from her business trip."

"Yeah, maybe." Riley went back into the shed and checked inside the various pairs of gardening gloves.

"What are you looking for?"

"Stolen jewelry. Hidden cash. Pretty much anything at this point." He stopped looking around the shed and folded his arms across his chest. "Did the kid tell you how long Sigfried was here?"

"No, but Preston will figure it out once she gets him in the box."

Riley frowned. "The kid could have blown you and Jack away."

"The vest would have saved me."

"Not if he shot you in the face."

"He shot the door, not me." I narrowed my eyes. "I'm okay."

"Yeah, I got that." He moved to a work table and scanned the random scrap materials. "What do you think Sigfried was doing here?"

"Hiding from us."

"Why did he take off? Who tipped us to his location?"

"It was anonymous, but I'm sure 9-1-1 can provide additional details."

"As soon as we get back, I'll look into it." Riley had a theory, but he wasn't sharing it. Still, I could see the wheels turning in his head. "As far as taking off, Sigfried must have had somewhere else to go. We need to figure out where."

I checked the time. "A liquor store? Someone's house? A storage facility?"

"I don't know, but maybe Jacob Miller will have some answers." Riley gave the shed one last look, snapped a few photos, and locked the doors behind us. "Let's head back. You don't want to keep Jack waiting."

We split up at the cars, and Lightman drove back to the station.

Pulling into the garage, he cut the engine and turned to me. "Miller fired a shotgun round at us. That's attempted murder of a police officer. They'll try him as an adult. He's looking at a few decades of hard time. Do you think he'll survive?"

I knew what Lightman was doing, and even if it was borderline unethical, I had no choice but to play along. "That's doubtful. Prisons are hard for even the toughest men, killers, rapists, violent offenders. Kids never do well." I glanced back at Miller. "Maybe his cousin will hear about it and put the word out that no one touches him."

"You really think Sigfried's got clout like that? The power on the inside resides with the street gangs and organized crime, not punks who think they're tough because they ride motorcycles and break into little old ladies' homes," Lightman said.

"Yeah, I guess you're right." I glanced back at the handcuffed adolescent. "I'm sorry, kid. Maybe you'll get a lenient judge. I hear juvenile detention facilities are improving. If you get a choice, that's what you pick."

By the time we opened the door, the kid was begging for a phone call.

"Nice save," Lightman whispered as we handed Miller off to be booked.

I nodded. "We need to find Sigfried."

"After today, we're straight, Sarconi. But next time you have some kind of misgiving about something that went down, find me, so we can talk about it. Bad cops are a blemish on the entire department, but it's worse when a good cop gets wrongly accused." He moved closer, whispering in my ear, "Don't cross me again. I've dealt with enough misunderstandings recently and will not tolerate another one."

"You got it," I said.

Lightman gave me a long look. "Call the kid's mom and find out how long it's going to take her to get here."

# TWENTY-EIGHT

Hours later, Ms. Sheila Miller arrived at the station. Her son, Jacob, was waiting inside an interrogation room.

"Jacob's a good kid," she kept saying. "I don't understand."

"Do you keep firearms in the house?" Lightman asked.

Ms. Miller shook her head. "I don't like guns. I've read all the statistics on accidental shootings. I'd never have one in my house."

Lightman held up the shotgun which had been tagged and processed. "Your son had this in his possession. He blew a hole through your front door. He nearly killed me and another officer. Where did he get it?"

"I don't know." She tore her eyes away from the weapon. "I swear, I've never seen that before."

Lightman put it down on the table. Instead of bringing the distraught mother into one of the interrogation rooms, he spoke to her in the break room, hoping she'd be more cooperative in a friendlier setting. "When's the last time you spoke to your nephew?"

"Nephew?" Her worry lines deepened.

"Alfred Sigfried." Lightman pulled out the most recent ID photo we had. "He's quite a bit older than your son."

She glanced at the photo before looking away, disgust on her face. "We are not in contact. I haven't seen or spoken to him since his last parole hearing."

"You were there?" Lightman asked.

"My sister asked me to go. She wanted the moral support."

"Did you speak on his behalf?" Lightman asked.

Ms. Miller shook her head. "What is this about?"

"Has your son been in contact with Alfred Sigfried?"

The reason for our questions dawned on her. "That's his gun, isn't it?"

"Answer the question, ma'am."

"I don't know. Jacob always idolized Al. That's partially my fault. I didn't want him to know how terrible that side of the family is, so I always downplayed it. I said Al was troubled or misunderstood. I didn't know they were in contact. I had no idea."

"What day did you leave on your business trip?" Lightman asked.

"It was supposed to be a ten day trip. I was scheduled to come back tomorrow, so eight days ago. What was that? Wednesday, I guess."

"You left your underaged son alone the entire time?" Lightman made a tsk sound.

"His father was supposed to check on him, but as usual, he flaked. So the neighbors were watching out for him. Jacob's a good kid. He doesn't throw wild parties. He doesn't drink or use drugs. I trust him. I filled the fridge and freezer with easy meals to reheat, made sure he had money for pizza and snacks, and gave him strict instructions on letting me know what he was doing and who he was with after school. He didn't skip or miss. The school would have notified me. Plus, I'm in a carpool, so I know he got picked up every day."

Lightman pushed a pad of paper toward her. "I need names and numbers for everyone who kept an eye on your house and your son while you were away."

Ms. Miller started writing.

"No one mentioned Alfred Sigfried was staying at your house with your son?" Lightman asked.

"Of course not. If I had known that, I would have done something to stop it. Al is not welcome in my home. He knows that. He knows I think he's a bad influence on Jacob." She scowled. "That gun must be his. That's the only explanation."

"Your son discharged this weapon at police officers," Lightman said. "He's in a world of hurt right now."

"I'm so sorry." She scribbled more furiously before pushing the pad of paper toward Lightman, as if completing the task quickly would earn his favor. "What do I do? I have to get Jacob a lawyer. I have to come up with bail or something." She blinked a few times, her mind going in a million different directions. "You have to understand, Jacob's always been a good kid. What he did was wrong, but it was a mistake. A terrible, horrible mistake. Is this going to ruin the rest of his life? I'll do anything to keep that from happening."

Lightman looked like he wanted to say something snide. Instead, he said, "Convince Jacob to answer our questions. Your nephew's responsible for dozens of recent crimes, including murder. We believe he used your house to hide out. We need to know where your nephew is now and what he has planned next."

She nodded several times. "Okay. Can I see Jacob now?"

Lightman turned to me. "Officer Sarconi, escort Ms. Miller to interrogation room four."

"Right this way." I gestured at the closed door.

Ms. Miller stood, hugging her purse as she made her way around the table.

"It sounds like you have a complicated family life," I said once we were out of the break room.

She nodded, still clutching her purse. "I always tried to do what was best for Jacob. I should have never left on that trip, but he's never done anything like this before. You have to believe me."

"We need his help," I said. "He refused to answer our questions. He's caught up in acting tough. That won't help him here."

"I'll knock the tough right out of him," she said. "I can't believe he'd pick up a gun, let alone fire it."

"At least he was smart enough to surrender. Firing on the police is a good way to get killed."

"How did he survive?"

"He got lucky. So did we."

She turned, stopping me in my tracks. "He fired at you?"

"I was with Detective Lightman at your front door when he discharged the weapon."

"I am so sorry."

I nodded, continuing down the hallway. Being this close to the interrogation room made me anxious. It was still too soon. But I fought to keep my nerves in check, ignoring the cold sweat that erupted on the back of my neck and the sick feeling that filled my stomach. "Here we are." I opened the door, revealing Jacob Miller.

His left wrist was handcuffed to the table while he ate a sandwich with the other hand. An advocate had been assigned to his case, which probably explained the sandwich and juice box, but the cuffs remained on. Jacob needed to know we were serious.

"Mom?" He wiped his mouth with the back of his hand, tears springing to his eyes. "I'm sorry."

"Boy, you better be sorry." She went into the room. "Look at you. Look where you are. What were you thinking?"

"I—"

"Tell the police what you know. Tell them everything."

"But Mom," he glanced behind me, and I turned to see Preston with a stack of case files in her arms, "shouldn't we wait for a lawyer?"

Preston pushed past me and put everything down on the table. "You can wait. Or you can cooperate. Depending on how much you tell us and where it leads, we'll consider dropping the charges. Jacob doesn't have a record. He's never been in trouble before. If he agrees to keep his nose clean, we could forgive him this once."

"Answer this nice detective's questions," Ms. Miller said. "Or I will leave you here to rot."

I wasn't sure that was the best strategy for a concerned parent, but it should get us answers. The advocate excused herself and stepped into the hallway where I remained.

"She should have insisted on a lawyer." The advocate eyed me. "Is Preston's offer legit?"

"As far as I know."

"It better be."

"Relax, Dolores," Lightman said. "We aren't after the kid. We're after his cousin. We get him, and we'll let the rest slide."

"Why?" Dolores looked skeptical.

"From what little we know, Sigfried put that gun in the kid's hands and told him to fire. I don't think the kid would have done it otherwise, so I'd rather nail the asshole who's actually responsible."

"Have you always been this enlightened, Jack?" she teased. "I've never noticed."

"I'm learning."

"I bet you are." She let out a throaty laugh. "If you're planning on keeping that up, I'll let you buy me a drink."

"Depending on how this interview goes, I'll give you a call later tonight."

"I'm counting on it."

# TWENTY-NINE

Watching Detective Lightman flirt was almost as disconcerting as being inside an interrogation room. Almost. My heart raced, so I forced slow, deep breaths to fill my lungs, over and over. I wouldn't panic. There was no threat. The shotgun blast to the door hadn't made me as tense as this room. *Dammit, shake it off, Lexie.* But my internal monologue did little to quell the irrational fear.

"What was Alfred Sigfried doing at your house?" Lightman asked.

Jacob stared at the empty juice box. "He was hanging out."

"How did he know you were there alone?" Preston asked.

"We chat sometimes," Jacob looked at his mom, "on that video game."

"I asked you about that," Ms. Miller interrupted.

"Please," Preston motioned for the woman to remain quiet, "go on, Jacob."

"I told him Mom was out of town, and he asked if he could come over and crash. We hadn't seen each other since I was like six, but we talked sometimes over the game."

"What did you talk about?" Lightman asked.

"Al talked a lot about his bike and this bar where he hangs out with his friends. They always sounded really cool. I thought hanging out would be fun."

"Did he go into specifics?" Preston asked.

"Not before he showed up, but when he did, I knew something was wrong. He didn't have his bike. A friend dropped him off."

"What friend?" Lightman asked, nodding at the pen in my hand, reminding me to take notes.

"Al didn't say. He told me he was in trouble, that he pissed off a rival motorcycle club and they were looking for him. He needed a place to lie low for a while. No one knew we were cousins, so he said they'd never find him there. He said it'd be fine. But a few days later, when I got home from school, he had that shotgun." Jacob nodded to the photo of the weapon we had taken into evidence. "He said it was a precaution, but that's when I started getting worried."

"Why didn't you call me?" Ms. Miller asked.

"I didn't want to get in trouble," Jacob said.

Ms. Miller opened her mouth to berate her kid, but I cleared my throat and shook my head, saving the detectives from having to intervene. The woman caught my drift and swallowed her question.

"What else did Al have with him?" Preston asked.

"When he showed up, he didn't have much, just a bunch of money. He gave me some of it and told me to buy some stuff. Clothes, food, things like that."

"Where did he get the shotgun?" Lightman asked.

Jacob shrugged. "I don't know. When I came home from school, he had it. He took me in the backyard and showed me how to aim. I thought it was loaded, but it was empty."

"It wasn't empty when you fired at us," Lightman said.

"No, sir. I...knew it wasn't. But Al told me to be careful. When he left, he said someone might come for him. If they did, I should shoot them."

"Who did he say would come for him?" Lightman pushed.

"Um...I don't know."

I watched the kid squirm uncomfortably. "Did he say the police were looking for him?"

Preston hid her grin, glad that I asked the question, but Lightman looked like I had lit a bag of excrement on fire. The kid wouldn't admit to that.

"He said he had enemies. He never said who, but he was hiding out because they were looking for him." Jacob bit his lip. "I'm not stupid. I know Al doesn't always do good things. He's been arrested before. I've heard Mom talking to Aunt Verna about it. So when Al said he had enemies, I knew he couldn't go to the police for help, but I wanted to help him. We're supposed to help people in need, right?"

"Your cousin's been hurting people, stealing from them, assaulting them, convincing others to commit murder for him." Lightman spread out an array of photos from the various crime scenes. Thankfully, he withheld the bloody photos from Big Bill's demise. "He's going to keep hurting people unless we stop him."

"We don't want to see him get hurt," Preston said. "But the longer he's out there, the more likely it is to happen. And the more likely it is he will hurt someone else. That's why it's very important you tell us everything you can. Where did Al go? Did he take anything with him or leave anything behind? Did he mention anything to you about his situation?"

"He took a bag with clothes and toiletries, the stuff I bought for him, when he left. He said he wanted to make sure he got to keep what was his. He left me money, about a thousand dollars, and the shotgun. But that was supposed to be for my protection. He didn't want anyone hurting me when they came looking for him."

"Where was he going?" Lightman asked.

"I think he was going back to the bar. He said he wanted to see his friends and make sure his stuff was still there. He wanted to make sure no one messed with it."

"That doesn't give us much to work with." Lightman stared at the kid. "You have to do better."

"I don't know," Jacob said, his eyes growing wide with desperation.

"If he doesn't know—" Ms. Miller began, but Lightman shushed her.

"Who knew Al was staying at your house?" Preston asked, taking over.

"No one. He swore me to secrecy to keep that to myself." Jacob paused to think. "Obviously, his friends must have known, at least the one who dropped him off."

"And whoever brought him the shotgun," Lightman muttered.

"What about your friends? The woman who drove you to school? The neighbors?" I asked.

"I didn't tell anyone."

"Not even your best friend?" I asked.

Jacob shook his head. "Al kept saying it wasn't safe, so I didn't tell anyone."

"Give me a minute." Lightman led me out of the room. Once the door closed, he said, "Mike's looking into who placed the anonymous call that tipped us. See if he's made any progress. I want to know if the kid is lying. If he is, no deal."

"And if he's not?"

"Just find out."

Sucking in another deep breath, I forced myself not to run down the hall and back to the squad room. Instead, I kept a steady stride and marched into the gangs unit. Riley was at his desk, the phone to his ear. Hawking was clicking away at the keyboard.

"Are you here to help sort out the dozens of arrests patrol made?" Hawking asked.

"No." But I peered over his shoulder to see who had been brought in. "I'm curious if anyone was arrested at Big Bill's bar or near Sigfried's home address."

"I'll check." Hawking paused what he was doing and keyed in my request. "Units have been assigned to Sigfried's place since he disappeared. No one's been in or out. As far as near the bar, we made six arrests in that neighborhood. Do you want the list of names?"

"No." I pointed to the map. "Sigfried lives around here, right?"

"Yep."

"Was the unit assigned to sit on Sigfried's place rerouted to deal with the sweeping arrests?"

"They provided backup, but they weren't gone more than thirty minutes," Hawking said. "When they returned, they swept the perimeter, but nothing had changed."

That we knew of, but I had my doubts. I waited for Riley

to get off the phone before I passed along Lightman's question.

"9-1-1 dispatch traced the anonymous tip back to Platt's Pawn. It was on our list. I've been trying to get surveillance footage pulled from the store, but in the meantime, traffic cams may have caught something. I had to figure out which cameras covered that block, and," Riley clicked a few buttons on the computer, "I should be getting access in a matter of seconds."

Once the video filled his screen, he backed it up to the correct timestamp. Two minutes later, Alfred Sigfried emerged from the pawn shop.

"That son of a bitch called in the tip on himself," Riley said.

"I figured." The pieces had come together. "He left the shotgun and money with his younger cousin and set him up to eliminate whatever cops came knocking. Sigfried must have assumed we'd come looking for him. It fits his M.O. He set a trap to kill a couple of cops and planned to pass the blame on to someone else."

"It's another one of his damn misdirects." Riley cursed. "While we were busy figuring out why a kid murdered two cops, Sigfried would be a million steps ahead. Any idea what he's planning?"

"Not yet, but I'm hoping Jacob can shed some light on that." I took a step back, anxious to tell Lightman the verdict. "Thanks for this."

"It's called teamwork."

By the time I got back to the interrogation room, Lightman and Preston looked like they were wrapping things up. After filling Lightman in on what I learned, he returned to the interview, and I went into the observation room to watch.

Even being in here made me jittery, but I had to get over it. The more time I spent in this part of the building, the more desensitized I'd become. And since I planned to pass the detective's exam, I'd have to conduct my own interviews and question suspects on a regular basis. It wouldn't help matters if I was always freaked out to be here. So I sucked it up and ignored my fight or flight response.

Jacob Miller didn't know much more than what he already told us. He couldn't believe his cousin had set him up to become a cop killer. Thankfully, that plan had backfired. However, even through the hurt and rage, Jacob only came up with one additional detail.

"He spent a lot of time out in the shed. I don't know why, but he said he liked it out there. It gave him time to think."

I pressed the intercom button, hoping Lightman wouldn't reprimand me for interrupting. "Ask about the gardening equipment."

Lightman had no idea what I was talking about, but someone had clued Preston in on the situation. "Ms. Miller, why do you have so many gardening tools when it doesn't look like you spend a great deal of time maintaining your lawn?" she asked.

"Gardening tools?" Ms. Miller raised an eyebrow. "I never garden."

"What about you?" Preston asked Jacob.

"No, but I know what stuff you're talking about. Al was into all that. The stuff in there, the little shovel thing and the dirt and all that, he had me buy that for him. I completely forgot. I thought it was weird, but he said that was his hobby. He liked spending time outdoors and planting stuff because he couldn't do any of that when he was in prison."

"So you bought that stuff?" Lightman asked, a look of disbelief on his face.

"Yeah, Al sent me to the hardware store, and I got what he wanted. It was mostly plant food and little pots. He wanted to grow things. Flowers or something. He said that's how he liked to relax."

"What was Al doing with all that stuff?" Ms. Miller asked.

"I'll have to double check," Preston said, "but I don't think we found any plants at the scene."

"He must have taken them with him. He had six. They were in these ceramic pots," Jacob said. "They weren't very big."

"Did he ask you to buy seeds or bulbs?" Preston asked.

Jacob shook his head. "I kinda thought he already had that stuff with him, like he wanted to grow his own herbs."

"Herbs?" Ms. Miller asked. "You mean marijuana?"

"I don't know, Mom. But I thought maybe."

"Lexie?" Riley appeared in the open doorway. "What did Lightman say about your theory?"

"He agrees, but the kid still can't tell us what he doesn't know. But you were right about the gardening tools in the shed." I filled him in on what he missed. "We'll have to run it down. But I never pictured Sigfried as a gardener."

"He's not nurturing. But if he's on the run, why would he be growing his own? That makes no sense."

"A lot of things don't make sense."

"Maybe the V-7s will be able to shed some light on this. We have them all in custody. A few bikers have already squealed on their pals' involvement in the home invasions."

"That gives us something to work with," I said.

Riley smiled. "You sound like a detective."

"Stop." I turned to face the glass.

"We don't have Sigfried yet, but we've brought in everyone he controls. In essence, we've disbanded the entire MC, at least for now. This should count as a win. Police department, one. V-7s, zilch."

"It's about damn time, but I don't think Lightman will see it that way."

"See what what way?" Lightman asked, stepping into the room.

I kept my mouth shut while Riley updated him on the situation.

"We have to follow up with the hardware store. Once we verify Jacob Miller's story, we'll offer him and his mom protective custody until Alfred Sigfried is apprehended," Lightman said. "But the kid repeated one thing over and over. Sigfried wants to make sure no one takes his things. He must have another stash hidden somewhere. I'd bet my badge one of the bikers we arrested knows where it is. So we'll let them sweat tonight, and tomorrow, we make one of them talk."

"You think that's where Sigfried went?" I asked. "To get the rest of his stash?"

"Let's put it this way," Lightman said. "Where else would he go?"

"His apartment." And then I shared my suspicions on the other reason Sigfried tipped us off. He didn't just want to kill us. He wanted the patrol car pulled off his place so he could go home.

"I'll send units to check it out," Lightman said. "In the meantime, get me whatever you can from that hardware store."

# THIRTY

Footage from the hardware store supported Jacob Miller's claims. He purchased gardening equipment, some nails, and a few other supplies. Most of those items were found in the shed, but the six small flowerpots were missing, along with whatever Sigfried decided to plant inside them.

"He didn't buy seeds or bulbs," I said. "The footage didn't show it, and when we spoke to the clerk, she corroborated what we saw. So what in the world could Sigfried have so desperately wanted to plant?"

Riley examined our copy of the receipt. "He sent the kid to pick up plant food, fertilizer, flowerpots, gardening tools, lots of gloves, pruning shears, some pieces of wood, a saw, and nails. It reads innocently enough."

"Do you think that was intentional?"

"Probably." He squinted into the distance. "We need to find out what else Big Bill and Sigfried have stashed. He could be hiding whatever valuables that have yet to be pawned inside the planters for safe keeping."

"Like what?"

"I don't know."

I tried to recall the list of items which had been reported stolen, but besides jewelry, nothing else was small enough to conceal in the flowerpots. "Do you think a gun would fit in there?"

"Not in the pots the clerk showed us. Not without the handle or muzzle sticking out of the dirt, and at that point, it wouldn't be safe to fire. It'd probably explode in someone's hand." Riley checked the time. "Maybe Jessalyn Belknap can answer some of our questions."

"Wouldn't the Millers be a better bet?"

"Do you think Jacob or his mom withheld anything during the interrogation?"

"Jacob might have if he thought it'd keep him out of trouble." I was pretty sure Sigfried told him there was a chance the police would show up at the door. And even if he didn't, the kid must have suspected it. But he had been smart enough to keep that to himself for fear of prosecution for attempted premeditated murder of a police officer.

"All right." Riley leaned against the hood of the car. "What do you think we should do?"

"Why are you asking me?"

He chuckled, shaking his head. "You make the call this time, Lex."

I wasn't sure I liked this new game he was playing, but arguing would waste valuable time. After considering our options, I said, "We should see if anything turned up at Sigfried's apartment first."

Riley pointed at me. "Nice."

"Don't patronize."

He hopped off the hood and went around to the driver's side. "I wasn't, but I'll have to remember there's no winning with you."

"I wasn't—"

He winked. "I know."

I gave him a playful shove. "Oh, now you're busting chops?"

"Seemed fair." He reached for the radio, requesting information on Sigfried's apartment.

"It looks like Sarconi may have been right," Lightman grumbled. "The place looks like it got cleared out in a hurry. Drawers were dumped out. The closet doors remained open. We can't be sure when it happened, but a few of Sigfried's neighbors heard noises coming from his apartment around the same time we were busting into his cousin's house. I doubt that's a coincidence."

"What about security footage?" Riley asked.

"I'll check the cameras outside the building. That's the best we can do. But he wasn't supposed to get back inside.

That's why we had units sitting on the building."

"Sigfried knew it," I said. "He knows all our plays."

"I'd like to know how the fuck he got to be so damn smart." Lightman barked something at someone else. "We searched his place the moment we got a warrant, but we didn't find anything damning." Someone said something to Lightman, who cursed again. "Guess we didn't search that well. He had a false bottom in one of his drawers, and we just found a few loose floorboards in his closet beneath the carpet. Shit. How did we miss this?" He yelled at whoever was nearby.

Riley gave me a look. "I'm glad we weren't assigned to search the apartment."

"Me too."

He waited for Lightman to get back to us on the radio before he requested permission to interview Jessalyn Belknap again. After Lightman agreed, Riley put the radio back in its rightful spot and started the car. "Whatever Sigfried retrieved from his apartment must have been whatever he was afraid someone would take. I wish we knew what could be so valuable."

"Do you think he had a go-bag?"

"We've been working under the assumption Alfred Sigfried would never run."

"What choice does he have? We've arrested every member of his biker gang and all the former Street Bishops. He must realize someone's going to roll on him. And it'll only take one before the rest turn on him too."

"Maybe you're right. Maybe he wants to get out of Dodge." Riley grabbed the radio, making sure every train station, bus depot, and airport knew to be on the lookout. Then he called Lt. Peterson to see about setting up roadblocks. "Do you think we're too late?"

"I don't know. He has the money John Wolfe paid him for the pawned items, but that's not enough to start over. That's enough to get away. But he wouldn't have access to any other assets."

"Unless he had money stashed or more stolen merchandise to hock." Riley reached for the radio again, making sure the pawn shops on our list were still under surveillance. "This guy should have been a professional chess player. He's always three steps ahead."

When we got closer to the safehouse, which was a motel by the highway, Riley instructed me to turn off my phone. So I did. Like Preston said, he was a stickler for following protocol, but we kept the radio with us. Too much was going on to run silent for even a few minutes.

After executing a few maneuvers to make sure we hadn't been followed, he pulled the unmarked into a self-serve car wash across the street which appeared to have been out of service for the better part of a decade. He kept his eyes on the mirrors, grabbing my wrist when I reached for the door handle. Silently, I waited for him to let go.

"We're clear," he finally said.

"Is this paranoia or extreme caution?"

"Both."

We made our way across the parking lot, keeping our heads on a swivel. A single motorcycle was parked near the motel office. It had Wisconsin plates. We passed the man who'd ridden it here. He had a long, gray beard, a beer gut, and a jolly laugh. He took his room key and headed up the steps.

Riley and I followed behind, eavesdropping on his phone conversation which appeared to be with his wife. Apparently, the man was meeting up with some old friends to go to a revival concert for a rock band who'd been big decades before I was born. He let himself into his room and closed the door.

Before I could ask, Riley keyed his radio, requesting a check on the bike. When it came back clean, Riley let out a sigh, the tension in his shoulders easing. "We can never be too careful," he said.

After going up one more flight of stairs, Riley led me to the room on the other end and knocked on the door. "Jess," he said, "it's Michael." He waved to whoever was in the silver car beneath us, and I realized that was the protection detail.

Jessalyn Belknap cracked the door open, leaving the chain on it to see out. Once she realized it was us, she shut the door, unhooked the chain, and opened it wide. "Did you get him? Can I go home?"

"Not yet." Riley led the way inside. As soon as I entered behind him, he locked the door. "Sigfried called in a tip to lure us away from his apartment. Any idea what he kept in there?"

"I don't know. All I know is he found everything Big Bill had hidden."

"What did Big Bill have?" Riley asked.

"I told you already. He kept some things from the jobs his crew pulled."

"What about cash, fake IDs, or passports? Anything like that?"

"I'm sure Big Bill had cash on hand, but I don't know about the rest."

"Did you ever hear anyone talk about Alfred Sigfried or the V-7s?" I asked. "Do you know what they were into?"

"Everything. Anything. They didn't follow the same rules as the Street Bishops. They had no problems dealing. Drugs, guns, it didn't matter."

"What about women?" I asked.

"I wouldn't be surprised. It's why I wanted to get out of there after they took over Bishop's Bar. I didn't want to turn tricks for them."

"Were you turning tricks before?"

"No. I danced. That was it."

Before I could ask anything else, Riley put a hand on my shoulder, reminding me this wasn't vice. This was gangs. We had a different goal in mind. "Jess," he said in that soothing way, "do you have any idea what Alfred Sigfried would take with him if he decided to flee the city?"

"Probably whatever he could strap on his bike."

"What about plants?" I asked.

She looked at me like I was crazy. "What?"

"Plants? We believe he had six small flowerpots with him."

"The V-7s were in the drug biz. I never heard they were manufacturing their own product, but the Bishops didn't know who Sigfried's connection was. As far as they knew, he didn't have one."

"So you think they could have been running their own

operation?" Riley rubbed his chin. "That would explain why we didn't have any details on them or known connections to cartels or other crime organizations. But plants, like poppies, coca, and even marijuana, would have to be monitored closely for temperature and moisture. All sorts of factors go into it."

"Maybe he got that stuff so he could transport them more easily. Then once he arrives, he'll worry about getting an indoor greenhouse going. He just needs the plants to stay alive until he gets settled," she suggested.

I looked from Jessalyn to Riley. "Even if that's the case, that still makes very little sense to me."

"I don't know," Jessalyn said. "I'm just telling you rumors I heard about the V-7s. If it's not something like that, I don't know why Sigfried would have anything to do with planters or gardening."

"We're missing something," Riley said.

"Jacob suggested the same thing," I said. "It makes no sense, but it's the only theory we have."

"All right," but neither Riley nor I was convinced, "any idea where Sigfried would go if he left town?"

Jessalyn dropped onto a chair and stared at the floor. "I have no idea. His boys should be able to tell you that. They'd know where he likes to go or would like to go. But I'm guessing, he won't leave his bike behind."

"We haven't found his bike," Riley said.

"Every member of any MC that I've ever met always has one passion, and that's his bike. Sigfried would have wanted to make sure he put that somewhere safe, somewhere you wouldn't find it." Something flitted across her face. "I'd say if he leaves town, that's going with him." She reached for a pen and the tiny pad of paper the motel provided. After scribbling down a few things, she handed Riley the list. "These were the latest parts he got for it. You should ask the other members of the MC. They may be able to tell you what garage he uses. But if you find his bike, I'll bet you find him." She stared up at Riley with big doe eyes. "Do me a favor. When you see him, kill him. That's the only way it'll be safe for me to go home."

# THIRTY-ONE

After returning to the station, Riley requested Deacon Reynolds be brought back for another round of questioning. I wasn't sure why he opted for Reynolds when we had dozens of other suspects in custody, but I didn't ask. While we waited for Reynolds to be transported from central booking, Riley worked his way through the former Street Bishops.

"Where does Alfred Sigfried keep his bike?" Riley asked.

Most of them couldn't answer. A few provided smartass remarks, varying in creativity, but Riley kept his cool, even after the fifth, "At your mother's house," response.

"What's your parents' address?" I asked while we waited for the next one to be brought into the interview room.

Riley gave me a look. "If you're looking for Sigfried's bike, I can assure you it's not there. However, if you're looking to meet my folks, then I say let's do it."

I hadn't expected him to turn the tables on me, and he grinned, satisfied with his slick answer.

Isaac Bertrand entered the room, escorted by a uniformed officer. This was the first time I'd seen him in person. From the look of recognition on his face, I had no doubts he'd been in the car when Riley almost went splat.

Instead of asking the same set of questions, Riley pulled out the chair across from Bertrand, flipped it around, and straddled it. Resting his wrists on the back of the chair, he stared across at the handcuffed man. "Alfred Sigfried sent

Stryker King into this very interrogation room to kill Big Bill. He shot him in the head. His body was slumped over the table right where you are."

Bertrand gave the table an uneasy look, pulling back and leaning away from it.

"Don't worry," Riley said, "we mopped up."

This wasn't the same interrogation room, but hearing those words made me a little queasy. I sucked in a silent breath and tried to think of something else.

"Why are you telling me this?" Bertrand asked.

"Because you'd do anything for Big Bill, including mowing down a police officer."

Bertrand stared at him. "You can't prove that."

"It doesn't make it any less true." Riley stared at him with a ferocity I'd never seen before. "But that's not why you're here. I'd say for someone willing to put it all on the line for Big Bill, you wouldn't want the man responsible for his death to get away with it."

Bertrand gave the table another uneasy look. "I'm listening."

"Sigfried's planning to run. He's going to leave the Bishops and the V-7s holding the bag. He's going to let you all go down for the crimes he forced you to commit while he rides off into the sunset."

"That fucking bastard's gonna get his," Bertrand spat.

Riley drummed absently on the chair back. "It'd be easier for you to dole out some street justice if Sigfried was in lock-up with you."

Bertrand stared at him. "What do you want?"

"We're looking for Sigfried. We know he went back to his place to get something."

"I wouldn't know anything about that."

"I wouldn't expect you to," Riley said. "But maybe you know where he works on his bike or where he stores it."

Bertrand stared at the table, attempting to control his facial muscles which kept twitching and contorting in disdain. "The V-7s had a few garages they liked to use. I don't know if he'd keep it there."

"Let us worry about that." Riley slid a legal pad and pen across the table.

After Bertrand made a few scribbles, he got sent back to holding. Riley picked up the legal pad and tore off the top sheet.

"What do you think?" he asked.

I read the three garage names which appeared to have been scrawled by a kindergartener. "I'll run them down and get us locations." I searched his eyes, wondering if he'd meant what he said to Bertrand, but his face gave nothing away. "He tried to kill you," I finally said.

"Yeah."

"Are you okay?"

Riley filled his lungs and tilted his head to one side. "Yeah."

I gave him one last look, but he'd pushed the chair in and paced at the rear of the interview room, getting ready for Reynolds to show up. "Are you good in here by yourself?" I asked.

He watched me through the reflection in the glass. "I'm not by myself. Sam's on the other side."

A faint knock sounded on the glass. I didn't know how he knew that, and I didn't ask. Instead, I took the page he had handed me and went to the door. "I'll be back as soon as I have something."

When I emerged from the interview room, I found Detective Preston waiting for me in the hallway. She gave me a reassuring nod. "You guys did good in there."

"Is he okay?" I asked.

She glanced at the door that had closed behind me. "He's fine. He's just Michael." She reached for the page, so I let her see it. "This doesn't give us much. Bubba's, Lloyd's, and Piston's. You'd think they'd come up with something more original for garage names. See if any of these are legit businesses. I doubt they are, which means you'll have to get creative. Cross-reference them with the assholes we've brought in and their known aliases. More than likely, these garages are run by members of the MC. That's usually how they do it."

"I'm on it."

The search didn't take long. Preston's assumption had been partially incorrect. Bubba's and Piston's were real businesses with websites and everything. I wrote down the addresses and phone numbers. Then I did a quick search on the ownership and management, finding Bubba's was owned by one of the bikers we'd arrested. Piston's wasn't held by anyone we arrested, but that didn't mean the management didn't have close ties to someone in the MC. In fact, it looked like Piston's had lots of ties to various MCs. They specialized in custom parts and bodywork.

The only garage I couldn't find was Lloyd's. So I followed Preston's instructions to the letter. Lloyd Cartwright, a founding member of the V-7s, paid rent every month for a warehouse. That had to be the garage Bertrand had referenced. But it wasn't an actual garage. More than likely, it was a place where his brothers in the MC went to work on their bikes.

I raced down the hallway, slowing as I approached the interrogation rooms. Preston wasn't waiting in observation anymore. A quick peek through the two-way mirror showed she had joined Riley inside the interrogation room while he spoke to Deacon Reynolds.

Drumming my fingers against my thigh, I wondered if I should wait for them to finish, but this seemed too important, so I opened the interrogation room door. "Detective Riley, I need to speak to you."

"Hold that thought." Riley gave Reynolds a hard look before joining me in the hallway. "What did you dig up on the garages?"

I told him everything I found and what I suspected. He took the list from my hands, along with the notes I'd jotted down. After giving it one last look, he tucked it into his shirt pocket.

"You're thinking Lloyd's?" he asked.

"It makes the most sense, but we shouldn't dismiss the other two possibilities."

"Then let's find out. I'll see what Reynolds has to say about this. Find out if Jacob Miller has anything to add about Sigfried's bike or these garages."

"You want me to fly solo?"

"You're more than capable, Lex. I'll catch up with you in a few minutes."

I wondered what Detective Lightman would think about this, but I had my orders. If Lightman didn't like it, it'd be Riley's head on the chopping block. That should have provided some comfort, but it didn't. Instead, I hurried to the break room, where the Millers were patiently waiting while a uniformed officer kept an eye on them.

"Jacob," I said, entering the room, "I need to ask you a couple more questions."

"I already told you everything."

I looked at his mom, seeing the annoyance on her face. She understood the danger her son was facing, even if he didn't fully comprehend what could happen to him if he failed to hold up his end of the bargain and we revoked his deal.

"You mentioned your cousin spoke a lot about his bike during your chats."

Jacob's ears perked up. "Yeah, but he didn't say much about it once he showed up."

"Did he ever mention where he kept his bike?"

"Kept it?" Jacob wasn't following along.

"You know, when it rained or the weather was bad. Where did he keep it?"

"I have no idea."

"Did he ever mention having to get it fixed?" I asked.

"He did most of the work himself. He said that's what he and his friends did. I always pictured it was like those car racing movies, where they all hang out together in a garage, drinking beer, and fixing shit." The kid glanced at his mom, but she didn't scold him for cursing.

I smiled. "Right, a garage, just like that one. I bet that's exactly what it was like for Al."

"Maybe."

"Did he mention where the garage was or what it was called?"

Jacob shook his head, his gaze dropping to the floor. "That's what I imagined. I don't know if he ever said."

I needed to come at this another way, so I redirected my attention to the vending machine and reached into my pocket for some dollar bills. After getting a bag of candy-coated chocolates, I took a seat at the table across from

Jacob and opened the bag.

"Why didn't you ask him where his bike was when he showed up at your house?" I popped a handful of candies into my mouth.

Jacob eyed the bag in my hand. "I did."

Since he was cooperating, I offered him the bag. He held out his palm, and I poured a few into his waiting hand before retracting the bag.

"What did Al say when you asked?"

"He said a friend dropped him off."

I ate some more chocolate. "But that doesn't answer your question. Where did he leave his bike?"

"At a friend's."

I poured more candy into the kid's waiting hand. "Which friend's?"

"Um..."

"He must have said," Ms. Miller insisted. "Think, Jacob. This is really important."

I could see it in the kid's eyes. He didn't want to get his cousin in trouble. "We need to find Al's bike," I said. "He told you he has enemies. If they find it, they're going to use it to lure him out and hurt him. We don't want that to happen."

"But you want to arrest him," Jacob said. "You're going to do the same thing."

"Al's done a lot of terrible things," Ms. Miller interjected.

"We don't want to hurt him," I said. "We want to bring him in safely. He can tell us his side of things. He'll get a fair trial."

Jacob looked torn.

"Tell her what you know," Ms. Miller insisted.

I ate another piece of candy while I waited.

"I don't remember. It was a funny name," Jacob said.

Putting down the bag of candy, I reached for a pen and wrote down the three garages along with several other random names that popped into my head. Then I pushed the list toward him. "Do any of these ring a bell?"

Jacob read the list carefully. "He talked about working on his bike with Lloyd."

"You're sure?"

Jacob nodded.

"Thanks." I handed him the candy and went out the door. Hopefully, Riley had gotten the same answer.

# THIRTY-TWO

Undercovers had gone to the other two garages, Bubba's and Piston's, to make sure we weren't missing anything, but they didn't spot Sigfried or his bike. A judge had signed court orders for their records, but as far as we could tell, the only business Alfred Sigfried ever did with them was buy parts. That left Lloyd's warehouse.

Lloyd Cartwright had vehemently denied our allegations, claiming he didn't run a garage or store any bikes inside his warehouse. But once we took a closer look at his financials, the big ticket purchases said otherwise. Lloyd had retrofitted the interior with the machines and equipment needed to repair and rebuild motorcycles. Of course, Lloyd claimed those purchases had been personal in nature, since he owned a fleet of bikes.

"He's so full of shit," Riley said as we waited at the edge of the perimeter. "Lloyd Cartwright knew damn well Sigfried stowed his bike here. But he had no intention of ever telling us." He passed the binoculars to me.

"He was one of the founding members of the V-7s. It was him and Sigfried from the start. Did you really expect him to squeal?"

"I guess not." Riley waited for SWAT to move into position. "I'm just glad Reynolds did."

"What did you offer him as an incentive?"

"I said I'd try to get his charges bumped down to felony murder. It'll shave years off his sentence. He was the only one we had in custody who was willing to deal. The rest weren't facing anything nearly as serious, and the uncertainty of our evidence and lack of eyewitnesses made it hard to give teeth to the threats I wanted to make."

"You can't threaten suspects," I said.

Riley snickered. "I meant promises."

I handed him back the binoculars. Even though we'd gotten the intel, Lightman didn't want us involved in apprehending Alfred Sigfried after our previous failed attempt. Instead, we'd been sitting on the garage for days, waiting for Sigfried to show. And now that he had, SWAT had moved in to assist the gangs unit in the takedown.

It was an all-hands situation, but Riley and I were keeping our distance. If Sigfried fled, we'd see it happen. An airship was on standby, and we'd be able to point them in the right direction and take part in the pursuit, but I didn't think it'd get that far.

"Execute." The command came over the radio, followed by a sharp crack.

"Flashbang," Riley said while we watched armored officers storm the garage.

Thirty seconds later, the radio went off again. "Suspect in custody."

A moment later, Lightman verified it was Alfred Sigfried. From our spot, Riley and I watched Sigfried get dragged out of the building in handcuffs and shoved into the back of a squad car. Once I heard code four, I put my seat belt on.

Riley smiled, clicking his own belt into place. "We got him."

"It's about damn time."

"I'll say." He gave me that sexy grin of his. "I'm not sure we would have done it without you."

"Yeah, right."

He put the car in gear and headed for the garage. Now that Sigfried was in custody, we'd help clean up the mess, starting with evidence collection.

We swept the entire warehouse, top to bottom. Every item we found in that retrofitted garage, we bagged and tagged. I didn't know what the other teams collected. But I heard mention of more stolen goods and firearms found in the garage, in the saddlebags on Sigfried's bike, and on his person. This was it. Now we just had to put all the pieces together.

We returned to the station, which was in utter chaos. So much had to be sorted. We worked for a few more hours, but I never came across the six flowerpots Sigfried had taken with him from the Millers' house.

"What's wrong, Lex?" Riley asked, that secretive smile back on his face.

Before I could answer, Lt. Peterson entered the squad room. "Listen up, people. You did good today, apprehending the ringleader of this crime wave. But we have a lot more work ahead in the days to come. So tonight, I want everyone to go home, get some rest, and come back fresh and recharged. We've got paperwork to do and interviews to conduct before we hand everything over to the DA's office."

"You heard the man," Lightman said. "Sigfried's waiting for a lawyer. We're going to hold him here until we're finished with him. We don't want him anywhere near his buddies who've been moved to central booking."

"Looks like we've been ordered to get out of here," Riley said. "What are you doing tonight, Lex?"

I wondered if this was a trick question. "Nothing."

He waited for the area to clear before he bent down beside me, as if studying my computer monitor. "You're coming to my place for dinner. And if you happen to bring an overnight bag, I won't tell Amber."

"Didn't you say you weren't allowed to have guests in your apartment?"

"I said my place was too messy for guests, but that was before I cleaned. I did it just for you. Something told me today would be a good day." Riley caressed my arm. "It's a good thing I changed the sheets before coming to work this morning, put groceries in the fridge, and have an entire meal planned. I even bought a bottle of wine."

"You heard the lieutenant. The case isn't closed yet. We have a lot of work left to do."

"Paperwork. Once we dot the 'I's and cross the 'T's, you'll be back in uniform. Sure, we could wait, but I feel like celebrating. Don't you?"

Again, I could hear my superstitious aunt's words in my head. "Aren't you afraid we'll jinx it?"

"Sigfried's in custody. He's not going anywhere. And you still have to eat. C'mon, I hardly ever cook. This may be your one and only opportunity to see what I can do in the kitchen. What do you say?"

"I don't know."

"Don't overthink it. Come over for dinner and stay for breakfast." He saw the hesitation on my face. "If you're not ready, that's okay. I'll settle for cuddling. I can be patient, even though you've basically molested me on two prior occasions."

"Are you sure? I don't remember that ever happening."

"I'm pretty sure that was you, unless you have an identical twin or a clone." He pecked my cheek and stepped toward the door. "Seriously, there's no pressure for dessert. Dinner and breakfast are okay with me."

"What time?" I asked.

"Seven."

"I'll see you then."

# THIRTY-THREE

"Taste it." Riley put his hand on the back of my head and pulled my mouth closer. "Lean forward. I don't want it to drip down your shirt."

"Oh my god," I put my hand to my mouth, licking my lips, "your sauce is amazing. Where in the world did you learn to cook like that?"

"My mom." He placed the spoon on the counter. "I should have warned you not to wear white when I was making her infamous red sauce."

"Why is it infamous?"

"It always stains an article of clothing. Mom said it's because it spatters while it simmers, but I think it drips off the bottom of the spoon when being tasted." He lifted the spoon off the counter, revealing an oval patch of tomato sauce stuck to the countertop. "That's why I'm a detective."

"I thought it was because you look sexy in a dress shirt."

"That too." He filled a pot with water and set it on the stove, next to the sauce. "If you want an apron or splatter guard, I'll get you one of my shirts to wear. But the safest thing to do is take off your clothes and hang them in the closet. The tomatoes aren't wily enough to get to them in there."

"What about my bra?"

"You might want to lose that too, just to be on the safe side. Is it white?"

"What do you think?"

He scrutinized my chest, enjoying having permission to ogle me. "Nude."

"You really are a detective. I guess that badge didn't come out of a crackerjack box, after all. Does that mean the handcuffs are real too?"

"Everything's real, babe." The sexual innuendo and tension crackled between us. "Why don't you grab a glass of wine and relax? Once the pasta cooks, we can eat."

"I can't believe you made your own pasta from scratch. And my parents claim we're Italian. What a joke."

"I'm not looking to start a family feud. I'm not claiming anything other than my mom is an awesome cook. She worked in a few restaurants when I was growing up. She always made sure there was extra at work, so she could bring it home to feed the five of us."

"Wow. Three sons, a police officer for a husband, and a full-time job. She sounds amazing."

"She is. And whenever you meet her, you'll have to tell her that her son is a terrific cook. Whenever I tell her that, she doesn't believe me."

"Perhaps it's because you use her sauce as an excuse to get women to take off their clothes."

"Maybe." He stirred the pasta. "Is al dente okay? I don't want the noodles to turn to mush."

"That's great, but don't call them noodles. That's why she doubts your cooking skills. And never call sauce gravy, unless you happen to be in one of those households that feels completely different on the subject." I giggled at the absurdity that had been a few of my family gatherings.

"Are those Italian family secrets you're sharing?"

"Yes, and if you tell anyone where you heard them, you'll be sleeping with the fishes."

"You need to work on your *Godfather* impression. You sound a little too *Jersey Shore*."

"Is there a difference?"

"I hope so." He put the serving bowl on the table. Then he took a napkin, unfolded it, and tucked it into the top of my shirt. "It's for your own protection. Trust me."

"I do."

He met my eyes and smiled. "It took you long enough."

He sat across from me, offering the serving utensils. "Dig in."

It was delicious. At this rate, I might never leave Riley's apartment. He knew how to cook. He had excellent taste in wine, and he kept me amused. Maybe this should count as our first date.

"Hey," he ran his fingers over my hand, "you zoned out on me again. Is everything okay?"

"Fine. I was just reliving the great sauce versus gravy debate. It's scary how adamant my uncle can be."

Riley looked like he didn't believe me, but he didn't push the issue. Instead, we finished eating, and he cleared the table, picking up the pot to pour the leftovers into a container. When he returned, I burst out laughing.

"What?"

"You weren't kidding. Those tomatoes are damn sneaky." I pointed at the red splotches covering his shirt.

He sighed. "Another casualty in the battle of man versus tomato. And again, the tomato is victorious."

"Take that off," I insisted, standing up and working on undoing the top buttons. "The trick is to rinse the stain out before it has time to set."

"Oh, I thought the point was to convince you to rip my clothes off."

"Was it?"

He grinned. "A little bit."

Once his shirt was off, he grabbed my hips and held me close, the heat building between us. I ran my hands along his chest. Somehow, a few specks of tomato sauce had bled through his shirt and onto his skin. I reached for a napkin and wiped at the spot on his sternum.

"The shirt can wait." He kissed me, long and slow. "You can say stop anytime you want, okay?"

I didn't say anything, and he grasped my chin, refusing to kiss me again until I nodded. He lifted me onto the table and stood between my legs as we made out. When his hand moved to my belt, I broke away.

"Your shirt," I whispered.

"I'll buy another one."

He laid me back against the table, my hands running

through his hair. He kissed down my neck, nipping at my earlobe. Damn, he was good at that.

A timer went off in the kitchen, but he ignored it. However, the constant beeping followed by the smell of something burning indicated something was wrong. "Michael, stop." I pushed against his strong shoulders. "Is the oven on? You're going to burn down your apartment."

He leaned back, so he could look at me. "I am that hot."

I laughed, and he gave me a final quick kiss before straightening up. While he went into the kitchen, I climbed off the table. Our first time wasn't going to be on his kitchen table.

When he didn't return, I got curious. "Do you need help in there?" I stood in the doorway, finding Riley staring at a tiny potted cactus on his window sill. I knew what he was thinking. "We never found the flowerpots."

"They weren't at the garage or Sigfried's apartment. So why did he buy all that shit? There has to be a reason." He rubbed a hand down his face and turned to look at me. "Sorry. I got distracted." He moved closer, grazing my sides with his fingertips. "Where were we?"

I spotted a tray of bread, which had burnt to a crisp in the oven. "Did you forget something?"

"You didn't want bread, did you?"

I laughed. "No, I'm good."

"Great." He moved to kiss me, but I turned my head away. "Are we moving too fast?"

"It's not that."

He nodded, grabbing his shirt and holding it strategically in front of his body. "You want to wait until you transfer out of gangs." He sighed. "I get it. It's okay. After all, this feels like our first real date."

"This is our first real date."

"Unless we count the hot dogs in the car. Then we're up to, I don't know, a few dozen dates."

"That was not a date. Work doesn't count as dating." I grabbed the shirt from his hands and went into the laundry room, which was a large closet connected to his kitchen. Turning the dials on the machine to presoak, I searched the cabinet for a stain remover.

"What about the night we made out inside your apartment?" he asked. "Shouldn't that count?"

"That wasn't a date. It was something else."

"Phenomenal?"

I exhaled. "It was, but I still feel bad about it."

He watched me hunt for the stain remover. "Don't. I had fun, but I wish the events leading up to it had been better."

"Yeah," I said, distracted.

"What about the morning I first spoke to Amber?" He reached into the cabinet and hooked his finger around the handle of a plastic container before pulling it free. "Is this what you wanted?"

"Maybe you should do your own laundry," I suggested.

He rested his hips against the machine. "I didn't ask you to do it."

"I feel like I should do something." I sprayed the stain remover on the tomato sauce and gave it a gentle rub. "That morning shouldn't count. It was the result of our first fight."

"I'd like to pretend that didn't happen." He pulled the detergent out of the cabinet and poured some into the machine.

"Me too."

"Okay, so I guess this really is our first date. And I'm already half-naked. You move fast, Lexie."

I laughed. "Shut up."

"Shouldn't you strip so we'll be evenly matched?"

"Not a chance, buddy. My clothes are staying on because if they come off, I don't know what will happen."

"I have a pretty good idea."

Yeah, me too. But I didn't say it. "You're that sure of yourself?" I searched his eyes, surprised to find something more intense than excitement or lust.

"I'm that sure of us."

"Does that usually work for you?"

"I've never tried that line before. Why don't you tell me?"

That surprised me. "Really?"

"You're different, Lex. I've told you that. I don't invite women here, and I sure as shit don't cook for them unless we're in a relationship. But whatever this is between us, it's not going away. It doesn't matter if tonight's the night or we wait three months or six months or however long it's going to take because I'm not going anywhere."

His words terrified me, but they also excited me. "Don't you think we should try to speed up that process?"

This time, he didn't make a joke. Instead, he ran a hand through his hair. "We need to figure out what all that damn gardening equipment's for. Until we do, it's going to drive us crazy."

"Us? You're the one thinking about it in the middle of our make-out session."

"This is why I try not to take work home with me. It pops up at the most inopportune times."

That wasn't the only thing that popped up. "I doubt we'll figure any of that out tonight. Maybe I should go."

"Please don't." He wrapped his arms around my waist. "I promised you breakfast, remember?"

"Yeah, but—"

"But nothing. Let me take you on a tour of the apartment." He led me through the living room and into the bedroom. He opened the door and pointed. "That's the bed."

"Okay."

"That's the dresser and television." He looked around. "Nightstand. Closet." He picked me up and tossed me onto the bed. "That's pretty much it."

"Remote?"

"I can't believe I forgot the most important part." He tossed it to me. "Anything else?"

I snuggled against the pillow. "No, that does it. Now don't expect me to move from this spot."

"I wouldn't dream of it." He left the room and brought my overnight bag to me. "Do you mind if I take a quick shower on account of the sauce?"

"Are you sure it's not gravy?"

"You told me it wasn't."

"And you listened. That's a quality most men don't have."

"In case you haven't figured this out yet, I'm not like

most men."

I noticed, but I didn't say anything. "I'll get changed and put on a movie. Did we finish the wine?"

"Not yet."

"Then take your time. A girl needs a chance to get her drink on."

Riley returned ten minutes later. His dark brown hair was still wet, and he shook his head like a dog, earning a round of giggles. We only made it fifteen minutes into the movie before our conversation turned back to the case.

Riley grabbed a few notebooks and pens and poured us each a large glass of wine. Then we went over every aspect of the case again. But Sigfried's gardening obsession didn't factor into any of it. We were missing something. Whatever it was had to be important. Sigfried wouldn't have gone to all that trouble unless it fit into his plan.

# THIRTY-FOUR

The phone rang again, and I gave it a dirty look. It had been doing that almost nonstop for the better part of an hour. Apparently, there was some issue with the power grid which had resulted in outages, which always brought out the crazies. This was the last thing we needed today.

"Hey, Lexie," Kemper said, "have you seen who Alfred Sigfried hired to defend him?"

"Who?"

"Howston and Rollins."

"Shit. How can he afford them?"

"I guess he's been pinching his pennies." Kemper glanced down the hallway. "Lightman's not happy about this."

"I'm sure no one in the prosecutor's office is either." I gave the paperwork another look. "But we built a solid case, collected evidence, and went by the book. It shouldn't matter who's defending him. He's guilty, and I'm pretty damn sure we can prove it."

"Let's hope so." Kemper went back to sorting through his part of this mess while I tried not to let this latest tidbit distract me.

Our case would be a lot more solid if we had some eyewitness accounts. A few of the Street Bishops had agreed to testify against Sigfried in exchange for leniency, but I'd heard enough horror stories to know how shyster defense attorneys would spin that on the stand. The last thing we needed was Alfred Sigfried to get away with his crimes. Jessalyn Belknap's warning came to mind.

While I worked, I watched the detectives take turns in the interrogation room. This case was too important, so I didn't think Kemper, Hawking, or I would be invited to participate. Not that I had any desire to spend more time in an interrogation room, especially after all the interviews we conducted yesterday, but I didn't like feeling left out either.

"Hey, Sarconi," Lt. Peterson called. "You've earned yourself a break. Go downstairs and help the desk sergeant while Pickins is getting lunch. The Sarge is overwhelmed with redirecting all the calls that are coming in today. I don't want to leave her by herself, even if it is only for an hour."

"Yes, sir."

I saved my files, made sure everything was organized that needed to be, and headed for the stairs.

"Where are you going?" Kemper teased when he saw me leaving.

"The LT asked me to fill in downstairs."

"Peterson doesn't normally speak to us. You must have really screwed up."

I knew he was messing around. "The Sarge needs help with the phones."

"Even a trained monkey can do that."

"Obviously not, or they would have asked you," Riley said, his tone icy. He'd just returned from watching Lightman take a stab at Sigfried and had no idea what was going on. "And I don't want to hear any more disrespect coming out of your mouth. It's one thing to joke around, but you never know when to quit. Should I recommend they send you for sensitivity training or personal communication skills classes?"

"No, sir," Kemper replied.

Riley looked fit to be tied. "Good."

"Are you okay, Detective?" I asked.

"Just waiting my turn to take a crack at Sigfried." His expression softened when he looked at me.

"I won't be gone long. An hour tops, but if you need any of my notes, they're on my desk."

"Get going, Lexie." Riley jerked his chin toward the stairwell, winking at me.

It was sweet he defended me, but I didn't want that to turn into something either. He didn't say anything else, but I felt his gaze on my back.

When I got downstairs, calls were coming in left and right. The technicians couldn't figure out what was going on with the power grid, so they were shutting down power to parts of the city in an organized pattern to identify the source of the glitch in order to fix it.

"We're in a blackout zone," the desk sergeant said. "The generators should hold, but let's not take any chances. Reroute any non-emergency calls to a different station."

"Yes, ma'am."

While the desk sergeant called all off-duty personnel to prepare for a possible citywide blackout, I fielded the calls we were receiving. Some people had questions about the blackout. Others had security concerns. Several were reporting crimes, mainly robberies, looting, and car accidents. Apparently, the call center was flooded, which is why we were getting so many calls that usually went directly to 9-1-1.

"What is this? Friday the thirteenth?" I asked.

The desk sergeant snorted. "Obviously not since it's Tuesday. But I bet my ass it's a full moon."

"I wouldn't doubt it."

In the midst of the madness, Riley came down the stairs. "Lex," he sidled up to the front desk, seeing how jammed we were, "Jack said I'm next to take a run at Sigfried. You want in?"

"I'm a little busy. Do you have everything you need?"

"Yeah." He glanced at the desk sergeant who was too busy to pay attention to our conversation. "Jack hasn't asked a single thing about the stripper or the gardening. I'll see what Sigfried has to say when I hit him with it."

"Let me know what you find out."

He tapped the desk as he stepped back. "When you finish down here, meet me upstairs. I'm guessing I'll be a while."

"Did Lightman give us the okay?"

Riley nodded. "You earned your spot, Lex."

"All right. I'll try to join you, but don't get your hopes up. Things are crazy."

"They're always crazy when the city has power issues. The dark brings them out, like vampires or zombies," the desk sergeant said, catching the tail-end of our conversation.

"See you later." Riley nodded to the desk sergeant and headed back up the stairs.

After he left, I went back to answering phones, hoping Officer Pickins would return from lunch so I could see what was happening upstairs.

"You want to join him, don't you?" the desk sergeant asked. She shook her head making a tsk sound. "I do like watching him walk away." She was in her mid-forties with graying hair. From the gold band around her finger, I assumed she was married. "I don't think I've ever seen him personally invite someone to join him for an interrogation before. That's new."

"We were partnered together on this case."

"The biker thing?"

"Yeah."

The phone rang again. "Dammit." She spoke briefly to the person on the other end before hanging up. "The commissioner wants us to transport everyone we have in holding to central booking in case of anything. Since we're in the blackout zone, he wants the crooks gone before the lights start flickering. We don't need any lawyers saying the power outage counts as cruel and unusual punishment." She picked up a phone to call for a transport vehicle.

"Does that include suspects we're currently interrogating?"

"It should, but there might be ways around it." She realized where my mind was. "Inform Detective Lightman and the rest of the gangs unit what's going on. They'll want to prepare since keeping your suspects apart is vital to your case. I can handle things down here."

"Thank you, ma'am." I raced upstairs, glad to find Lightman in the squad room.

"Alfred Sigfried isn't going anywhere. I'll take care of it."

Lightman headed for Lt. Peterson's office, and I went down the hallway to find Riley.

# THIRTY-FIVE

I knocked on the door before opening it. Detective Riley had his palms on the table, standing over Alfred Sigfried who looked so smug I feared Riley would knock the look off his face. Mr. Rollins, Sigfried's attorney, maintained a perfect poker face, almost too perfect. Something told me he wasn't pleased with whatever his client had just said or done and wanted to make sure he remained outwardly unbiased.

"It'd be best to help yourself here," Riley warned.

"Oh, you'll see exactly why my gardening is so important in due time." Sigfried sat back in the chair and smiled. "Your case is bound to crumble, Detective. This is your last chance. Let me go and save yourself some trouble."

"Detective," I said, causing Riley to look up, "may I have a word?"

Before he could move an inch, the lights flickered a few times before turning off. All four of us stared up at the fixture, waiting to see if the power would come back. After thirty seconds and a loud mechanical whine, the generator kicked on, causing the lights to return, slightly dimmer.

"Interesting. Did you forget to pay the power company?" Sigfried asked.

Riley ignored it and joined me at the door. "What is it?"

I jerked my chin skyward. "The commissioner wants everyone moved to central booking until the fluctuations and outages in the power grid are fixed. I informed Lightman. He said he'd make sure that didn't happen, but he wanted you to get the heads-up in case you have to stall."

"Since you're here, you might as well stay."

"If you insist."

Riley went back inside the room, and I followed him.

Sigfried looked up at us. "Did I hear something about getting moved?"

"No way." Riley gave him a contemptuous smile. "You're not going anywhere."

"I wouldn't be too sure about that." Sigfried studied me. "I don't think we've been introduced."

"Officer Sarconi," I said.

Sigfried mentally filed it away which left an uneasy feeling in my stomach.

"Let's get back to it," Riley said, folding his arms and staring at Sigfried. "You were just about to tell me what you were doing at your cousin's place."

"Visiting family," Sigfried said.

The lights flickered again. "Shouldn't those in custody be moved to a central holding facility when a station is experiencing difficulties?" Mr. Rollins asked.

"We've got it covered," Riley said. "If you're afraid of the dark, we can pick this up at a later date."

Sigfried looked up at the lights. "Maybe you should be afraid of what happens in the dark." He gave Riley an icy look before making a kissing sound at me.

"Did you have something to do with this?" Riley asked.

"How could I have possibly done that? Do you think I did something to the main relays or the transformers? That would have been something, huh? Or are you saying I hacked into the power system and turned everything off? I've been here the entire time. Obviously, I have nothing to do with any of this." Sigfried jerked his chin at the ceiling before turning to his attorney. "I'd say they are trying to railroad me by coming up with even more bogus charges."

Rollins reached into his briefcase and pulled out a file. "The case against my client is circumstantial at best. You have no evidence or proof that he had anything to do with what other members of his motorcycle club were doing. He simply ran a club, meant for recreation and enjoyment by fellow motorcycle enthusiasts. He can't control the other members' actions."

"That's bullshit. We can place Sigfried at the pawn shop. He sold stolen property and ran from us."

"He was afraid." Rollins slid a signed statement across the table which his client had previously written. "He feared for his life."

"He feared for his freedom," Riley said, barely glancing at the paperwork.

"He didn't know the items were stolen."

"He had illegal firearms in his possession when we arrested him."

"He discovered those hidden inside the warehouse and was on his way to turn them in when you found him. As you know, that warehouse does not belong to my client. It belongs to another member of the V-7s. One would assume anything contained within is the property of that man." The lights went out again, and it took another twenty seconds before they returned to full power. "You should release my client now," Rollins said. "I'd hate to point out the harsh conditions in which you are holding him. His basic rights are being denied."

"Fluorescent lighting isn't a basic right." Riley narrowed his eyes. "What did you do to the electricity, Sigfried?"

Sigfried smiled. "It's not the power you should be worried about."

"What does that mean?"

Before Sigfried could reply, a loud boom sounded outside the window. It was strong enough to shake the building and plunge the room back into darkness. This time, the power didn't return.

"Lex, are you okay?"

I nodded, peering out the permanently attached metal slats which allowed the slightest bit of light to filter in from the window. It looked like something exploded.

"Where there's smoke." Sigfried sighed. "It looks like your clock's a little slow. You might want to fix that."

"You can't continue to hold my client here. Not with a

power failure and who knows what happening outside. It's not safe. I request he be moved immediately," Rollins said.

"Until we know what's going on, for everyone's safety, we'll be locking down the building." Riley turned to me. "Sarconi, find out what's going on. I'll keep an eye on things here." The last thing he wanted to do was give Sigfried a chance to escape.

Dashing out of the interrogation room, I only made it halfway down the hall when I spotted Detective Devereaux heading toward me. "Was that an explosion?" I asked.

"The generator blew up. One minute it was fine, the next it was a fireball, spitting shit out everywhere."

"Was anyone hurt?"

"Not seriously. We have guys checking it out now. Jack wanted me to make sure the interrogation rooms were locked down. No unauthorized personnel in or out. We don't want a repeat of the Big Bill incident or something worse."

"That's what Riley said."

"Mike knows what he's doing, at least some of the time. C'mon, let's get back there and help him out. Sigfried's the only suspect we have in the box right now. Everyone else is in the process of getting cleared out."

Riley looked at us when we returned. "What happened, Frank?"

"The generator," Devereaux said.

Sigfried smiled. "Ka-boom."

"If I find out you had something to do with it, you're going to be facing a world of hurt," Riley said.

Sigfried snickered. "Now you're threatening me. You can't do that."

"Wanna bet?" Riley lurched forward, and Devereaux grabbed his shoulder before he could do something that would jeopardize our case.

"Easy, Mikey." Devereaux waited for Riley to nod before he let him go. He turned back to Sigfried. "Looks like it's just the five of us alone in this room. If you don't want to talk, maybe I'll remind everyone of all the wonderful things I heard and saw you do."

Sigfried sneered. "I knew you were trouble, which is why

I kicked you out."

"You tried to have me killed," Devereaux said.

"I said I wanted you gone. I had nothing to do with whatever those men did in the alleyway."

"They have a very different story to tell." Devereaux took a seat across from Sigfried and put his feet up on the corner of the table. "But you know that. And you know there's no way out of this mess. You're caught. Confess or don't. That's up to you. Personally, I hope you keep your damn mouth shut. It'll make it that much sweeter when the judge throws the book at you."

Sigfried stretched as best he could while handcuffed and settled into his chair. "You're holding me in a building with no electricity, that seems like it could explode at any moment, or catch fire, and you think you're going to come out on top. I don't think so."

Rollins had been quiet for most of the interview, but he pulled out his phone to check some things. "This won't reflect well on the police department. I will be filing a formal complaint and petitioning the court to have the charges dropped for insufficient evidence and police bias. In fact, I have several judges on speed dial."

"Good for you," Riley said. "Make whatever calls you want, but this is an extreme situation. The steps we are taking are meant to ensure everyone's safety, including your client's. You can't prove otherwise."

"You'd be surprised." Rollins started to dial.

Sigfried hadn't taken his eyes off me since I returned to the room. "Are you scared, baby?"

I knew better than to engage. So I gave him an icy stare. "I suggest you refrain from speaking unless you plan on answering questions or confessing."

"How about we make a deal?" Sigfried asked. "You let me go, and I make sure nothing else in this city goes boom."

Riley stopped pacing. "You mean to tell me you had something to do with the generator going up?"

"My client didn't say that," Rollins said, putting his phone down when he found the circuits jammed. "And until the power comes back, he will refrain from speaking at all."

But Alfred Sigfried wasn't a man who took orders. He was one who gave them. "Actually, I have it on good authority six devices have been hidden throughout the city, which are set to go off in the next few hours. I'll make sure that doesn't happen, but only if you sign these papers and let me go."

"Again, my client isn't admitting to having any involvement in anything," Rollins said, but panic entered his eyes. I didn't think he knew what his client had intended to do, but he was stuck defending him.

"The six flowerpots," I said. "The fertilizer and nails. He built bombs."

Riley met my eyes. "No wonder we didn't find them."

"And you won't, unless you let me go." Sigfried looked convinced he'd won.

"For the record, my client never made those purchases and had nothing to do with constructing or hiding the materials. That was all Jacob Miller."

"Miller says otherwise," Devereaux corrected.

"Common sense says otherwise," I retorted.

"Jacob's lying," Sigfried said. "The kid has always been troubled. Maybe that's a byproduct of a nasty divorce. You can't believe a word he says. But I know how he thinks, what he'd do. I can prevent mass casualties, but only if you let me go."

"That's not how this works, you lying sack of shit," Riley said. "Miller's been in custody for days. He's cooperating. This is all you. No one will ever believe otherwise. Tell us where you planted the devices, and we'll consider not charging you with domestic terrorism."

But Sigfried couldn't care less about the bombs. He was determined to come up with a feasible scapegoat, and he had settled on his juvenile cousin. "Think about it. Jacob has disdain for authority. Didn't I hear whispers that he tried to kill two police officers who came knocking on his front door? Why would you make a deal with someone like that or believe a word he said? He could have easily set those devices with timers. Drop all charges, and I'll help you find them."

"How about you tell us where they are and we make sure you survive long enough to make it to trial?"

Sigfried jerked his chin toward the window. "I'm guessing one of them was right out there. Go see for yourself, and when you're ready to let me go, I'll tell you where you might find the others."

# THIRTY-SIX

"I can't believe he'd do this," I said.

"Why not?" Riley ran a hand through his hair. "This asshole always has a trick up his sleeve, some way to redirect our attention. He must have realized how close we were when we arrested everyone in the MC. He's using the IEDs as another misdirect and a bargaining chip."

"If he's even telling the truth," Devereaux said. "I have a hard time believing him."

"Is that a gamble we can take?" Lightman asked. It took forty-five minutes for power to be restored. After that happened, Sigfried was taken to one of the empty holding cells where a few armed officers were keeping an eye on him. Mr. Rollins had left to file those complaints he threatened, but I suspected he wanted to get out of the potential blast zone. "The bomb squad searched high and low around the generator, but the search was inconclusive. They swept this building and didn't find anything. It could be a lie, but even if it isn't, we don't negotiate with terrorists. The first thing we have to figure out is if Sigfried is telling the truth. For all we know, he bought that shit and tossed it in the first dumpster he passed."

I glanced at the clock. We were almost an hour into the six hour deadline. We hadn't received any reports of explosions. The bomb squad had swept every nearby police station, and officers were on alert to keep an eye out in public areas which were deemed high-value targets.

Bomb sniffers searched central booking, figuring Sigfried might have wanted to take out everyone who could testify against him in one fell swoop, but I couldn't figure out how he would have gotten access to the holding cells or why he would have wanted to be transferred there when the lights went out if he was going to detonate a device inside the building. And as we suspected, that search turned up nothing.

"Are we sure there isn't a device inside this building?" I asked. "Sigfried was all about getting transferred out of here."

Lightman looked at me. "We checked and got the all-clear."

"Yeah, but Sigfried wanted out. There must have been a reason he wanted to be transferred," Riley said.

"Maybe he was hoping to make a jailbreak before he ended up in jail," Preston said.

"There's no bomb. The generator exploding could have been a mechanical issue. I never liked those things. A few too many sparks, a build-up of carbon monoxide, and it's goodnight, folks." Lightman shook his head. "But we can't bet that's the cause, so for the next few hours, we do everything we can to figure out if Sigfried is telling the truth or if he's using the situation to his advantage."

"How do we figure out what's what?" Kemper asked.

"We'll retrace his steps," Lightman said, "revisit the places we know he's been, question his associates again, and see if anyone has anything new to add given the changing circumstances." He muttered something to himself. "I'd love to put that asshole attorney in the hotseat."

"Attorney-client privilege protects him," Preston said.

"Mr. Rollins looked just as shocked as we were when Sigfried started spouting out crap about bombs," I said.

"But even if he knew," Preston said, "we'd never be able to prove it without violating privilege."

Lightman didn't look deterred. "If this was Sigfried's plan all along, he must have made arrangements before he was arrested. Let's pull every camera feed we can find near the law office and warehouse." He reached for the phone to make the call. "Sam, help me with this. Hawking and Kemper, I'll need you working on the footage as soon as we get it. Frank, go check Sigfried's hangouts. You know them better than anyone else. The garages have already been checked, but I'll have the bomb squad sweep them again for explosives. While they do that, Mike, you and Sarconi will check Bishop's Bar and anyplace else Big Bill considered sacred. Blowing up a dead rival's favorite hangout seems like something Sigfried would do."

"You should also have someone check the Millers' house," Riley said. "Sigfried wants to pin all of this on Jacob. What better way than having an accident happen over there?"

"Good call." Lightman dialed, and the rest of us dispersed.

"Be careful, Michael," Preston said. "You too, Frank."

I followed Riley down the stairs and out of the building. Even from here, I could see the remains of the generator. Shrapnel had blown into a few parked cars and marred the nearby sidewalk and street. Luckily, the injuries sustained hadn't been life-threatening.

The sun hadn't set yet, but I didn't notice many interior lights as we drove past businesses. The last thing we needed was the insanity that came with power outages. All I could think about were those flowerpots. They weren't very large. If Sigfried had made some sort of improvised explosive device using fertilizer and nails, the damage would be contained to a small area, but it might have had enough bang to take out the backup generator.

"Do you think Sigfried orchestrated the blackout?" I asked.

Riley glanced at me, his shoulders and jaw tense. "I'd say yes, but there's no way he possesses that kind of access. He's an ex-con who runs a motorcycle club. More than likely, he's full of shit. He's desperate, so he'll weave whatever tale comes to mind, and since I spent a good deal of time asking about the gardening supplies, he may have decided to turn the tables and use them against us."

"But he had Jacob buy them for a reason."

"Yeah, which is why I'm not sure if he's full of shit. I

hoped Frank would be able to get a more accurate read on the guy, but he doesn't know either. The generator blowing up at the station doesn't feel like a coincidence to me."

"Me neither."

He parked outside Bishop's Bar and turned to look at me. "We have to be careful. I don't know what we're walking into."

"I wish you did."

"That makes two of us."

# THIRTY-SEVEN

After circling the bar and checking for signs of foul play and finding none, Riley grabbed a set of non-regulation lock picks from the glove box and crouched down to unlock the front door. I kept my head on a swivel. The neighborhood was getting darker by the minute. The sun was on the verge of setting. Already, I noticed a broken window in the building across the street.

"Were you a burglar in another life?" I asked when the door popped open.

Riley tucked the picks away and reached for his weapon and flashlight. "I have some stories."

"I bet you do." I gave our surroundings one last look, wondering if our car would be in one piece by the time we got out, reached for my own weapon and flashlight, and followed Riley inside.

In the dark, the bar looked eerie, as if it were haunted by the ghost of the dead Big Bill. Maybe it was. Dust motes floated in our flashlight beams.

"Check over there," Riley gestured toward the other side of the room, "and watch your step. I wouldn't put it past Sigfried to have set a trap."

"Copy." I kept an eye on the ground in front of me as I moved toward the back of the room while Riley checked the bar and the nearby booths and tables.

"No flowerpots over here," Riley said.

"None here either." I crouched down beside the rickety

stage that held the stripper's pole. "But I may have found something." I put my flashlight on the ground beside me while I examined the scarred crevice separating the top of the stage from the side. "We may need a crowbar."

"Hang on." Riley grabbed a slim jim from behind the bar and joined me. After a few tugs, he yanked one of the wooden planks out. Underneath the stage was a hollowed out area. "This must have been where Big Bill kept his secret stash." He pointed to a bag that remained wedged in the far corner. "Looks like someone forgot some of his loot."

"Or it's booby-trapped."

"I'll call it in." Riley reached for his radio. Once we were told a bomb sniffer was on the way, Riley straightened. "Until we know for sure, let's give the stage a wide berth, but we should check the rest of the bar."

"You mean upstairs."

On our way to the hidden staircase, Riley examined some of the décor and checked behind the dartboard, but there was nothing else to find. "Stay behind me."

"For the record, I hate it when you do that macho thing."

"I let you go first last time," he said. "It's my turn. Plus, I'm lead. Once you make detective, we can revisit this argument."

"You're lucky you have a nice ass."

He snickered, but my comment didn't distract him as we made our way behind the curtain. While he went up the stairs, I checked the remaining areas in that hidden hallway.

"Clear," I said.

"Hang back one second." Slowly, he turned the knob, keeping as much distance between him and the door as he pushed it open. When nothing went boom, he peered inside the room, sweeping the beam of light from right to left. "Okay, let's see what we have here."

I made my way up the stairs and joined him inside Big Bill's apartment. The funky smell from last time had only gotten worse, but I didn't spot the milk container on the counter. The dishes were no longer in the sink, and the bed had been made.

"Did someone hire a cleaning lady?" I wondered.

Riley pointed to the right, so I moved that way, finding tons of knickknacks and clutter on every surface. "The Street Bishops must have cleared the place out after Big Bill's demise. My guess would be the bartender tried to straighten up."

"Detective Devereaux said the bartender loved this place." I searched every inch of my side of the room, but the only planter I found was a container that had once held mixed nuts and now contained nothing but cigarette and cigar butts. "We've had eyes on this place since Sigfried disappeared. We would have noticed if he'd resurfaced here."

Riley stood frozen in the doorway to the bathroom. "Are you sure about that?" On the bathroom counter was a small flowerpot, like the ones Jacob had purchased from the hardware store.

"Is it armed?" From where I was standing, it didn't look much like an explosive.

Riley moved closer, finding it filled with what appeared to be soil. "I don't know." He examined it more closely. A thin piece of twine ran through the center.

"I'll call it in," I said.

Riley peered around the rest of the bathroom. "I don't see anything else."

I answered the bomb disposal expert's questions, passing the ones I couldn't answer off to Riley, who gently picked the pot up to examine the area beneath it. Whatever it contained was inside the pot.

"Lex, stay out there."

"What are you—" Before I could finish asking my question, Riley dumped the pot into the sink. Thankfully, nothing went boom.

"Son of a bitch."

"What?" I edged forward, wondering if the pot contained some sort of corrosive or chemical agent. Instead, it contained nothing but dirt and roots from a dead plant. "False alarm," I said into the phone.

Without waiting, Riley marched down the stairs,

grabbed the slim jim, and used it to hook the corner of the bag from beneath the stage. Inside, he found a black, hooded jacket. Inside the pocket was a note with the Stanfields' storage unit number and instructions on where to find weapons, jewelry, and cash.

"What a fucking waste." Riley shoved the items into an evidence bag. "That bastard still has us chasing our tails. He really thinks he's going to get away with this."

"He's not."

Riley gestured at the bag. "Except this points the blame at Big Bill. And we still can't connect Stryker King to Alfred Sigfried."

"Besides the V-7s' connection."

"Lex—"

"King's dead. We don't have a paper trail, but we know Sigfried was using the MC to do his bidding, carry out his orders, and perform his hits."

"Lex—"

"It's all on him. We have him, and while we've gotten a few of the Street Bishops to talk, it may not be enough. We need a victim to shed light on this. Sure, we have the Millers, but Sigfried's already working on spinning that. And I'm sure Rollins thinks that's an ace up his sleeve since the kid shot at us. After all, Jacob bought these damn flowerpots, which is why we're on this wild goose chase."

"Lexie, stop." Riley put his hands on my shoulders. "Damn, and I thought I'd seen you worked up in your apartment that night."

I shook my head. "We've had eyes on all these places. This bar, Sigfried's apartment, the garages, everywhere we knew to look. Sure, Sigfried slipped back into his apartment but that was because he created an opportunity by distracting us with the anonymous tip, but that was the only time he had that chance. Jessalyn will cooperate, maybe, but the last time we spoke to her she sounded iffy." I nodded down at the evidence bag which contained the hooded jacket and note we found. "Lightman probably won't go for it, but I think we should go on the offensive. We approach the Stanfields again and see if they'll cooperate. What do you think?"

He looked around the bar, where we had wasted over an hour. “Okay.”

# THIRTY-EIGHT

As the sun set and the sky grew darker, more reports started coming in. The rolling blackouts brought the lunatics out of the woodwork. Every available officer was responding to calls. Grand larceny division seemed to be the busiest. But everyone was tasked with assisting, which meant manpower was being diverted from our hunt for the alleged explosives.

"This is what Sigfried wants," Riley said. "We're spread so thin, he must think we'll give in to his demands."

"If the threat's real, maybe we should. Saving lives is more important than making a case, but he's killed before. And he'll do it again. I don't know that I believe him, particularly after what we found inside Big Bill's bar."

"My thoughts exactly." Riley turned down the next street which was brightly lit compared to the block we'd just left. "I guess we're looking on the bright side now."

I laughed. "How long do you think it'll take for the power company to get this situation handled? It's already been half a day since we received the warning."

"The last report said they found the glitch and are resetting the system. Everything should be back to normal within the hour."

"Doesn't that coordinate with the timeline Sigfried gave us for the potential detonations?"

"It does."

"Again, I don't see that as a coincidence."

"Me neither," Riley admitted.

He parked in front of the Stanfields' apartment building, just as a call came in on the radio. A neighbor reported a fire at the Millers' house. The fire department arrived to find the house decimated, as if it had exploded. They suspected a gas leak, but they didn't have all the intel.

"Arson and bomb squad are on the way," dispatch informed us.

Riley's phone rang, and he grabbed it. "Where do you want us, Jack?" He drummed his hand on the steering wheel while he listened. "Fine, we'll finish up here and head over. Is Frank okay?" He waited for the caller to respond. "Good."

"What happened?" I asked.

"Frank finished checking Sigfried's hangouts, so he went to the Millers' place. He was halfway up the walk when everything went boom. He got thrown back a few feet. His ears are still ringing, but he's okay."

"He was there when it happened? Dispatch said a neighbor called it in."

"A neighbor did call it in, but when the fire department arrived, they found Frank on the front lawn. That's when Frank called Jack." Riley fidgeted, looking uneasy.

"If you'd rather we go—"

"No. We find a way to stop this, and since Sigfried isn't going to tell us what we need to know, then we squeeze him until he does. I just hope we can convince the Stanfields to tell us everything we need to know." Determined, he got out of the car, marched up the steps to their floor, and knocked on the door.

When they didn't answer, he banged a little harder.

"This is the police. Open up," Riley announced.

"Something's wrong," I said. "I thought I heard a noise inside."

Riley tried again. "Do you want to give it a go?"

"Kathryn? Stuart? This is Officer Sarconi. Let us in." I tested the knob, surprised to find it unlocked. "Mr. and Mrs. Stanfield?" I pushed the door open, only to be knocked backward when something exploded against the door, slamming it against me and knocking me onto my ass.

"Lexie?" Riley ran to me, his focus split between me and the slightly ajar door which was now impaled with two dozen nails. "Are you okay?"

Shaking off the jolt, I nodded. That was all Riley needed to hear to enter the apartment. He did a quick sweep, finding the place had been cleared out. The few things that hadn't been stolen during the home invasion were gone.

"It looks like they fled." Riley studied the front door, finding pieces of shattered ceramic on the ground. "I'd say we found one of Sigfried's flowerpots. The damn thing sprayed nails like a porcupine." He turned back to look at me, making sure I didn't get hit.

"The blast was small and contained. Dispatch said the Millers' place was decimated."

"Maybe he attached one of these devices," Riley tapped the toe of his shoe beside the ceramic dust, "to the gas line. He would have had more time to plan things out with Jacob at school all day. Maybe he set up something even more elaborate, a fertilizer bomb or something to that effect."

"He must have used a timer."

Riley crouched down. "This was a trap. No timer. He was waiting for someone to enter the apartment. He probably wanted to take out the Stanfields, figuring they'd return after news of his arrest spread. But again, we can't prove it. And after Mrs. Stanfield was released from the hospital, she refused our protection. We had too much going on to maintain eyes on her." Riley gave the place one last look and phoned Lightman.

~*~

"I told you," Sigfried said, smug as always, "more devices are out there, and you have twenty minutes to get to them before they go boom. Do you really want to risk more casualties?"

"There were no casualties," Lightman said.

"Not yet." Sigfried jangled his wrists in front of the detective. "My offer's still on the table. Take these off and the city will be safe."

"Anything but." Lightman glanced at the police captain standing in the doorway. The commissioner had insisted we play along, fearing our inaction to stop an attack would result in a lawsuit the city couldn't win. "If you take us to the other devices and help us disarm them, we won't charge you with terrorism."

"Correction, you won't charge me with anything," Sigfried insisted.

Lightman worked his jaw.

"Don't do it, Jack," Riley said from behind the two-way mirror.

"Only if you come through. Then you have a deal." Saying those words caused Lightman physical pain. In fact, it caused all of us physical pain.

Sigfried looked at Rollins, who gave his nod of approval. "Okay, great. Let's get going. We're on a clock."

"I never should have reported the second detonation," Riley said. "Sigfried doesn't deserve a deal. His first two targets were empty dwellings. We have no reason to think the next four, if there are even four, are going to cause harm to anyone else."

"We can't take the risk." Frank rubbed the bandage at the side of his face where he'd sustained a mild burn. "We keep people safe. And we haven't been able to do that at all with the way this clown's been running his MC and taking over Big Bill's turf."

I watched Sigfried climb to his feet, holding out his bound hands.

"Not until you prove yourself," Lightman insisted.

"Fine, check the back patio at John Wolfe's house. My cousin left him a surprise. But you might want to hurry." Sigfried nodded at the clock. "If I remember correctly, that's running slow."

Within minutes, patrol verified another flowerpot had been located. This one concealed a pipe bomb filled with nails, like the one Riley and I had encountered. Stepping onto the back patio from inside the house would have triggered it, just like opening the front door had triggered the detonation at the Stanfields' apartment.

"The other two are trickier. You'll need me there to disarm them." Sigfried held up his wrists. "And I'll need my hands free to do it."

"Where?" Lightman asked.

Sigfried shook his head. "I'll give you directions once we're on the road. Or you could let me go alone. I don't really need you cramping my style."

"He's a psychopath," Frank muttered.

"That's only five," I said. "Where's the sixth?"

Riley stormed into the hallway as a group of armed officers and Lightman escorted Sigfried and Mr. Rollins out of the interrogation room. "Where's the last device?"

"Last device?" Sigfried snorted. "Learn to count. The first one took out this building's generator. How else would I have known your clock was running slow?"

"You set these yourself," Riley said.

"I did no such thing. I told you, it's my cousin. I fully expect you to charge him for these heinous crimes, or I'll go to the press."

Riley fumed, but one warning look from Lightman and the captain forced him to back off.

"Keep an eye on Mike," Frank whispered to me. "When he gets like this, all bets are off."

"Lex, let's go," Riley called, watching as Lightman got behind the wheel. Mr. Rollins slid into the passenger seat, and two armed officers sandwiched Sigfried into the back. "I'm not letting that bastard out of my sight."

"I'll hold down the fort here," Frank said. "Jack told me I have to sit this one out. But I'll make sure Sigfried didn't leave us any other surprises."

# THIRTY-NINE

Sigfried led us to a bar. It wasn't near the V-7s' turf. In fact, it had never been on our radar. Sigfried's financials never showed he had been here before. The place wasn't crowded, but it wasn't empty either. Twenty people were inside.

"Wait here while we clear everyone out." Lightman grabbed Sigfried's shoulder and shoved him back against the side of the car.

"What about the cuffs?"

"I'll take them off after the bar's empty."

"Fine, we'll wait. But you better make it quick. We only have a matter of minutes. Maybe two. Maybe five. Maybe less than one." Sigfried rubbed his face. "I held up my end of the deal. If you fuck this up, that's not my fault."

"Every damn bit of this is on you. You're a fucking psychopathic killer. I'm going to enjoy watching you burn." Lightman pressed his lips together, but I could see the wheels turning. "Riley, Sarconi, help the bomb squad clear the place. Officers Evans, Gallo, and Treste, get the civilians out. Don't cause a panic, just take care of it." Lightman turned back to Sigfried. "As soon as they find these devices, you're going to tell the bomb squad how to disarm them, and I'm going to make sure you're standing right in the blast zone while they do it. If you think you're going to put one over on us, you're mistaken."

"I wouldn't dream of it. Like I've been telling you, I had

nothing to do with any of this. You already arrested everyone who participated in criminal activity, but I'm innocent, like a virgin on prom night."

I followed Riley inside the bar. The dog handlers had already spread out, but all the liquors and perfumes made it harder for them to detect. That would slow things down. Meanwhile, three other members of the unit conducted a thorough sweep as they made their way through the place.

For the most part, the patrons paid little to no attention to the intrusion, which was making the officers' jobs much harder. Part of me wanted to yell fire or bomb to get them to clear out, but I knew a panic was the last thing we needed, and given the volume on the stereo, I didn't think they'd hear me anyway.

Riley flashed his badge at the bartender while I went down the side hallway and checked the office and kitchen. When I came to a closed door, I hesitated, afraid opening it would lead to another detonation.

"What's behind here?" I asked the bartender.

"The storage room."

"Have you been inside today?"

"I just went in there. We ran out of whiskey."

Cautiously, I turned the knob and eased the door open a few inches. When nothing exploded, I went inside. Hidden behind a large metal keg, I found the two remaining flowerpots. Several different colored wires connected them together while duct tape held what I could only imagine was a battery to the front of the contraption. A red digital timer was counting down. 2:57. 2:56. 2:55.

"Michael, I found it. It's on a timer."

He appeared in the doorway behind me, yelling for the bomb squad. That commotion caused the few remaining drunks to take notice, but they didn't seem scared or worried. They turned on their stools, ready for a show.

"Get these people out of here," Riley ordered the officers. "Drag them out if you have to."

Two of the bomb techs turned to us. "With all this alcohol, this room is a powder keg. If that goes off, it'll take down the building, not just the bar, but the entire building."

Nodding, Riley grabbed my wrist and yanked me out of the room. "Get out of here," he told the bartender. "As far as you can." Then we tried to push our way outside. The patrons hadn't wandered far enough from the front door. "Get back. Everyone get back," Riley ordered.

I worked the crowd to the left, hoping to clear a path. As soon as I could see past the people who'd basically created a wall around the front door, I spotted Lightman on the ground beside the car.

I ran to him. He shook himself. His throat was bruised and swollen from the chain and swivel from a pair of handcuffs. "Where's Sigfried?"

"That way," Lightman choked out, clutching his neck and coughing. "Go."

I took off in the direction he pointed. I knew this had to be another distraction. Sigfried had planned his escape from the beginning. He orchestrated the entire scenario in order to get away. But the bomb inside the bar didn't look like a misdirect. It looked real. And since this neighborhood hadn't even been on our radar, we weren't prepared for this.

Spotting Sigfried, I willed my legs to go faster. Everything else turned into a blur as I ran after him. I didn't see so much as feel Riley behind me. He was close. His presence reassured me, but I didn't slow. I was going to catch that son of a bitch.

Sigfried ran down an alleyway. I chased after him, gaining, even as my lungs burned and the muscles in my legs threatened to cramp. But I kept moving.

He yanked open a side door into whatever building this was and disappeared. I reached the door before it had time to close and slipped inside. I caught a glimpse of him turning the corner. He couldn't be more than ten feet away.

I charged forward, aware of the door slamming behind me. I didn't hear any footsteps. Then again, I couldn't hear much over my pounding heart and ragged gasps.

Rounding the corner, I was shocked to find a nearly empty furniture store. Only a few dim lights on the ceiling provided illumination. "Give up, Sigfried." I scanned my surroundings. I was right behind him. He couldn't have gotten far. Not more than a few feet, which meant he was hiding. But where?

I forced my breathing to slow as I held the flashlight beneath my firearm, slowly sweeping the light over the furniture displays. A shadow moved behind the oversized sofa. Cautiously, I moved toward it.

A battle cry sounded from behind the armoire. I spun, glimpsing Alfred Sigfried coming at me with an iron fireplace poker raised above his head. Riley darted out of the shadows. The whoosh of air hit me before I even had time to properly aim at Sigfried, but the lethal blow never landed. Instead, Riley tackled him. The sound of flesh slamming into flesh echoed as the two crashed into a hutch. Glass shattered around them as Riley fought to subdue Sigfried.

My body moved on its own, training taking over, as I attempted to help. But with the way they were locked together in battle, I couldn't risk firing for fear I'd hit Riley. Holstering my weapon, I grabbed Sigfried and tried to haul him off Riley.

Sigfried reared back, knocking me into a tall bookcase. We hit hard enough to cause the bookcase to rock. Locking out Sigfried's left arm, I reached for my cuffs, getting one bracelet clasped around his left wrist before he broke free from my grip.

The bookcase tipped over, crashing into my back and pinning me to the ground.

"Lexie," Riley bellowed, drawing on Sigfried before firing one shot and then another. He raced to me, struggling to get the heavy piece of furniture off of me. "Lex."

"I'm okay." I stared through the darkness at Sigfried. He wasn't dead. He was still moving, crawling toward the exit. I wasn't sure where he'd been shot, but Riley hadn't executed the traditional double-tap. One in the shoulder and one in the leg, maybe.

After a Herculean grunt, Riley freed me from beneath the bookcase. It banged against the ground, bits of wood chipping and breaking away. He let out a few deep exhales and checked my back. "Stay still, Lex. You could have spinal cord damage."

"I'm fine. See?" I moved my legs and arms as I pulled myself up and moved to where Sigfried had crawled. "You're under arrest, asshole. And there's no way you're getting out of it this time." I yanked his right arm up and finished cuffing him.

Riley was beside me, his gun back in its holster.

"It doesn't matter. You're too late," Sigfried said, a maniacal laugh overtaking him.

I saw the look on Riley's face. "Michael, don't. It's over. We got him." I peered out the front door, but we were facing the wrong way. "We should have felt the blast. Maybe they disarmed the bomb."

Sigfried continued to laugh, and then he started to gurgle.

Riley returned to his senses. "Shit." He crouched on the ground beside me and administered first aid. Sigfried may have deserved to die, but we'd prefer if it didn't happen on our watch.

I grabbed the radio, announcing the suspect was down, and requested an ambulance while Riley fashioned a tourniquet and tied it around Sigfried's leg.

"Copy," Lightman's gruff voice came back. "We're code four over here."

I sighed. "And I thought working vice was hard."

# FORTY

Now that I was no longer buzzing from the adrenaline surge, I realized just how much we could have lost. First, the explosion at the Millers'. Then the close call at that bar and the fight with Sigfried in the furniture store. Any one of them could have proven fatal.

After backup and the ambulance arrived and Sigfried had been carted away, Riley had been forced to hand over his firearm and speak to the scene investigators. Firing on an unarmed man was never a good thing, but given the circumstances, I hoped he'd be cleared of any potential wrongdoing. Thankfully, a cache of hidden firearms had been discovered in one of the storage chests inside the furniture store. They had been reported stolen during the crime spree.

Sigfried had hidden them inside the store. He had everything planned out. We even found a second go-bag with a thousand dollars and a fake ID. That had been his contingency in case he got caught at the garage. I just wondered when he had time to plant the bombs.

I'd already spoken to the detectives assigned to investigate the shooting, and I'd written my report. There was nothing left for me to do. But I couldn't leave. I had to know if Riley was okay.

A skeleton crew remained at the station to handle any walk-ins, but with the earlier power problems and the potential bomb scare, it wasn't business as usual. But it would be by the morning.

"Sarconi," Lightman whispered, his throat still sore from nearly being crushed, "shouldn't you call it a day?"

"Any word on Sigfried?"

"Hospital said the bastard will pull through. Maybe if Mike hadn't been so quick with that first aid, things would be different." He shrugged, and I wondered if he meant what he said.

"What about Riley?"

"He'll be fine. This is routine. Bastard tried to kill a cop, so Mike shot him." His eyes narrowed. "Isn't that what happened?"

"Yes, sir."

"I heard you found the bomb in the bar. The bomb squad disarmed it with less than twenty seconds to spare. I'm glad you were quick about it. And I'm even more impressed you were so quick to catch Sigfried. I swear, if he got away again, I'd—"

"You'd what, Jack?" Preston asked. "Try to force him into submission by letting him wrap something else around your neck?"

"There was so much going on between the bomb and the evacuation. I pulled out the handcuff key, and that's when he attacked. Then he grabbed the key, tossed the cuffs, and took off running. It could have happened to anyone. I doubt you could have done better."

Preston gave me a sly smile. "Of course not, Jack."

He glowered at her. "I'm calling it a night. Make sure you do the same."

Preston swiveled her chair around to face me and waited for Lightman to leave before she asked, "What are you still doing here? Are you worried about Michael?"

"Is it that obvious?"

"It's procedure. Believe it or not, we deal with this type of thing on a semi-regular basis." She gave me a long look. "Make sure you treat him right. Michael's one of the good ones."

"We're not—"

"Don't finish that statement. We make it a point not to lie to each other in this unit." She pulled her purse from her drawer and headed for the door. "Good night."

"Night."

I remained alone in the squad room, knowing I should leave and unable to make myself go. A million questions went through my mind. Would Sigfried confess to everything now that we had him? Did it even matter? We had him for attempted murder of police officers, and given the number of security cameras near that bar, we'd be able to pin the explosive device on him too. Rollins wouldn't be able to deny either of those things, not when Riley and I would testify against his client.

A phone rang in the distance, getting louder and closer. Riley emerged from the stairwell, glancing at his phone and then at me. He hit answer and held it to his ear. "Hey, I'm gonna have to call you back." Then he put it into his pocket.

I rushed into his arms and hugged him. "Are you okay?"

"I'm fine." He didn't sound fine. "Are you?"

"I am now."

"Good answer." He scratched his head and edged toward his desk, glancing at the security camera and reminding me we weren't truly alone. "I got my ass handed to me, but they cleared me." He pulled out a notepad and started writing in the dim light. "At least we got Sigfried. It took us long enough. Let's just hope he doesn't have another escape plan."

"Don't even say that."

I watched him write his report. He was stressed. I could see it in the way his shoulders tensed and the white-knuckled grip he had on the pen. When he finished, he threw the pen down and let out a frustrated growl.

"Hey," I said softly, pushing away from my desk and crossing to him, "you're okay. Everyone made it out of the bar okay. That's all that matters."

"It's not that. You should have waited for backup. You should have waited for me before you went inside that furniture store."

"There wasn't time."

"I know. But you scared me today, just like that day with Stryker King. I don't want to lose you."

"You won't." I glanced at the cameras, aware they didn't record audio. "But maybe don't shoot the next person who assaults me."

"He came at you with a deadly weapon and then he knocked a bookcase on top of you. You could have been killed or paralyzed. I needed to end it before things got worse."

"He had a hidden stash of guns," I said, unsure if Riley had heard the news.

His eyes went wide. "That's why I got cleared so quickly."

"Uh-huh. But you didn't know."

"Still, it was the right call." He stared into my eyes. "And I won't apologize for that. If someone hurts you, so help them."

"In that case, we probably shouldn't work together."

"Maybe not." He moved closer. "Now that this is over, you can do whatever you want. It's your call, Lex. You decide."

"Whatever I want?"

"Yep."

"What I want is to go back to your place and finish what we started in your kitchen."

"The sauce?"

"Uh-huh."

His blue eyes ignited. "Get going. I'll be right behind you."

~*~

We barely made it inside his apartment before his mouth was on mine. He kissed me hard, needing to feel grounded after the day we had.

"Michael." My voice was barely a whisper as he kissed down the column of my neck and his fingers undid the buttons on my shirt. But I had no intention of stopping him.

He pulled my tucked-in shirt free from my pants and smiled at the front-clasp on my bra as he unhooked it, watching the material fall to the sides.

I threw my head back as his mouth explored my newly exposed flesh. When his lips moved back to mine, my hands made fast work of his shirt, rubbing random patterns against his abdomen. His skin scorched my fingertips.

He ran his hand along my stomach before undoing my belt. I quivered, and my legs shook as I stepped out of my pants. He smiled at the effect he was having on me.

"Lexie," he met my eyes, and I saw just how badly he needed this, "please."

"Condoms?"

He lifted me up, my legs wrapping around his waist as he walked us into the bedroom and dropped me onto the bed. "Good thing I bought a box the other day."

"Did you think you'd get lucky?"

"Never this lucky."

# FORTY-ONE

I stretched out in Riley's warm bed, watching as he entwined his fingers with mine. "I didn't think it was possible, but you definitely outdid yourself."

"I warned you what happens to the male anatomy when things get dicey at work." He pressed my hand to his lips. "So what happens now?"

"I guess I call Amber and tell her I have a boyfriend."

"Oh, wow. That makes it official and everything. We should post it online." He snorted, enjoying the mockery.

"Sure, except neither of us uses social media and we've agreed that no one at work needs to know about us, not until I figure out what I want to do."

"No problem, but Kemper better keep his distance. And he better be nicer to you."

"And you better be a little less alpha male. I'm capable of taking care of myself and fighting my own battles."

"I wouldn't have it any other way," he replied, finding the phrase amusing given the context. "How do you feel about constant sleepovers? With the way work is, the only chance we'll have to see each other will be at night, and you know how often we get late night calls."

"Toothbrushes. Deodorant. Body wash." I listed the toiletries I'd need to buy. "Do you have conditioner?"

"Why?" He ran his free hand through his hair. "Does my hair seem dry or unmanageable?"

"No. You have great hair."

"It's because I condition." He rolled onto his side. "I'm exhausted. We'll work on the shopping list tomorrow." He watched as I tugged on his t-shirt and settled back on the bed beside him. "Oddly enough, I'm guessing you'll have fewer things to keep at my place. After all, you can sleep in my clothes, but I can't say the same."

I inhaled sharply, the familiar unease of a new relationship washed over me, but this time I forced it away. This relationship was different. I was different. And Michael Riley was unlike any man I'd ever met.

"Is everything okay, Lex? You got quiet all of a sudden. Am I boring you?"

"No, I'm good." I smiled. "We're good."

**Don't miss the second book in the Lexie Sarconi series, Break-ins and Bouquets.**

***One bad night will change everything...***

Officer Lexie Sarconi is preparing for the detective's exam and finding her footing with a new unit. However, everything that she's worked so hard to achieve is about to crash and burn. The criminals have declared war on the police. No one is safe, and when Lexie ends up trapped in an ambush, nothing will ever be the same again.

But as a police officer, Lexie knew the risks. She swore an oath to uphold the law, but her boyfriend, Detective Michael Riley, feels differently. If he had known what was going to happen, he never would have let her near that crime scene. And now he's willing to break all the rules to get the men who hurt her.

Lexie fears the lengths Riley is willing to go. She and the rest of the unit want to stop these criminals from striking again, but she'll have to keep her eye on Riley to make sure he doesn't do something that will land him behind bars or worse. There are only so many lines a person can cross, and Riley's ready to cross them all.

# ABOUT THE AUTHOR

**G.K. Parks** is the author of the Alexis Parker series. The first novel, *Likely Suspects,* tells the story of Alexis' first foray into the private sector.

G.K. Parks received a Bachelor of Arts in Political Science and History. After spending some time in law school, G.K. changed paths and earned a Master of Arts in Criminology/Criminal Justice. Now all that education is being put to use creating a fictional world based upon years of study and research.

**Elisa Archer** has always loved reading, writing, and romance. On most days you can find her hiding behind a computer screen, frantically typing away at her latest story. She's always been an avid reader and enjoys everything from technothrillers to steamy romance. In fact, there isn't a genre of book she doesn't like. Writing just seemed to be the natural progression of her passion for books.

You can find additional information by visiting our website at
www.gkparks.com

Sign up for the e-mail newsletter for the latest information on upcoming releases, sales, free promotions, and more.
www.gkparks.com/newsletter

www.ingramcontent.com/pod-product-compliance
Lightning Source LLC
Chambersburg PA
CBHW020743250626
47155CB00003B/893

* 9 7 8 1 9 4 2 7 1 0 3 8 7 *